The Abbey of St. Mary Magdalene

Greville Wilday

Copyright © 2020 Greville Wilday
All rights reserved.

Front Cover by bellydraft@blueyonder.co.uk

**Prayers from *Common Worship: Services and Prayers for the Church of England* © The Archbishops' Council 2000.
Published by Church House Publishing.** Used by permission.
copyright.copyright@churchofengland.org

Fiction Disclaimer

This is a work of fiction based in East Anglia, around the ancient port of Lowestoft. At the time of writing, there was a substantial plot of undeveloped land adjacent to Lake Lothing, which is where I have sited the fictional abbey. Any similarity between my characters and any living or recently deceased person is purely coincidental. However, some of the distant historical references are real.

Acknowledgements

Many thanks to the Reverend Garry Ward, vicar of the medieval parish church of All Saints, Claverley, in south-east Shropshire. Inspirational Garry has helped me with some of the practices, protocols, and principles of current Anglican worship. However, any mistakes are mine. His ancient church, is very well worth a visit, especially for its hatchments and unique early thirteenth century wall paintings. The village of Claverley is famed for its community spirit, whilst a warm welcome from the parishioners is assured.

The Author

Greville Wilday served as a deck apprentice and junior deck officer for a major shipping company. Injured in a shipboard industrial accident, he left the sea but has always retained a love of, and deep interest in, matters nautical. He lectured in Nautical Physics for several years at the University of Southampton School of Navigation. He kept a Neptune motor-sailer at Brightlingsea and explored the Thames approaches.

A student of the natural world and human behaviour, he spent several enjoyable years at university. He has lectured to degree level in Physics and Computing, and practised as a Psychological Counsellor and Hypnotherapist.

A keen golfer, he is also a county hockey umpire. He lives with his wife and a number of cats on the borders of Staffordshire and Shropshire in the United Kingdom.

Books by Greville Wilday

Fiction

Jutland Bank

The Abbey of St. Mary Magdalene

Non-Fiction

Help Yourself to a Little More Happiness (In Preparation)

1

Across the water, a blue-hulled, rig-support vessel eased in towards Lowestoft's North Quay. Three short blasts of her whistle pierced the stillness of early evening as her engines went astern. In the low April sun, the dark blue waters glistened to the east, where Lake Lothing stretched towards the swing-bridge and the outer harbour beyond.

'I've caught something, Dad!' drew my attention towards an excited boy, of about twelve, fishing from the worn dockside to my right. He pushed back the hood of his parka and started winding in his line as his rod twitched.

'Keep the end of your rod up,' Dad stood up from his seat, grabbed a landing net, and moved closer to help.

'Well done, Bob. We'll have that for tea tomorrow.' Proud Dad dispatched the foot-long fish with a blow to the head.

Several yards beyond the boy and his father, two drifters lay alongside the quay. Hulks now, seaweed trailed sadly from their drooping mooring ropes, once-black hulls streaked with rust. Softened by the rays of the low sun, their dead and rotting bodies still spoke of the port's past trade. As with many parts of the town, they mourned a previously thriving marine history. A small motor cruiser glided quietly upstream, heading for one of the marinas.

A whisper of breeze ruffled my hair and brought odours of

seaweed, mud, and dead fish. I felt at once at ease and yet challenged by the place. It reminded me of South Shields, where I grew up. My dad, a naval architect, used to take me fishing off the inside of Shields' pier-head. With the closing of the pits and the move towards containers and flags of convenience, shipping generally, and Tyne traffic particularly, had also declined substantially.

Glancing at my watch showed the time was five-twenty. I had stayed too long and only just had time to get to the abbey. Turning, I crossed Magdalene Road where it ended next to the old quayside, and walked into the grounds of the abbey of St. Mary Magdalene. The grounds stretched from the edge of Lake Lothing, all the way back to Waveney Way, almost a quarter of a mile inland. Now largely an expanse of wild bushes and grass, there were a few low runs of exposed ancient stonework, the highest being the walls of a long building to the north-east of the remaining main structure. The abbey church was nearer to the main road. It stood solid and proud against the low sun. So far, I had discovered only a little of its history. The Abbot of St. Benet's abbey, a Benedictine community next to the River Bure near Horning, had founded our abbey on a small hillside in 1245. Our area bore the name 'Queensholme'; in past times, water must have surrounded the abbey frequently. I thought of the original monks making their way by boat down the River Bure to Yarmouth, then through Breydon Water (an inland sea) up the River Waveney, and into Lake Lothing. It was now eight months since my induction to the parish. After a long interregnum, the regular congregation had fallen to a handful. It had now risen to twenty.

Picking my way past moss-covered stone fragments, I tingled as I felt the presence of the past monastic community.

Lord, send your blessing on those who served you here in the past. I give thanks for their love and care. Please forgive my lateness and mistakes and guide me in your work.

The main entrance to the abbey was through a porch and

doorway into the south transept. The current building was in the shape of a cross with four nearly equal arms. The nave to the west of the transept, or north-south crossing, was approximately the same length as that of the choir. As far as I could discern, the building had originally boasted a substantially longer western nave. The remnants of walls to the west of the current nave, suggested a partial destruction during the dissolution of the monasteries. Lighter stonework and a small rose window in the west wall of the nave indicated a later partial restoration.

The vestry jutted out as an architectural carbuncle on the east side of the south transept. I let myself in and heard the sound of soft organ music floating on the air. Father Rex was playing before we held compline. We had introduced compline two months ago at his suggestion, holding it at five-thirty p.m. I had started approaching local businesses in the area offering help in the event of any personal problems. I hoped that this short service of compline would offer a way of winding down for workers on their way home, as well as some of those from the residential area in our parish, largely on the far side of Waveney Way. We highlighted it in the local press and were now drawing three or four people.

Rex was one of a few lucky finds since my induction as vicar, serving the two parishes of St. Mary's, and neighbouring Coxton St. Giles. A bald, portly, jovial man, in the Friar Tuck mould, he had retired two years ago as a parish priest in Yarmouth. His wife had died of cancer ten years before. A man steeped in east coast salt, he was born in Lowestoft, served in Hull, Felixstowe, and Yarmouth before heart and arthritis forced retirement. He now lived in a four-storey terrace house on the sea front. The house was left to him by his father, the owner and skipper of a large trawler. Although the abbey heating system was on, I felt sure his fingers, now gnarled with arthritis, would be hurting.

Dear Lord, please help us to find an organist soon.

As I gathered a taper and matches to light the candles on the altar, the vestry door opened and in stepped a tall well-built man.

The Abbey of St. Mary Magdalene

A strong and fine-boned face was topped by a good head of white hair.

'Evening, Brother John. Sorry I'm late. ' he smiled as he removed his thick fleece, revealing a black clerical shirt and clerical collar. Jeans and warm boots completed the picture.

'Hi, Paul. I've only just arrived, too.'

Father Paul, C.R., was another lucky find. Now seventy-two, he had retired from active out-placement work for the Community of the Resurrection to live with an unmarried younger sister in Lowestoft. Following many years of work in the industrial north, his last parish attachment was in Yarmouth where he had met Rex.

'See you presently. Thanks for your help.'

I let myself into the body of the church and lit the altar candles. Paul was taking the service tonight. A little later we sang a version of the ancient compline hymn:

Now in the fading light of day,
Maker of all to you we pray.

As the hymn continued, my eyes wandered along the soft white roof with its crisscross of gold trusses. Lowering my eyes, I scanned the congregation, ashamed that I had been too late for more than a cursory 'Hello' and welcome words. Tonight, ten were spread out in the misericord seats of the choir. Two months ago, when we started compline, there were only the two retired clergy, the long-suffering churchwarden, Jim Pike, and myself. Jim had held the place together during the interregnum. For our main Sunday morning service, the numbers had risen to an average of twenty. I felt that we were making progress.

Jim wore a maroon waterproof blouson revealing the navy top of a polo sweater. He usually wore jeans unless it was a Sunday service or he was on official duty. Then he was always tidy in jacket or suit. His thinning hair topped a strong weather-beaten face, proof of his many years at sea as skipper of a beam trawler. Retired now, he and his wife, May, were often to be seen at the local bowling club.

On the other side of the choir, opposite Jim, a tall thin man bent over his service book, like a gaunt windswept tree on an exposed moorland ridge. Heavy black-rimmed spectacles and broad dark eyebrows gave him a serious demeanour. A white shirt and waist-coated black suit matched his role as a deputy bank manager. George Parslew was our treasurer. He was a kindly generous man and a keen cricketer. With his fussy manner, I suspected that he had been passed over for higher roles in the bank.

Next to George stood a tall lithe white-haired woman in a bright red trouser suit. A single woman of sixty-eight, Alice Broad was a retired matron from Lowestoft's Brandon Hospital. Still full of energy, she ran an afternoon Zumba class in the community centre and played cello in the county orchestra. Alice organised our church flowers and cleaning.

There were two faces I had not seen before: a woman and a man. I guessed that Jim had deliberately sat nearby to make them welcome. The woman appeared to be in her mid-fifties. Either she wore yellow in her make-up or she was jaundiced. Her eyes seemed partially closed, as if she was sad or had been crying. The man next to her looked ten years or more, younger. In contrast he seemed alert and spent much time looking around at the windows, walls, choir stalls, and roof. He wore cords, an open-necked shirt and a light sports jacket with elbow patches, and was topped by a head of luxuriant sandy hair.

Snatches of the service registered with me as we approached its end:

May your holy angels dwell with us and guard
us in peace — .

Soon, Paul and I stood near the south door to say farewell to those leaving. The two newcomers were last to leave, which often signified a wish to talk. I greeted the woman who approached first:

'Good to see you. I don't think we've met before. I'm John.'
'Hello, I'm June.' Her shoulders were raised in what I

assessed as tension. She hesitated.

'I've got to dash now — Jack's tea — but I wondered if you would have a moment free, sometime?' A tear slipped from one eye.

'Of course. Tomorrow? When would suit? Shall we sit down for a minute?'

June had no time just then as she was on her way home to get her husband's tea. He was a police sergeant. We made a date for Tuesday, the following week, when she had an afternoon off from her job. She worked as a supervisor at the large supermarket nearer to the swing-bridge. She had seen my notice of services and offer of help on their staff notice board. Aware that we had services on Tuesday and Thursday evenings she had arranged to do morning shifts on those days. I gave her a copy of the parish news-sheet and my card.

'You need to have a word with our vicar,' Paul was speaking to the new man. They walked over.

'John, this is Ben Fillingham. He's Head of History at Coxton Endowed School.'

I was aware of engaging with Ben in the exchange of introductory gambits that social intercourse conventions demanded before addressing the principal issues.

'I'm about to start a Middle Ages project with our Lower Sixth. I wondered whether we might be able to use the abbey as our focus: survey the ground and building, explore and follow up any old records we could lay our hands on. I'm also a member of the Lowestoft Historical Society and would probably like, in due course, to present a talk to them.'

'It all sounds very exciting to me, Ben. I'm very new here and have a lot to learn. I'll search the vestry, although it's very likely any really old records went to the diocesan archives. Tomorrow, I'll ring the archivist and see if he or she can help. There is a list of abbots and vicars on a board in the Lady Chapel in the north transept. Perhaps you and your students might be able to put on an exhibition of your work in the abbey in due course?'

Ben agreed to prepare his head teacher for a visit that I was planning to make. We exchanged telephone numbers.

A little later I locked the vestry door. Paul, Rex, and I stepped out into the fading light.

'Thank you, brothers.'

I appreciated their friendship and help. They enjoyed the ancient atmosphere of the abbey, and our worship.

'Oh, John. I meant to tell you,' Paul turned towards me. 'A friend of mine in the Beccles' team ministry told me that a certain Heaven's Angel is planning an off the cuff visit to Lowestoft sometime soon.'

My heart sank. He was referring to the Venerable Imogen Rodgers, archdeacon of Lothingland, within whose purview the abbey fell. She was the bishop's lieutenant for a good third of the diocese. Imogen was a keen motorcyclist, and was frequently to be seen showing the flag around her archdeaconry, dressed in leathers and on a loud and shiny Harley Davidson. She appeared to hold the impression that she was an angel of the Lord and that a loud exhaust made her a woman of the people and nearer to her flock. The diocesan website showed that she had a degree in sociology and had been an army officer before entering the priesthood. She seemed to have made very rapid progress. In the few months I had spent in the diocese I gathered that many of the male priests felt that his grace, the bishop, had gone too far towards equality and diversity; two of our three archdeacons were women.

I worked hard to feel love and charity towards Imogen. The evangelical, folk-guitar playing Imogen, disapproved of our moderately high church practices. Incense incensed her. She had also made it clear that I had a limited, but unspecified, time to build up an economic congregation at the abbey. There was a rumour of deconsecration and sale of our land for local development. The abbey had been represented as a holy barrier between lake and road in the middle of a partially redeveloped area. I preferred to see the abbey as an inspiration in regeneration.

Our parish of Queensholme extended a little on the far side of Waveney Way. Beyond that was our related team parish of Coxton St. Giles. The original church of St. Giles was flattened in a bombing raid on the docks in the latter stages of the Second World War. Our team now used a multipurpose building that served as a small community centre most weekdays and evenings, and as a church on Sundays. It belonged to the local authority. Our use was intended to be a temporary measure sixty plus years ago. I had hopes that in the future both parishes might come together and use the abbey for worship, releasing the community centre for purely secular use.

'OK. Thanks for the warning, Paul. I don't think we can work much faster on our plan for engagement with the local community. Good night, chaps.'

Paul and Rex set off towards their respective homes on the Esplanade. I crossed over Waveney Way heading for the vicarage, a detached house in Coxton.

2

'Hello, I'm Sally Foster.' The tall, attractive, energetic woman in her forties, wore a charcoal grey trouser suit. She held out her hand in welcome. Smiling, she continued, 'Dare I say: "take a pew"?'

She clearly had a sense of humour. The head teacher's room was light and spacious. The walls were pale green. A wide window looked out across playing fields. The light-coloured meeting table at the inside end of the room was surrounded by a dozen chairs. Nearer to the window, the head's desk, with a glass-fronted bookcase beside it, rested against a wall. A further bookcase and two filing cabinets graced the opposite wall.

I sat in one of two easy chairs near the desk. They were distinctly lower than the office chair on casters in front of the desk. Sally sat in the other easy chair: no power play there. A good start.

'Right then. How can I help? I gather from Ben that our Lower Sixth historians are to centre a medieval study on the abbey. Thanks for that.'

I had the impression that Sally didn't tolerate time-wasters. I presented my visiting card.

'Coxton Endowed School is in the parish of the abbey church of St. Mary Magdalene. St. Mary is, of course, symbolic of the contribution that women make to the world.'

'"Sinful women" do you mean?' Her face was a combination of frown and smile.

'No. I don't mean that at all. I agree that some claim a tradition of an earlier looser life style. However, I have never seen any suggestion of this in the bible or any credible historical source. Quite the opposite. Several bible references place Mary before the apostles in precedence.'

Time to move on.

'This is partly a pastoral visit and partly to offer other resources. We have a beautiful and ancient building with ample room, wonderful acoustic properties, and a tuneful historic Harrison organ. You might like to consider the abbey for seasonal school services, choral or other appropriate musical events. On the pastoral side, perhaps you would kindly display this A4 laminated notice in your staff room. The notice gives concise details of our services and also an offer of counselling for anyone who is distressed. Equally, I would be happy to conduct or contribute to any school service.'

'I notice that you have a doctorate,' she glanced down at my visiting card. 'Is that in theology?'

'No. I originally trained in clinical psychology and worked in that area for a couple of years before training for the ministry.'

'I see. That possibly explains your weekly healing service.'

'Indeed. My thesis studied aspects of expectancy, belief, and the placebo effect. There is plenty of evidence that belief can affect the immune system.'

Sally proved ready to chat a little longer. It transpired that she was a mathematician. She was keen to develop and inspire her staff and pupils in the traditional arts and sciences, alongside a few of the more rigorous vocational courses. She had little time for soft options. English Literature, Music, and Art were preferred to Media Studies.

Shortly, recognising she was a busy person, I expressed my thanks for her time. Sally stood, turned, and led me to the door. I couldn't help but admire her fit firm figure and natural curves.

Oh Lord, why did you make some women so attractive?

Apart from visiting the school it was a very ordinary day. A mixture of challenge, self-expression, and routine. I spent the rest of the morning largely on pastoral visits, cold calling on residents in the nearer parts of Coxton within the abbey parish. Mostly there was no one in. Those I met were retired people or young mums. In the afternoon I spent time ironing and thinking about ways of developing the parish of St. Mary's. The ironed clerical collars and shirts in the airing cupboard increased in number. Next Sunday's sermon was planned. My evening meal was over: cold ham, tomatoes, green leaves from a supermarket plastic bag, and some boiled potatoes, sitting at the kitchen table.

My ordination vows required me to say evensong daily. Tonight, I'd done this alone in the abbey, although some days, especially if it was cold, I would do this at home. It was now 7.00 p.m. Wearing my black cassock, I stepped outside, and closed and locked the vestry door. The air was still and the sky cloudless and golden towards the west. Sunset was approaching. Drawn by my fondness for water, I headed along the path that led to where the abbey grounds bordered on Lake Lothing.

I heard laughter ahead. Nearing the water, I saw three teenagers. One with blond hair threw a stone towards the water. The other two laughed and one shouted

'Got it! Good shot.'

Striding faster, I broke into a run as I saw a second youth searching for another stone. The tide was low and the water's edge out of sight. The second youth, dark haired, threw the stone he had found. I was in time to see the stone just miss a small Labrador. It was swimming along the water's edge frantically trying to climb out, only to be pushed back into the lake by a red-shirted third boy who was wielding a long stick. The boy tried hard to push the dog under the water but the stick slipped off. The boys were clearly trying to kill the dog.

'Stop that!' I shouted, incensed.

'It's just a queer in a black frock,' shouted one.

The others turned and at last saw me. I paused briefly, deciding what to do. Gathering myself up, I stood, a tall silhouette, black against the setting sun. I raised my right hand in the traditional sign of blessing, recalling words from our Lord to his disciples: 'Whosoever sins you retain, they are retained, and whosoever sins you forgive, they are forgiven.' The 'apostolic succession' is the tradition of many varieties of Christianity that this authority is passed down through the ages through bishops and the priesthood.

'When you have learnt and positively show kindness to animals, may our Lord bless you and keep you — but until then, beware.'

Then, stripping off my cassock, I ran towards the water's edge as the boys fled. The edge was lined with thick mud, where the dog was struggling to climb ashore. It was stuck a metre out unable to progress further, clearly weakening. Tentatively, I put one foot out towards the dog and sank up to my knee. Cautiously, reaching forward, I grabbed it by the scruff of the neck, and pulled the creature shoreward until my hand slipped off. Leaning over I was just able get a good hold with two hands. A pair of eyes looked gratefully and wearily at me.

'Come on old chap, nearly there.'

The dog came clear with a rush. I swung it ashore onto the grass, and fell sideways into the mud. Scrambling out on all fours I sat, covered in a sticky grey-black layer. The dog coughed and brought up some muddy water. It struggled over to me and licked my hand. We both sat for a while, recovering from the experience.

'Right. Time you trotted off home.'

But the dog, who looked to be a Labrador crossed pup, was recovering quickly and showed no willingness to leave. It had no collar and hence no name tag.

'In that case we'd better go home and have a shower. I wonder what your name is?' Determining the dog's sex, I continued 'I think we'll call you Moses.'

Wiping my hands on the grass, I picked up my cassock, and set off homewards through the abbey grounds. The dog trotted close behind. Crossing Waveney Way, Moses relieved himself on the first lamppost.

Back at the vicarage, Moses and I stripped off and went in the shower. I reckoned a bath might be too traumatic for the dog after his experience in the lake. A little later, whilst he explored the house, I rang the police. Not much interest there. There was no report of a missing dog, so they would just put his details on file in case of any enquiries. The kettle boiled. I made a cup of coffee and took a biscuit from its tin. Within a few seconds there was a small black creature sitting just in front of me, looking up with big wide eyes and licking its mouth. I gave the dog my biscuit and it rapidly disappeared.

'I guess I'll have to get you some proper food.'

Nine-thirty. A quick trip to the twenty-four-hour supermarket and I was back, better prepared for my new companion: a bag of dog biscuits, two metal bowls, a collar, lead, and a packet of poo bags.

'OK, Moses. Here's your supper and some water. You're sleeping on the kitchen mat tonight, with this lovely red collar. Night, night.' Closing the door behind me, I headed off to bed.

Lord, for the sake of Saint Francis, please bless this little chap and help me to do my best for him.

3

From the edge of the supermarket car park one could see two ways along Lake Lothing. To the east, you could just see part of the road swing-bridge, to the north, the opposite shore presented a long dockside with cranes, a few buildings, and evidence of the railway line to Norwich. The blue rig support vessel, which I had seen mooring a few days earlier, had now gone. A large police or Her Majesty's Customs' vessel drew the most attention with her suggestion of speed and power. Several whip aerials stood smartly to attention near her bridge. I liked to leave my car at this part of the car park. The water-scape evoked interest and happy memories.

I locked the ten-year-old Golf estate and compared it with the clean but old green Land Rover Discovery parked nose in on the opposite side of the lane. It sported a tow-bar ball. It would have some difficulty reversing out as the car park lanes were quite narrow. Approaching the supermarket entrance, I passed a row of wider spaces with parent and child signs. A bulbous black pickup, with 'Animal' in large sign-writing, swept into one of those spaces, just missing me. A fit-looking man in a sleeveless vest stepped down from the driver's seat and an amply endowed woman in very high heels emerged from the passenger side. The driver clicked his key fob, and they swaggered off together. No children then!

Inside the automatic doors I gathered a trolley and entered the fruit and veg' section. This seems to be the starting point in most supermarkets. Checking my shopping list, I picked up a netting pack of 'sweet and juicy' Spanish oranges. These were followed by four bananas (slightly green), a pack of medium sized tomatoes, loose broccoli (supposed to be good for the brain), and a pack of pre-washed potatoes. Yes, a luxury, but it didn't look good dispensing communion with grubby fingers. Milk, 50/50 sliced bread, ham, cheese, and sparkling water (more interesting than tap water and cheaper than cola or wine). A tin of braised beef, but avoid the baked beans, they could prove an embarrassment. A steak pie with a flaky-pastry top. My mouth salivated at the thought, this was my treat for the week. Three tins of dog meat as a treat for Moses in addition to a large bag of biscuits.

Job done, I headed for the checkout. Three ahead in the queue was a very attractive brunette with shoulder length hair, white trousers, a black top, and medium length high heels. Elegance! Wow! Her face was elfish. She showed an intriguing blend of pertness, beauty, kindness, and strength of personality. As she walked off I couldn't but admire the lithesome movement of her hips.

Forgive me Lord. It is so difficult to control the right balance between imagining a woman in bed, as a friendly open companion, as a potential parishioner, and as a fellow Christian. It isn't easy for a poorly paid bachelor priest to meet up with and present himself attractively to an agreeable, beautiful, and like-minded woman friend.

When I unloaded my trolley onto the checkout belt, the girl had paid and disappeared. After checking out my groceries, I fancied a coffee. The supermarket had a well-sited cafe with panoramic windows in a corner of the building. It partly viewed the car park but also looked out over Lake Lothing towards the swing bridge. A small Americano, with cream, shed a spiral of upward moving Columbian essence – the legal sort. Sitting in the corner window seat, I looked out over the disabled parking area towards the swing bridge. I relaxed and watched the world go by.

'Hello. Mind if I join you?' It was June, whom I had met at our evening service a few days ago. She was carrying a coffee.

Jumping up, I pulled out a chair for her.

'I'm on a short break,' she said as she sat looking out over the disabled parking bays.

'Somehow I feel just a little more at ease since we met at St. Mary's.

'Now just look at that!' She pointed at one of disabled bays. 'We see some really low life here at times.'

I turned to look and saw a well-dressed, fit-looking woman transfer her last shopping bag from her trolley into the boot of a shiny, new, large Audi, parked in a disabled bay. Closing the boot lid, she pushed the trolley onto the adjacent unused disabled bay and drove off.

'I find it hard to feel charitable towards a person like that!' June said angrily. 'Must go. I'm due back on supervisor duty shortly. See you on Tuesday.'

'Take care,' I replied.

Sipping the last drops of my coffee, I noticed a smart young man in an open-topped red Porsche drive past and stop beside, yes, Miss Gorgeous pushing her empty trolley to a trolley park. She stopped and chatted to the young man for a few minutes before he drove off. I recognised the chap as a Norwich City footballer.

Forgive me for feeling jealous, Lord, and help me to feel charitable. What chance would a poorly paid priest have with a woman like that?

On my way out I met churchwarden Jim. After a brief chat we reviewed the arrangements for a funeral to be held the next morning. I had secured the organist services of Father Rex. Jim would put out the 'No Parking' signs near the abbey entrance. He had also put ready the Common Worship Funeral Service leaflets.

We happened to be pushing our trolleys along the same route and came to my car first. Unless I had a big load for the boot, I always preferred to back the car into a space. It was then easier when driving out. It was immediately apparent that the car was now different from how I'd left it. The car was slightly angled to one side of the bay. The driver's side front wing had a circular indentation and had the edge pushed down against the tyre. Between the pair of us, we managed to pull the wing up and away from the tyre allowing the wheel to turn.

'Lost some of her beauty looks,' commented Jim. 'However, I know a reasonable body shop which will sometimes use breakers' parts to cut costs if needed.'

Most of the way home I experienced bouts of anger at the other driver who had damaged my car and hadn't stayed to exchange insurance details. The excess would probably cost me the price of the new coat I'd planned to buy. A tussle ensued in my mind.

Lord, I feel angry at the person who has damaged my car, and yet you say 'turn the other cheek.' I ought to love the other person, although I may disagree with their behaviour. I find this hard to do.

In turn, one minute I seethed, and the next endeavoured to pray for the well-being of the other driver. A little later I spotted a small card and scrap of paper fluttering under the wiper blade. Doubtless someone promoting a way to earn extra cash. I chuckled cynically. Was this a divine way of helping me to pay for the insurance excess?

Eventually, turning onto the vicarage drive, I switched off the engine, removed the ticket, and looked at it. It was a business card. The scrap of paper carried some writing in a fine hand:

'Sorry I couldn't stop. I had a business appointment. In legalese, our vehicles were involved in a collision. Please give me a call on the number overleaf. I'm so sorry, Marie.'

On the business card were the details:
Marie Webb,
    Director,
        BioSolutions.

There was an address at the nearby trading estate, and mobile and land line numbers.

4

Easter was two weeks away. Clumps of daffodils nodded cheerfully amongst remnants of the old monastic buildings in the abbey grounds. Escaping the gentle drizzle, I let myself into the vestry. It was a good-sized room. There were two wardrobes for vestments, and racks for the robes of the choir that we did not yet boast. Two locked filing cabinets held parish registers for hatches, matches, and dispatches. The old escritoire housed basic items of stationery, the roll top serving to keep dust off the writing surface. Two upright but padded chairs offered just a little comfort for visitors. I pulled out the ancient office chair on casters and settled down to await and prepare for June's appointment.

Time for reflection is an important ingredient in the life of both priest and therapist. At various times elements may include awareness of one's self and one's needs, developing empathy for, and sensitivity to, others, cultivating humility, and perception of the individual's place within society and the cosmos. I spent several minutes in reflection and asking for spiritual help before June knocked on the door.

With her agreement, I said a short prayer asking that we might know the near presence of God and that we were wrapped in his love. June looked to be in her early fifties. When she removed her short red waterproof jacket, she was wearing a sunny gold woollen jumper and black skirt. Her figure was slim, firm, and well-rounded in the right places. She wore a cherry red lipstick. I detected a hint of rouge on her cheeks. There was a slight tint to her skin as if she had some genes from a sunnier climate. Once again, her eyes were slightly hooded, as if the light was too bright, or she was tearful. I recalled that last week her first visit to St. Mary's had been to compline, an end of the day service. Was there possibly an association with endings in general, or even an issue about one more specific, like a close death, or a relationship finishing?

'I don't know quite where to start,' she lifted her right hand to her forehead for a few seconds.

'I saw your notice about healing services at work, at the supermarket. I wondered if you might be able to help.' She drew in a deep breath.

'In November I had a scan and some tests. The consultant told me I had liver cancer. I've been having chemotherapy. Just before Christmas, Dr. Marshall, my G.P., told me I had six months left to live. Now it's April, I've only two months left. I'm frightened,' she burst into tears.

Lord Jesus, please help this woman. Enfold her in your love.

I felt an urge to put my arms around her, but held back. I try to avoid physical contact with a parishioner or client in case it is misunderstood. I was aware that she was hooking a strong sense of fatherly or brotherly love from me. I knew Dr. Marshall was a partner at a local medical practice. I don't like to criticise a professional but felt a swell of anger at his bad psychology and callousness.

'June, I promise you that Dr. Marshall cannot know exactly how long you have to live,' I touched her gently on the arm.

'At the most, all he could predict from assessment of your condition, plus experience, would be that perhaps on average patients might live for six months. It's a statistical matter, and also depends on your own approach. Some patients might give up and die within two weeks. You clearly are not one of those. Some might live three years. A few may even get a total remission.

'A substantial physical factor in your health is how well your immune system works. It is well known that this will work better the less stress and anxiety, and the more happiness and relaxation you feel. I can't promise how long you will live, but the more you accept our Lord's love and will, the better and healthier your life will be, however long that is.

'There isn't generally a quick fix. Rather, it needs a continuing commitment of trust, acceptance of love, and giving of love. As you know, we have a healing service every Tuesday evening. This is an opportunity to be helped by the prayers of others, to give your help to others by prayer, and to accept our Lord's love.'

There was so much more that I wanted to say, but the way forward would be better if June could express her bottled-up feelings, thoughts and questions. I went quiet and calmly attentive.

'I'm frightened of pain and dying,' she said eventually. 'And there are so many things I wanted to do. I feel I haven't been good enough or useful enough in my life.'

There was an intensity in her eyes and voice, hinting at an inner energy, concerns about the past, and hopes for the future.

'Have you talked to your doctor about your fears and worries?'

'Huh!' She grunted. 'I started to talk to him but he told me to pull myself together and make a will.'

It seemed that Dr. Marshall was one of the, thankfully shrinking, school of medics who had little in the way of bedside manner or empathy with their patients. He was missing an opportunity to improve his medicine by showing psychological support and encouraging a positive expectancy. In fact, he was probably doing great harm using the 'nocebo' effect, like a witch doctor casting black spells that came to fruition due to the expectancy and belief of his victim.

'June, if the practice is a partnership, which I think it is, there's no reason why you can't see one of the other doctors. You could probably find one who was a lot less stark. It's worthwhile asking friends who they go to and what their doctors are like.

'I suggest that you come to our healing services for a while and that we meet again, possibly the same time next Tuesday, if that suits? Our next healing service is this evening.

'Can you tell me how church healing works, please?'

'Of course. It seems generally to require an opening of the heart and mind to God's presence and love.'

'How do I do that?'

'It usually helps to practice a little quietness. Talk to God. Listen and be aware for his replies and love. Find time to say thanks for the good things you have and continue to experience. Ask his blessings on other people. Tell him your worries and ask for his help and guidance. Know that he hears. Try to relax in gratitude and allow his love and peace to flow into you. Most people find that coming to Holy Communion at least once a week, helps. We have Holy Communion on a Sunday morning and also on a Tuesday evening as part of the healing service.'

'What happens at this service?'

'We thank God for the good things that have happened to us, ask his blessing and help for others, ask for forgiveness for the mistakes that we have inevitably made, ask and receive God's help for ourselves and any problem we have. For those that wish it, there is the special focus of the Laying On of Hands. It's probably best for us to have met again, and for you to have attended a couple of services to feel ready for that and to make the most of it.'

'How about the medical treatment I am receiving?'

'You should continue with that, using all the means available to help yourself.'

'I'm still not clear how this healing works.'

'When we are more aware and accepting of God's love, we are usually more at ease, and our immune system seems to work better. There is no guarantee as to how illness changes, or to how long we will live, but life should be better and more at ease than it would otherwise have been.'

'Is there any proof that it works?'

'Well, let me tell you of two quite different studies. One is about the effect of belief in general, the second is about the effect of spirituality.

'There was a study of a group of asthmatics who were exposed to a nebulised saline solution — that's a fine spray of salty water, which would normally be innocuous. They were, however, told that it was an irritant. Just under fifty per cent of the group experienced substantially increased difficulty breathing. Some of them experienced full-blown asthma attacks. Then they were given another spray and told that it was therapeutic. They were all relieved by the second spray, which in fact, was exactly the same as the first. That is the effect of expectancy, belief, or faith.

'Several studies have shown that people who regularly attend religious services (once a week or more often) are likely to live longer than those who don't attend, or who attend less frequently.

'You may like to try some of these activities.' I gave her a card with a number of suggestions:

- Make a list of some of the things that have happened in your life for which you feel grateful.
- What is happening in your life NOW for which you feel grateful?
- Is there anybody or any event at which you feel particularly angry? See if you can let it go.
- What are you doing to let the little boy or girl inside come out and play, to give you joy and happiness?
- What are you doing to help any other people?
- Is there anything that bothers you especially? Is there something about which you feel particularly ashamed? Let it come out and talk to God about it. You may find it helpful to talk to a priest in confidence.
- You may find it helpful to keep a private journal in which you write these things.

We talked a little longer, and then asked God's blessings and guidance for all who were ill and for June in particular. Then June left, after agreeing to meet in a week's time, and to try at least one of our services.

5

It was approaching lunchtime as I let myself into the vicarage to an enthusiastic welcome from Moses. Bending down, I returned the affection with a pat and stroke, and picked up the mail. Fortunately, Moses had not franked the post with his teeth. Neither were there any scratch marks on the door. A quick rifle of the fridge and bread bin and I headed out to the small metal table and chairs on the garden patio. Lunch was a cheese sandwich and a glass of sparkling water. The back of the vicarage faced south. I looked out over the lawn which had an offset cherry tree and a securely boarded perimeter with the odd flowering shrub: an economic pattern developed by the last vicar who was not a keen gardener. Moses trotted out to explore.

Taking out my mobile I switched off the silent mode. I'd set it on silent just before the funeral, which was a 10.20 service in the abbey, followed by interment in the council cemetery. There was a text message notifying a voice-mail a few minutes ago. I rang the voice-mail number.

'Hello Mr. Green. This is Marie Webb. Sorry to miss your call earlier today. I was with a client. I'm now clear 'til 3.00 p.m., if you care to try again. Otherwise I'll ring you later.'

Just before setting out for the funeral I'd dialled the business number on the card left by the person who damaged my car. A woman answered. She was briefed to expect my call, took my details, and promised that Marie would call back as she was engaged at that time. I finished the sandwich and dialled the number again. It went straight through.

'Hi Mr. Green? So sorry about your car. I'd just popped into the supermarket to get some drinks for a business meeting a little later. I would have waited for you but we'd had a number of problems and I was running late. You must have thought me terrible.'

Her voice was very clear. There was an intriguing mixture of warmth and femininity. Yet at the same time it was concise and business-like.

'Please call me John. Thanks for taking the trouble to identify yourself. A lot of people wouldn't have bothered. How would you like to progress this?'

'I suggest you get a couple of quotations for the job, send me copies, and give me another call. We'll pay for the repairs as a company expense, which is what it is. Once I've got the quotations, I'll do you a letter of authority to the garage we agree on.'

And that was that. Short and sweet. Direct and to the point. Reminded me of Laura, my girlfriend when I was a Ph.D. student and at the start of my clinical psychology career. She couldn't face the thought of being a clergyman's wife when I wanted to offer myself for holy orders. It would have meant living separately, engaged. Most of the small savings from my time as a psychologist had gone as a contribution towards theological training costs. A penniless priest was not much of a catch for a working professional woman.

OK, switch of the self-pity and be aware of the glow of satisfaction at the value I saw in my work. What better gift could I have than sharing in bringing the love of God to a wider group of people. The opportunity to bring healing to the suffering, and comfort to the dying. Joining in the important social events and sacraments of baptism, confirmation, and marriage, and aiding in the magical closeness of approach to our Lord in the Holy Communion.

I did face problems. Congregations at St. Mary's at Queensholme, and Coxton St. Giles, had dwindled under the last vicar. The situation was not helped by the poor worship facilities at St. Giles and the lack of a hall for social use. A few of the parishioners from St. Giles came to the midweek services at the abbey as there was no opportunity for these in the mixed-use community hall of St. Giles.

6

Visiting is an essential part of the work of a caring, and successful, parish priest. It can include house calls on both sick and well members of the congregation. I also regarded it as essential to visit many others in the parish as my job included caring for the whole community, not just those of my congregation. I asked my congregation to let me know of any who might benefit from my help. During daytime, one tended to meet the retired, the unemployed, and stay-at-home mums with babies or young children. Evenings until around seven-thirty were best left clear as people were eating.

I'd had a busy day today: the funeral this morning, and pastoral visits planned for afternoon and evening, hopefully ending with a pint at the Brandon Arms, by the lake. My first visit that afternoon was planned for Sasha, a young mum with a baby. One of the congregation, a community nurse, called Judy, had visited an elderly couple in the house next door. There she learnt that Sasha went out very little and seemed to cry a lot.

I turned off Waveney Way by a petrol station that had closed a few months earlier. It had been unable to compete with the prices at the supermarket not far away. The kiosk walls were covered in graffiti, and broken glass was scattered below sightless windows. One road further and I turned into a group of largely rented properties. Sasha lived in a small two-bedroom semi-detached house in the parish of St. Giles. The white weather-boarding around the top half of the house looked in need of a coat of paint. The small patch of grass at the front showed signs of a first cut, and the border had been turned over recently. The sun was shining on the blue front door as I knocked gently.

'Hello. I'm John Green, your local vicar from St Giles and St. Mary's. Do you have a few minutes to spare?'

The girl opening the door looked to be in her early twenties. She wore a yellow blouse, a pair of faded jeans, and sandals. Ginger hair reached down to her shoulders. She showed me into a living room that extended the depth of the house. Two budgerigars chattered away in a cage on a stand. There was a table with two wooden chairs, a couch, and a television that rested on bare floorboards. Through the rear window I could see a pram in the small, grassed, back garden. Sasha made two cups of coffee, and we sat down at the table.

'I can keep an eye on Emma from here,' she said.

'So how are you feeling in yourself, now that you have been a mum for a few months?'

'Oh. All right, I suppose.' Sasha stared into the distance for a few seconds. 'I ought to be on top of the world with a lovely healthy baby. She sleeps and feeds well. She doesn't cry much and has a lovely smile.'

'But?'

'But I get some terrible low feelings at times.'

'Low feelings? How low?'

'Well, if it wasn't for caring for Emma, I don't know what I might do. I feel so lonely, confused, worthless — at times.' Sasha burst into tears.

A tiny moth distracted my field of view as it landed and rested on the outside of the window, its white wings remaining open and placed very close to the glass. Just a centimetre of delicate wingspan, fine antennae sensing around, it was framed by the dark underside of a distant cloud. A fragile creature of beauty, it paused for a while on its short life's journey.

I resisted the urge to put my arm around the girl to comfort her. Instead I put my hand gently on hers and then withdrew it.

'The doctor said it was post-natal depression and normal, and gave me some tablets. I haven't taken any as I don't want them getting into Emma through my milk.'

'Sasha, in my experience there are usually perfectly normal psychological reasons for post-natal depression. It is not at all surprising that you have been feeling as you have, bearing in mind what has been going on for you. If you feel OK, we could talk about these and see what might be done to help. You said you feel lonely. Do you have many friends? How about Emma's dad?

I noticed that Sasha wore no rings.

'Danny? Well, he's stuck by me. Lives with me. But he's out most day times — at the job club, or trying to get a job, or with his friends. He's a carpenter and lost his job two months ago when the builders he worked for laid off a lot of staff. He trained as a cabinet maker but had to move to building to get a job.'

'How do you mean "He stuck by you"?'

'I think he blames me for getting pregnant. We were both working then and I wasn't on the pill, and we got carried away one evening. I used to work at a bookshop in the main street, promoted from the branch in Yarmouth. I occasionally see Anne from the shop. We shared a flat when I left home in Yarmouth and moved to Lowestoft for work.'

'So how about Mum and Dad?'

Sasha sighed and dropped her shoulders.

'Dad was rather a bully to Mum, my sister and me. That's really why I jumped at the offer of the job here. He was always very strict, wouldn't speak to me after I got pregnant — wanted me to have an abortion. He won't let Mum come to see me. I felt so released and free when I had a good reason to get away and move to Lowestoft. Now I feel cast out, worthless, tied, lonely. My family live too far away to baby-sit, even if Dad agreed to it. Danny comes from Ipswich, so his folks are too far away to help. We never get out on

29

our own. But I couldn't have had a termination, nor had Emma adopted. I sometimes feel God is punishing me heavily for a few minutes sexual activity.'

'Sasha, I think that most people who went through what you have been through would probably feel similar, pretty low. I don't think it is a matter of God punishing you. More likely, it's the circumstances around us, and sometimes the consequences of our own actions.

'We have a very small group of mums and babies or toddlers that meet in St Mary's abbey on a Tuesday at ten-thirty, we can't get the Coxton church room as it's regularly booked. You would be very welcome. They make a small charge for a cup of coffee, to cover costs. They are considering forming a baby-sitting group, where dad stays in and mum goes out to baby-sit maybe once a week. No money would change hands. You earn baby-sitting hours that way, which you could use to go out with Danny.'

Sasha brightened and thought that she might try the meeting next week. I pressed on.

'Have you thought about when you and Danny might have Emma baptised? It's probably the greatest gift that you could give her.'

'Would that be in the abbey? It's a beautiful old church. Much better than that communal room at Coxton.'

'I don't see why not. Perhaps it might be a way of getting your family and Danny's to visit. It might break the ice at home. Does Mum work? If not, and if the atmosphere thawed, maybe she could come over one day a week. She would get to see her granddaughter. You might even be able to go back to work on a part-time basis.'

Sasha's comment about St. Giles resonated. The room available for St. Giles was unattractive for worship. It was rarely available for worship or parish social use other than on a Sunday. Whereas, the abbey had an impressive atmosphere for worship. The plastic seats in the nave were admittedly ugly, but at least they allowed a flexible use of the floor space, as in the case of mums' and toddlers' meetings. A small block containing a kitchen, toilets, and a storeroom had been built onto the south side of the west end during the thirties. Architecturally it was rather a carbuncle, practically it was very useful. It made sense to me to combine the two parishes to use the abbey. A church hall would be a useful building project, if the money could ever be raised.

We chatted on a little longer. I left a visiting card and a copy of the combined parishes magazine, which detailed services, meetings, and their times.

7

I called at three more houses after leaving Sasha. The old couple next door seemed pleased to see me and thought they might try to get to church at Easter, which was only nine days away. I'd drawn blanks at the next two houses and retired to the Vicarage for evensong, a quick walk with Moses, and an early tea. It was about seven-thirty p.m. and I was out visiting again. A busy day, today.

Grange Road was a quiet cul-de-sac in the parish of St. Mary's. There was a touch of pink blossom on the cherry trees, interspersed with birch and beech. The houses looked mostly four bedroomed and generally sported two cars. I'd called on a number of residents previously and so started halfway along.

The first house I approached had a new looking estate car and a Mini on the drive. I could hear a TV as I rang the bell. The man who opened the door was wearing a tracksuit and clutching a bottle of beer.

'Hello. I'm John Green from St Mary's, your local vicar. Do you —'

'Sorry mate. Just got in after a hard couple of days. Not interested. Good night.'

The door closed quickly.

Forgive me Lord, there doesn't seem much point in pursuing things here at present. I pray that their hearts may be opened to become aware of your great gifts.

I walked around to the drive of a meticulously tidy garden next door. A green Ford, parked facing outwards, carried a permit for the car park of our local council offices. A pleasant young woman with shoulder length golden hair opened the door. She wore a red polo shirt and blue slacks. A faint smell of cooked fish caught my nose.

'Mum, Dad. It's a vicar,' she called, in response to my introduction. 'Come in, please.' She limped slightly as she led the way.

An artist's portfolio case and a folded wheelchair were tucked under the stairs, next to a rack of coats. I was shown into a light and spacious lounge. A gold-rimmed mirror over the mantelpiece caught my eye. It was full of colour from a painting on the wall behind me. I turned to take a better look. A schooner, with fore and mizzen sails set, was heading out towards the Lowestoft pier heads. The detail in acrylic was sharp and accurate, showing a vessel setting out optimistically from a secure haven, in good weather towards a clear distant horizon. A metaphor for life's journey?

'What a beautiful painting!'

'Yes. We're very proud to have it.' The reply came from a man in a light-blue shirt, navy tie, and neatly creased navy trousers. 'Rebecca painted it as part of her A Level portfolio.'

Don and Rose Coates introduced themselves. The young lady who had invited me in, Rebecca, smiled and disappeared. I could hear two girls talking and the sound of washing up. Don turned out to be the deputy planning officer for our local council. Rose worked as a teaching assistant, studied part-time, and was hoping to become a teacher now her children had all but grown up.

'Rebecca returned home today for the Easter break. She's in her second year studying Fine Art at Norwich University College of Art. Her twin brother Mark is doing Maths at Swansea on an R.A.F. scholarship. He won't be home for a week as he's doing a flying course.'

Don and Rose were clearly very proud of their children.

'I think Mark is more in touch with Rebecca than he is with us,' added Rose. 'Especially since her accident.'

My eyebrows must have crept up.

Rose continued, 'You might have noticed the wheelchair. Rebecca doesn't use it very often but keeps it handy in case her stump hurts. She has an artificial lower right leg and foot. She was knocked down by a drunken driver when she was sixteen.'

There was a knock on the lounge door and a thirteen-year-old girl entered.

'Would you like a cup of tea or coffee, or a cold drink?' She was introduced as Gail.

'Well, that's very kind of you. Thanks, but no. I really must be going very shortly.'

We chatted a little longer. Rose volunteered that she and Don were married at St. Mary's but had fallen away. I left the usual visiting card, magazine, and invitation. As I was stepping out, she added that they would join us for a service over Easter.

Dear Lord, thank you for a warm reception. Bless this family. May they grow in grace, happiness, and fulfilment?

Oh Lord, will you please excuse me, and indeed come with me, if I pop into the Brandon Arms for a pint, on the way home?

8

Lakeside, a road off Waveney Way, meandered through varied territory. On the left side, furthest from Lake Lothing, was a large area belonging to a developer. A number of small cul-de-sacs sprouted like alveoli off a bronchiole. Some sported smaller industrial units, others had larger two or three storey buildings. On the right, the boundary was initially the abbey grounds, before the road turned left running more or less parallel to Lake Lothing for some distance. Once past the abbey, there were disused old quays, workshops, and a derelict single storey shipping company office. The latter had stinging nettles growing in front of the boarded windows, and tiles missing from the sagging roof. To the side of an old slip, was a discarded rusting mast that looked as if it came from a large fishing boat. Nearby, a rusting submersible on chocks was a sign of more recent North Sea activity. At the edge of the yard was a cared-for bungalow, with a small but tended garden. It was probably originally a caretaker or watchman's residence, kept in use after the company closed. Next to it, the contrasting modern site of Southshore Boatbuilders, was the last on the right before I reached the Brandon Arms.

The whitewashed old lakeside pub was well supported. It drew on local businesses at lunchtimes, whilst the view towards the marina and Mutford Lock attracted a wide range of customers outside work hours. The main bar was an extension on the lake side of the main building. Beyond this was a patio with tables topped by square green umbrellas. A number of outside tables were occupied by people enjoying the mild late March evening. A quartet were playing 'Smoke gets in your eyes' as I made my way to the bar. I noted drums, bass guitar, violin, and a keyboard. An electric guitar rested on a stand beside the keyboard player.

'Evening, Vicar,' landlord Simon pulled me a pint.

'Evening, Simon. New group?'

'Yes, thought I'd try them out, just on a couple of Friday nights. They play dinner jazz, which suits our ambience. Seem pretty good, so far.'

I spotted Father Paul in conversation with a man at a table near the band. He waved. It was Paul who had alerted me to the band. I knew he played an old electric guitar as we'd had a couple of sessions with my keyboard. His guitar skill could prove useful as we hoped to get some youth activity going.

'Mind if I join you?'

He pulled a chair out as I approached. 'Martin, John. John, Martin.'

Martin looked to be in his late thirties.

'Martin's a boatbuilding supervisor at Southshore, next door.'

The band finished 'Smoke gets in your eyes' and the keyboard player made a joke about the 'No Smoking law'. They continued with 'Feelings'.

'Good, aren't they?' Martin turned back from looking at the group.

'Do you play, Martin?'

'I played saxophone in a small group for a number of years until two of the chaps moved away for other jobs. I gather you and Paul play occasionally.'

'Yes, that's right, occasionally. We'll have to see if we can get you involved in a local music event if we manage to get one going. Sort of "Queensholme's got Talent".'

We chatted on about music, the recent poor performance of

Norwich Football Club, and the latest banking disgrace.

'How's your business going in these hard, financial times, Martin?' I asked.

'Pretty good at present. The boss has just secured an order for four forty-foot semi-displacement boats for HMRC. This could lead to further business. Despite the poor economic climate, the private market in quality cruisers is holding up. We're actually looking for carpenters at present, particularly if they have cabinet making experience.'

That jogged a memory for me. I wondered about Sasha's partner, Danny.

'Strangely enough I heard of a young carpenter who is looking for work. May I suggest he contacts you?

Martin jotted down the name and telephone number of his company on a beer mat. 'Rupert Bishop is effectively the boss. He's a naval architect and involves himself in most of the major sales work. His father is technically our MD, but he is stepping back more and more through ill health. The grandfather started the Southshore business.'

I was vaguely aware of two women getting up from a table on the other side of the room. As they approached our table en route for the exit to the car park I recognised one as the rather special girl I had noticed in the supermarket. I stood and moved my chair to allow them more room.

'Thanks,' she said, as we exchanged glances and they slipped past.

Her face was oval with high cheek bones and dark eyebrows. There seemed an aura of care and confidence overlying a slight sadness. A woman at ease and yet a deep sparkle of passion and energy. I realised I was breathing deeply through my nose. Was I picking up pheromones or searching for them? There was a slight whiff of fragrance that reminded me of wild flowers. I nodded and we exchanged smiles. Then she was gone.

'Nice!' Martin commented as I sat down.

'Gorgeous.' I replied.

Paul glanced at me and smiled.

I was aware that she hooked a counter-transference of both fatherly love and desire to be closer. A pull to put my arms around her in comfort, but also to press my cheek against hers.

Dear Lord, please send your Holy Spirit to bless, guide, and protect this woman and her friend. I feel it inappropriate to call her sister or daughter. May she know the joy of your love?

The group took a break. Martin said he had to go and left us. Paul wandered over to look at the now idle instruments. The electric guitar was a later version of the old Yamaha which Paul owned. The keyboard was a newer version of my old Korg.

'We were just admiring your instruments' I commented, as the keyboard player returned.

He put his drink down on a nearby table. We introduced ourselves as interested amateurs.

'Would you be from the abbey?' he was looking at my dog collar. I nodded.

'I'm Mark Ransome. I teach music at the Endowed School. Our head mentioned your visit and kind offer of use of the abbey. Clare, our head of music, is due to contact you about staging a concert. Would we be able to use the organ?'

'If you play the organ, Mark, you'd be welcome. I doubt if we could provide an organist. We don't have a regular. One of my colleagues stands in at services but he suffers terribly from arthritis. I've been searching for someone who might be interested.'

Mark smiled, 'I studied organ and was organist and choirmaster at my last parish in Leicester. I moved to the school last September to be a head of house and teach music. Where I live in North Lowestoft, they have a regular organist. I help out very occasionally.'

'St. Mary's has a richly voiced organ with three manuals. You would be very welcome to come and try it. If you are free and would care to try being our organist, I have no doubt Father Rex would be very relieved. We don't have much of a choir as yet. They usually sing at Sunday evensong. It would be good if we could get them going for a sung Sunday morning Holy Communion as well.'

The rest of the musicians had returned and were waiting, so Paul and I took our leave.

'That was a very useful meeting,' said Paul as we left the Brandon Arms and headed homewards along Lakeside.

9

Steady rain fell outside. What a wet year we were having. The jet stream was more southerly than usual for this time of the year. It was feeding depression after depression over the British Isles. I was sitting in the vestry, reflecting, and waiting for June. She had been to the healing service after we met last Tuesday, and also to Holy Communion on Sunday. I had noticed her tears when she received communion, especially on Sunday. She agreed to meet with me again to talk things over a little further. I wondered whether there was an undisclosed concern that was causing additional anxiety. There was a knock, and then the vestry door swung open. June entered and removed her dripping raincoat.

'How are you getting on, June?' I asked after a few preliminaries and a short prayer.

'Very mixed. I sleep brilliantly some nights and terribly on others. This seems representative of how I feel in the day. I wonder if I'm a good enough person for God to help.'

'Actually, that sounds like a step in the right direction. If you were perfect, you wouldn't need help. Anxiety about old problems can cause a lot of stress. Is there anything you feel you could talk about?

June went quiet. Her eyes welled up. I waited patiently.

Please help her, Lord. Fill her with the grace and strength of your Holy Spirit. Please be with her.

'I find this very difficult to talk about. As a younger woman, I had a strong sexual appetite.' She paused, and took a deep breath.

'A year after we were married, Jack had to go on a three-month course. He was home at the week-ends, but stayed away during the week. Well, um, his best man came around to see if I was OK, at least that's what he said. Anyway, one thing led to another, and we had an intense secretive affair. It stopped a week before Jack finished his course. Steve got a promotion and moved away up north. I never told Jack, and I've not been unfaithful since. I haven't thought about it much for a long time. Somehow, recently, I've been wondering if the cancer is a punishment.'

She stopped, and sat quietly, looking down at the floor.

'June, it seems to me that sex is at times a wonderful gift, and at other times a great challenge and source of unhappiness. It is a measure of the boundless love of God, that when we admit our mistakes, he will forgive us. You may remember that St. John's Gospel tells us of the time that a group of scribes and Pharisees dragged a woman to Jesus and told him they had caught her in adultery, for which the punishment was stoning. Jesus said: "He that is without sin among you, let him cast the first stone." They all faded away and Jesus told her that he did not condemn her. He told her to go away and sin no more. Now that's a practically impossible thing to do. However, it often helps to focus on the positive side, consider what you can do that's helpful. After the incident with the woman, St. John reports Jesus as presenting a rather beautiful metaphor in this direction. Jesus said: "I am the light of the world: he that follows me shall not walk in darkness, but shall have the light of life." Amongst other things, following Jesus means largely doing things to help other people, even though others may mock you for that.'

'So, doing some sort of voluntary work might be indicated?' June looked up.

'Could be. It may help to ask God what you might do, and give him time to help you with some ideas. You may get a feeling towards more than one activity, but one may feel more rewarding to you than the others. It's not a matter of atoning for mistakes. Christ has done that in dying for us. It's rather about spending energy loving others, rather than being perpetually focused on feeling sorry about ourselves.

'There is a rich choice of opportunities to get in touch with God coming up over this Easter weekend. There may be one or more that appeals or fits your work schedule. Thursday evening, we shall have a Maundy Thursday Communion, rather than Compline. Friday at midday we have the Stations of the Cross which helps us to be aware, give thanks for, and meditate on Jesus' suffering and love for us. At 9.15 on Sunday we have a traditional Easter Family Service with Communion. And on Tuesday we have our Healing Service. You may feel ready to receive the Laying on of Hands.'

June looked a little more at ease and ready to go. We talked a little longer, said a prayer of confession, and then one of absolution and blessing.

June said thanks, and got as far as the door. There she paused, turned, and burst into tears.

'I'm so sorry taking up so much of your time —' she sobbed. 'there's something else terrible that I need to tell you.'

'Come and sit down and take your time.' I waited whilst June gathered herself to go on.

'I told you about my adultery, I feel I've broken a worse commandment, that of murder.'

I wondered what was coming. I didn't associate murder with her. She appeared a warm-hearted caring person. It came tumbling out.

'When I was eighteen, I found I was pregnant — I had an abortion — horrible word — termination. I was three months. I've felt awful about it ever since. It was so selfish of me. I've two grown-up children now. When each one was born, I thought of the brother or sister they might have had. I took a life. God might forgive me, but I can't. I feel I deserve to die.'

'June, many women who have a termination try to rationalise it.

In my experience, few, if any, totally succeed. Most feel at least a degree of guilt. So, what can you do? As before: admit to God what you feel you have done, or not done, that you feel was wrong — and know that his love is so great that he will forgive you and help you progress. And as before: listen to God's guidance and do something positive and constructive. You may remember the great Easter message of resurrection and the presence of Christ with us now, here. With this goes the consequence of life after death. From this it follows that your embryo child lives with God. Ask God to tell the child that you are sorry and to give the child your love. Endeavour to find more opportunity to pass on God's love to others through your life.'

I made a mental note to amend my Easter sermon to relate the Easter story to the souls of the departed as well as to the living. We said a formal confession and absolution again.

'Shall we say a prayer before you go? Will you say this after me?'

'Lord, I am not worthy that you should enter under my roof, but speak the word only and your servant shall be healed. Fill me with the healing grace of your Holy Spirit, and guide me in your ways.'

June left. I stayed a while longer, near to the reserved sacrament, to pray for our Lord's blessing on her.

10

It was just after eight-thirty as Moses and I walked smartly across Waveney Way in a break of the rush-hour traffic. He ran ahead a little, and onto the start of the abbey's grass surrounds. Moses proved a good companion and never strayed far from me when we were out together. Today I was expecting history and geography sixth formers accompanied by a few school staff, for most of the day. This was the second week of their summer term. They had started their abbey project last week.

The morning was mild and sunny, for a change. A few bluebells had appeared in the abbey grounds, almost overnight. Moses barked as a bumble bee swerved to avoid us on its way to spread the good news. I unlocked the south door, left it ajar to welcome visitors and allow Moses a wider degree of freedom, and put my bag in the kitchen. There was a sandwich lunch for me and some biscuits for Moses. Then I made my way to my stall to say the morning office.

I worked in turn through the collect for the second Sunday of Easter, and the readings of the day. I felt a nearness to the thousands who had worshipped in this great church ever since the monks had arrived nearly eight hundred years ago. At last I arrived at the intercessions which have always seemed one of the most important parts of the service to me. This was the place to give thanks and to ask our Lord's blessings and help for others.

Here, the Book of Common Prayer, around five hundred years old, rather disappointed me, when one read between the lines. It started with what I regarded as unchristian prayers of subjugation: prayers for the head of state, the government, bishops, — those in authority generally — and, I feel ashamed to admit, for priests and deacons. Only after that, might one be allowed to consider the rest of humanity. Put the people in their proper humble place, and exalt the high and mighty. As an ordinand in training I had bought a recommended book on intercessions by a leading bishop. It started off well enough, humorously pointing out the many mistakes made by those leading intercessions, and then moved on to suggested intercessions. To say the least, I was disappointed to find one of the first recommended intercessions was one asking for blessings on bishops.

My own strongest feelings and intentions frequently, and particularly at this time, were for peace in the world, and God's healing grace and comfort for the sick of the parish.

Within this I had special thought for June. The pageant of Easter had been and gone. June had come to our Stations of the Cross service on Good Friday, and also to the Easter Sunday service. She had not turned up for the Tuesday evening healing service in Easter week but had attended last night. She had presented herself for the laying on of hands. Paul, Rex, and I, jointly and gently laid our hands on June as she knelt at the communion rails and I said the words:

'In the name of God and trusting in his might alone, receive Christ's healing touch to make you whole. May Christ bring you wholeness of body, mind and spirit, deliver you from every evil, and give you his peace. Amen.'

June had seemed more at peace as she said farewell.

Morning office over, I felt a nose nudge my leg, and a gentle tug at my trousers. Moses led me away. Ten past nine. I followed him out through the south door to see three teachers and a number of sixth formers approaching the abbey.

'Morning, John,' that was Ben, head of history. With him were Jodie Fisher, a historical geographer, who taught both subjects, and Keith Booth, the head of geography. As well as those working on the history project, the school had chosen to use the opportunity for some work on surveying for students studying geography. A number of students were soon setting about the abbey grounds armed with clipboards, GPS', and theodolites. Several students with cameras were quickly at work recording both outside and within the abbey.

Keith came over. 'I've a friend who trains pilots at Norwich airport. He's been very helpful in the past. We hope to get some aerial photographs of the abbey grounds.'

He called together a group of students who were working between the abbey and Lake Lothing. 'Right Alan, tell the vicar some of what we reckon so far.'

Alan was a studious looking lad wearing black-framed spectacles. He was a little nervous.

'Er. Well. We made a rough sketch of the whole area last week and have been getting down to better accuracy. There are two groups of walls that make square shapes which we think are probably cloisters where the monks might have walked protected from bad weather. The larger one is just to the north of the original main body of the abbey and is rather longer than that section, the nave. We think this was probably the main cloister and that the nave of the abbey was originally longer than it is now.'

'Thank you, Alan.' Keith turned towards a girl in trews. 'Louise, what else have we noticed about the nave of the abbey?'

Louise was confident and clearly spoken.

'There are places where exposed stones indicate that the nave previously extended rather further to the west. Also, the west wall seems differently built to the other walls and has a relatively small stained-glass window and no door. So, we wonder if someone may have started to knock down the abbey, possibly at the dissolution of the monasteries, but then stopped, with a less than beautiful repair to a now shorter nave.'

'That's very interesting and well argued. Thanks.' I looked at both pupils and they smiled.

'OK, Alison, what about the smaller square? Let's walk over there.'

Keith led us due north from the north door, and then into a smaller grass square with surrounding wall remnants and the low walls of a building to its east.

Alison frowned and continued the story.

'We think that the remains of the building over there might have been an infirmary for the monks' work with the sick of their community and the neighbourhood. The walkway around this grass square would then have been the infirmary cloisters. We've been looking up other abbeys on the internet, and parts of Tintern Abbey are rather like St. Mary's.'

'Thank you, Alison. OK, Colin, tell us what you found.'

Colin, a tall blond boy, led us past the infirmary cloister remains and towards the lake. 'There are three rectangular depressions a little short of Lake Lothing, and the remains of a small rectangular building. It seems possible that these depressions may be the remains of three fish ponds, which the monks would have used to keep live fish in, as they didn't have refrigerators. The small building may have been a fish hut, possibly used for preparing fish for consumption or for smoking them.'

Colin looked a little nervous as Moses trotted past him, keeping well clear. I wondered if he might have been one of those who had originally been involved in abusing Moses.

'Well, thank you ladies and gentlemen, that's been very interesting. Thank you, Mr Booth.'

I watched them spread out and resume taking measurements and making recordings in their notebooks.

Later on, I watched Jodie inside the abbey, working with a number of students. On the western wall of the nearly central tower, where it rose above the transept was a coat of arms that was painted on a black rectangular board. Churchwarden Jim had turned up to watch proceedings and help where he could. He was rigging up an extension lead to the chancel where Ben was setting up floodlights aimed at the coat of arms. A little nearer to the transept was a camera on a tripod.

'I tried a photograph last week, John,' said Ben, 'but the light level was too low for a decent one. It's an interesting coat of arms. Mostly, the ones you find in old churches are from the late sixteen hundreds onwards, but there are a few, like this one, which date back to Henry VIIIth. They demonstrate the loyalty of the local people to the king rather than to the pope, after the dissolution of the monasteries. I even wondered whether this may be related to the west end of your nave. It looks as if the destruction of the building started but had then been halted.

'Whilst we've got the lights, I'd also like to photograph the frieze around the upper nave walls, if that's OK? I'll probably have to do three or four photographs on each side. Back at school we've a piece of software that allows us to join several overlapping horizontal shots into a panoramic view. The geographers have found it very useful for topographical photographs in their field studies.'

'Sounds great.' I replied. 'I would guess the frieze is quite old. It seems very much in the style of the Bayeux Tapestry but must be more recent. According to the board listing past abbots and vicars, the one in the Lady chapel, the abbey must have been founded around 1245.'

The frieze, that Ben mentioned, was in now faded pastel colours. It ran along both sides of the nave along the short depth wall that stretched over the pillars at both sides of the nave. It ended abruptly where the line of pillars met the west wall.

'The students will do the photography' said Ben. 'I hope this is all OK. We'll do some in the Lady Chapel. The raised tomb is very interesting: Admiral Sir Richard Brandon and his wife, 1595. I suspect he may be the Brandon of the 'Brandon Arms' and the hospital. Neither of the hatchments can be his. They didn't come in until roughly the end of the seventeenth century. But they may well be related to him, being located so near to him.'

I knew that hatchments, family crests on black square boards which had their diagonals horizontally and vertically, were funeral relics. This was the first church in which I'd served that had any. Which reminded me I'd given Ben the telephone number of the diocesan archivist?

'Have you had a chance to speak to the diocesan archivist?' I asked.

'Ah, yes. He said that all items of any significant interest were passed on to the county archivist in Norwich some time ago. I've spoken to the county person, and she put me on to their education officer, who has been very helpful. We've a visit planned.'

Lunchtime was soon with us. Both staff and students had brought packed lunches. Jim and I offered coffee from the kitchen to those who wanted it. I'd just finished my sandwiches, and Moses had demolished his biscuits and a bowl of water, when a man and woman walked in and nodded to the three members of staff. I recognised the man as the keyboard player from the Brandon Arms, Mark Ransome, and remembered that he taught music. The woman was short, plump, had a bossy bouncy walk, and blonde hair. She soon proved to be vivacious as well.

'Hi, John, if I remember rightly. This is Clare Parkinson, our head of music. I was asked to come over and comment on the abbey organ. I wondered if it would be OK to try it out as well. Clare and I have just popped over in our lunch break. Clare's keen to hear the acoustics here. We understand that you kindly offered the use of the abbey as a venue for a school concert.'

'Yes, indeed I did. I'll come with you over to the organ, but it's not locked.'

We walked over to the organ console at the entry to the north transept. Mark folded back the protecting doors. 'It's a relatively modern organ. There's even a date on the builder's plaque. "Harrison and Harrison. 1865." They're from Durham. This would have been a very early one of theirs. It looks as if there has been some renovation since the nineteen-eighties.'

He settled down and tried his feet on the pedals. Picking some music from his bag he switched on and selected some stops.

Clare watched as he as he started to play a piece I recognised as by Widor. Then she marched off down the nave, turning to listen every so often in various locations. She was soon back with Ben, four girls, and two boys in tow. Stopping Mark, she turned to me.

'Vicar, could we borrow you for a few seconds to join a small group of choral volunteers? You sound as if you have a fine tenor voice. I'd like to check how a choir sounds.'

She handed out some sheet music, Mark had his own and ran through the first few lines for us. It was John Rutter's 'Gaelic Blessing'. With that she pranced off down to the nave again. Mark was clearly watching her through the organist's mirror. She turned and waved her hand, and off we went. The accompaniment was deliberately very quiet and despite it being our first attempt together, I thought it sounded pretty good. After a minute or so, which seemed ages, Clare was back. She stopped the music and thanked everyone. Ben and the pupils departed.

'Beautiful acoustics, John, and not a bad tenor voice. Could we take you up on your kind offer to host a school concert, in July, after the exams have finished, if that's OK?'

We talked a while and agreed on a Friday evening, so as not to clash with our regular Tuesday and Thursday evening services. The school would also do some rehearsals, largely late afternoons.

'I wonder if I could ask another favour?' Clare had an appealing smile. 'I took over the running of a Lowestoft choir, the St. Cecilia Singers, a year ago. We are currently desperate for a rehearsal venue. We could of course do a fundraising concert for you.'

'As long as we keep clear of the regular services on Tuesday and Thursday evenings that should be fine. I'll have to officially clear both uses with the Parochial Church Council, but I'm sure they will be happy to help.'

Churchwarden Jim, who had been standing nearby and listening, nodded vigorously, 'It'll be good to have more use made of the abbey.'

A little later I wandered outside to watch the surveyors and photographers at work. As the sun had moved around since they started this morning, different directions were now favoured. Jodie approached.

'Would it be acceptable to chip a few samples of the building stone? There's just a chance that analysis might enable us to locate the type and origin of the material.'

I agreed, but asked her to be economic and use already broken-off elements where possible.

'Thanks. Of course.' She replied. 'Did you see the chap in the posh car stop along Lakeside. He approached a couple of pupils who were using a theodolite and asked whether they were surveying for land sale. He seemed to be relieved that it was a school project. The students were sensible and noted details of his car. It was a Bentley with the registration "A1 GB".'

I hadn't noticed the incident. Jodie marched off taking a geological hammer out of her back pack. I watched her with two pupils, instructing them in taking samples from the remains of various buildings. The samples were put in small food bags and tagged with the date and their location.

Before long it was time for students and staff to pack up. We said our farewells. Some headed back to school to catch coaches. Others headed directly for home. It had been an unusual and different day for me. I thanked Jim for his help and headed back into the abbey to say evening prayer, with Moses beside me.

11

It was three p.m. as I turned the recently repaired Golf out of the vicarage drive towards Beccles. I'd spent the morning at Lowestoft's Brandon Hospital, ostensibly to visit two parishioners, but in the end, there were also three non-parishioners whom I hope I was able to help. The first parishioner was a seventy-year-old man from Queensholme, who had recently been diagnosed with advanced prostate cancer. The second was a thirty-year-old woman who'd given birth the previous day to a little girl. It had been a difficult birth and the underweight baby was struggling with a serious blood disorder. I had spent some time listening and endeavouring to provide comfort to all. All chose to receive communion. After the hospital visit, Moses and I had lunch and then a quick walk amidst the rain showers that were clearing away eastwards.

    The built-up area of Carlton Colville at last gave way to the green farmland of Suffolk. To my right, the terrain dipped gently down to the Waveney valley, once a major water thoroughfare for trade. On my left, low hedges revealed light green fields of young wheat shoots, interrupted by the occasional copse. I felt my shoulders easing and breathed more deeply for a while.

    I planned to have a look around Beccles, some eight miles away, and then meet up with Mark Ransome, dinner jazz player, music teacher, and now our organist, I hoped. His group were playing at a riverside restaurant called The Wherryman. I intended to look around the waterside, have a bite to eat, and stay on a while to listen to the music.

Rounding a left-hand corner, I had to brake suddenly and stop for oncoming traffic. There was a green off-road vehicle on my side of the road. Its hazard lights were flashing and a woman was standing on the grassy verge looking at a very flat near-side tyre. Perhaps I could and should stop to offer help? I put my hazard lights on and pulled in behind.

'Anything I can do to help?' I asked as the woman looked up. She seemed vaguely familiar, pleasant looking and a few years younger than me.

'That's kind' she smiled. 'My colleague's phoning the rescue organisation we're in and they'll send a technician. Unfortunately, we were on our way to a meeting at the farm.'

The driver's door opened and a second woman got out and came around to the back. I recognised her very clearly as the attractive girl I'd seen at the supermarket and at the Brandon Arms. She looked at my car and then at me with a wry smile.

'I heard your kind offer. If you could be good enough to get one of us to a farm about five miles away, a little way off the Beccles road, that would be very helpful. There's someone on the way to deal with puncture, but by the time he's here and changed the wheel, we'll be a bit late. We're due at a meeting to check off some alterations we're having done to the labs.'

'I think you should go' said the other girl. 'The car is insured for both of us to drive. I'll follow on when the wheel has been dealt with.'

And so, it was agreed. Collecting a brief case from her vehicle, my passenger stepped past the door I held open and sat in my car.

'See you later, Anne.'

As I signalled and pulled out, I took in that the punctured vehicle was a green Discovery and noticed the registration number: 'B10 SOL'.

Turning to the girl, I caught a whiff of fragrance. I felt my pulse increase somewhat.

'I'm John.'

She smiled. 'I have a feeling we've sort of met before. You look younger than I expected, but are you a vicar?'

The registration number of the Discovery suddenly clicked: 'B10 SOL' stood for 'BioSolutions'. I smiled this time.

'You must be Marie?'

'Yes. Our cars must have been destined to meet again. At least I didn't prang yours this time. Sorry to digress but take the next left. I hope I'm not taking you too far off-route.'

We turned off onto a rather narrow road and soon caught up with a large tractor. We followed it for a mile before it turned into a farm yard. I told her of my intention to have a quick look around Beccles and take in some music. Marie explained that she and Anne worked in a small scientific business. She was a biological ecologist, whilst Anne was more on the botanical side. They had met as students. Anne's interest was in vegetables and fruit trees, whilst hers was in insects, and bees in particular. As research students they had done some work for a farmer. Now they had a mutual arrangement with him. They had continued to monitor his crops and help improve crop health and productivity. He had loaned them an old barn for an office and laboratory. They shared a flat in Beccles. The barn had just been renovated. This was the object of the meeting this afternoon. At the farm she had started to build up a number of hives of bee colonies. They would shortly be moving the business to the farm, from a laboratory and office off Lakeside in Queensholme.

'And you must work at that beautiful abbey that I drive past most mornings,' she reflected. 'The farm's on the right just around the next corner.'

I pulled up near to a builder's van parked outside a converted low, red brick and tile barn to the left of the drive in. At the right hand end a neat plaque identified the company. A sign over the adjacent strong wooden door said 'Reception.' A similar barn lay further away from the first and parallel to it. Both had clearly been refurbished and had double glazing and stout doors. A car park area lay between the further brick barn and a newer looking barn. Some way to the right of the barns lay a small farmhouse with flint covered walls, a steep tiled roof, and tall brick chimneys at each end.

'Thanks ever so. Perhaps you'll come back some time and I'll show you around. I hope I haven't delayed you from where ever you were going.' Marie grabbed her brief case and closed the car door behind her.

'You're welcome. I'm off to browse around Beccles and have a snack at The Wherryman, where our organist's dinner jazz group is playing this evening.'

We said farewell and shook hands. She didn't snatch her hand away. There was a firmness in her hold, feminine not crippling, altogether very pleasant.

'Until the next time,' I smiled and drove away.

Fifteen minutes later I was negotiating a complex of narrow one-way streets having entered Beccles from the north, almost parallel to the river. I'd missed the earlier turning recommended by Mark, instead following the routing signs for Beccles. Despite living in Queensholme for several months I'd never ventured into Beccles, having bypassed it on the few occasions I'd been to Norwich. The narrowness of the streets and the many vintage buildings suggested that a strong influence of the eighteenth and earlier centuries had survived. I endeavoured to park near to an imposing large church with a strangely separate bell tower, but the one-way system led me off in a different direction. At last, between two buildings I spotted a glimpse of moored boats and the sparkle of sun on the water. Shortly, I pulled onto The Wherryman's car park.

On foot, I picked my way uphill towards the town centre. There was a strange aroma in the air. As yet I have not discovered its origin, but it reminded me of rice and Chinese restaurants. Perhaps it was from the waste products of a brewery. Eventually I arrived at the town hall, a very precise and geometric building. Symbolic of officialdom and complicated byelaws, I wondered?

Almost opposite, on the highest land in the town, was the building that dominated Beccles: the parish church of St. Michael, the Archangel. I just had to cross over and have a look. It was impressive and yet strange. The tall and substantial bell tower stood defiantly alone and separate, several yards to the south of the east end of the main church building. The green carpet of churchyard swept around the occasional tree, and dropped steeply away from the west end of the church, towards the river. There was a hubbub of children cutting through on their way home from school.

Inside, the church was cool and spacious. Somehow it seemed plain and disappointing in comparison with the abbey. I put this down to the windows. Apart from the east window, they were nearly all of plain glass. I was spotted by a colleague of the cloth, who was carrying a prayer book. He was limping and looked to be approaching retirement, but there was a sparkle in his eye. He explained that the church was old, there was a thirteenth century font, but had been badly damaged by a fire in the late sixteenth century, a little before his time. He was about to say the evening office and invited me to join him, sitting in the choir. Afterwards, we chatted for a while. He turned out to be a Franciscan, and a friend of Paul. He eventually mentioned Archdeacon Imogen.

'I believe that she of the motorbike may visit you before long. She seems to have been doing the rounds of some parishes with high or slightly high church practice. I don't think she approves. One of my parishioners is her secretary. It appears the Venerable Imogen has gone on holiday in Majorca. She is staying in a hotel but knows someone with a motor yacht. So, it's interrupted her schedule.'

'Thanks for the warning. Paul did mention a possible visit. I'm off for an amble along the waterside.'

The earlier showers slipped away as the cold front tracked eastwards, being replaced with a clear blue sky and a drop in temperature. After a teacake and pot of tea at a riverside cafe, I'd pulled my coat tighter and set off for a walk downstream. As the sun slipped lower, I'd followed the riverside path at first northwards and around a long curve to the east. As the evening approached, the breeze dropped with patches of fine cats' paws ruffling the water surface. There were a few early holiday makers with their boats moored up along the river bank. A few were fishing, although I had a feeling it might be the close season as there were no riverbank anglers around. A herd of grazing cows gave me an occasional glance. I experienced the waterscape as invigorating, inspiring, and yet calming, perhaps related to my boyhood by the Tyne. After three-quarters of an hour, I'd turned and retraced my steps until I ended up back at The Wherryman.

At approaching nine p.m., I was finishing a tasty plaice and chips washed down with a light lager. Mark and his group had played for an hour. My reverie was interrupted by a pat on my shoulder,

'May we join you?'

It was Marie, Anne, and an athletic looking chap with a round smiling face. He was introduced as Jake, Anne's boyfriend. We joined a nearby empty table onto mine. Marie and Anne insisted on getting the drinks, and I accepted a coffee. Jake and I chatted whilst they were away. He proved to be a local solicitor, thespian, and rugby player. He'd met Anne at an amateur dramatic society.

'Anne said this was a good group which she'd heard before. It makes a change from kids bashing away on guitars with a loud and distorted output. These chaps have melody, harmony, and improvisation; altogether more sophisticated.'

'Do you play anything, Jake? Apart from rugby.'

'No. Although both Anne and I have made the occasional choral contribution when our society puts on a musical.'

The girls returned with a tray of drinks. Anne sat next to Jake, Marie sat next to me and turned towards me.

'We usually eat out on a Friday night. We're a bit late tonight after getting the puncture repaired.'

I caught a brief hint of that fragrance in the air and realised I was drawing more heavily through my nose than usual. Pheromones? There was the very pleasant excitement of having an attractive woman next to me, combined with the warmth and uncertainty of temporary companionship. The amplification was turned up on my senses.

After a short break, during which Mark came over for a brief chat, the group restarted with a slow tempo 'Moonlight becomes you.' Jake and Anne took to the pocket-sized dance floor. I turned towards Marie

'The title of that tune always seems a dubious compliment to pay a woman. It might be interpreted as "You look better in the dark."'

We chatted inconsequentially for a while. Then she asked whether I had always been in the church.

'No. I trained and worked for a couple of years as a clinical psychologist, before I felt I could help the people more through faith.'

The music changed to 'Have you met Miss Jones?' I noticed that both our feet were tapping. I plucked up courage.

'Would you care to dance?'

It was only a pocket-sized dance area, shared with Anne and Jake, and another couple. We started ballroom style which had the benefit of allowing me to hold Marie. With the lively tempo and little room to progress, we frequently changed to freestyle on a ha'penny. I noticed Mark smiling at me and chatting to his fellow musicians. The piece concluded shortly after. It was followed by a similar tempo tune 'Love walked right in.' Marie was a lithe and fluent dancer. We moved in and out of hold. The next tune was a slower tempo. I searched my memory and recalled the tune was 'Li'l darling.' I noticed Mark and his boys smiling and watching us. I reckoned they were engaged in a musical leg pull. After that we returned to our table.

'Thanks,' I said. 'You're a very good dancer. I hope I didn't stand on your toes too often.'

'Thank you, kind sir. I did do ballet until I was seventeen.'

It was turning out to be a very pleasant evening. Then my mobile vibrated.

'Sorry about this.' I looked and saw it was the hospital calling. 'I'd better take the call, if you don't mind?'

I walked outside. The hospital was calling to say that the mother of the baby struggling to live, that I had seen that morning, had asked for her baby to be baptised as she was not expected to survive that night. With heavy heart for two reasons, sadness for the mother and disappointment at the curtailment of my time with Marie, I made my way back to the table.

'I'm so sorry but I need to go. It was the hospital about a mother wanting her dying child baptised.' I looked at Marie. 'Would it be all right to give you a call next week? I still have your card.'

'I'd like that.' She smiled and held out her hand, which I held for a second before giving it a gentle squeeze, which was returned.

12

It was a cold sunny Monday morning as I walked along Lakeside on my way to visit Rupert Bishop of Southshore Boatbuilders. I had unlocked the abbey and said Morning Prayer. High on my list of intercessions was prayer for Jane and Brian Lowe and their infant, who had been christened as 'Mary Elizabeth' late on Friday night. It was doubtful whether Mary would survive the night, although her consultant was intending to do a blood transfusion. This was expected to be in the early hours of Saturday morning when the blood, of a rare group, arrived from another hospital.

Inland, away from the lake, stretched the business park with its mix of office buildings and industrial units. A green noticeboard proclaimed in gold letters that this was the Lakeside Business Park operated by Blacke Holdings (Lowestoft). To the side of one of the entrances to the park was another green noticeboard carrying the names of the companies and their unit addresses. Amongst these I noticed 'BioSolutions' which I remembered as Marie and Anne's company.

I wondered what Marie was up to. On our journey to her new lab she had said that this week she would be staying with her grandparents near Ipswich for a little over a week, studying fruit trees on a large farm in south Suffolk. Somehow it was hard to visualise her in wellingtons, taking samples of soil and fruit tree blossom, and trapping insects.

Approaching Southshore Boatbuilders I passed the remnants of a deceased shipping company yard. The disintegrating building had window high nettles. A once proud board carrying the designation 'Office' now hung vertically on one end with paint flaking off it. Grass and brambles sprouted through the concrete yard and quayside in nature's battle to reclaim the site.

In contrast, Southshore's car park had recently been resurfaced with tarmac. A gardener was weeding flower beds which were covered in yellow and blue crocuses. A modern industrial building stretched back towards the water, its sides punctuated by large sliding doors. Signs pointed the way to the reception office near the Lake Lothing end of the building. I paused to take in the company's considerable waterside frontage with its marina pontoons, a slip, and a large crane. There was even a relic from Lowestoft's more substantial boat building days: two men were jet-washing below the waterline of a large white motor yacht which was perched precariously on blocks at the bottom of a small dry-dock. It all reminded me of the Tyneside yard where my father worked as a naval architect.

Rupert Bishop's office looked out over the yard towards the lake. Two computers, one with a large display, a large printer, and a long table took up most of one side of the office. I suppose that these days most of a naval architect's work is done using computer aided design. Two low-level cupboards, a chair on casters, three easy chairs, and a coffee table completed the furnishings. Two photographs graced the walls. One showing a pilots' power boat at speed was complemented by a second of a trawler-styled motor-sailer in a stiff breeze.

'Thanks.' I looked up as the secretary placed two cups of coffee and a plate of biscuits on the coffee table.

'Good to see you,' Rupert Bishop paused to quickly check my card, 'John. Karen only gets out the chocolate biscuits when we have visitors.'

The girl smiled and withdrew.

The man sitting next to me looked to be in his early forties. He wore a bright red open-necked tailored shirt and navy-blue trousers with a sharp crease. He had long artistic fingers.

'I'm Rupert, naval architect and acting MD. I gather it was you who introduced Danny Murray to us. He's settled in well and seems to be just the sort of chap we were looking for. But — how can I help?'

'Well, technically your company is a parishioner of the abbey church of St. Mary. It seemed only polite to call and offer any help we can. Staff sometimes run into distressing times. They might find it useful to be able to access speedy local help. This could save your company on sick leave. A number of local organisations now display our notice of service times, groups, and help numbers. Perhaps you could display this notice on yours.'

I paused to pass Rupert a laminated notice.

'Additionally, you, or your staff, may find our Tuesday eight a.m. service helpful. A slim Morning Prayer is the base, with intercessions specially arranged. It's designed to help people be inspired in their work, to open their minds to new ideas in the service of others, to reduce undesirable stress, and to give thanks for success. Of course, if you need any new vessels blessed, I would be happy to do that.'

'Might I ask where you studied Naval Architecture?' I added, changing tack.

'Southampton University.'

'My father did too. He reckoned they had a very good course in his day. I believe they have a testing tank as well. I notice that you have photographs of both power and sailing boats. Do you build both types?

'No. As you possibly recognise, the motor-sailer is a Fisher 37, mine in fact. We largely specialise in semi-displacement power boats. They overlap two markets, work boats and pleasure craft.'

We chatted a short while longer. I shared my sailing experience on my Dad's slightly smaller motor-sailor, and then stood to take my leave.

'Have you had any approaches from Gregor, yet, for sale of the abbey land?'

'No.' I shook my head alarmed and perplexed. 'Who is Gregor?'

'Gregor Blacke. He's a wealthy local developer. He owns the business park on the left of Lakeside, as you drive towards Southshore. I know he's just acquired the derelict yard next door. I hear that he's approached the Brandon Arms. He's contacted us with a view to buying our site. He seems to be in cahoots with the local councillor, Bruce Jackson, who is chair of the authority planning committee. They appear to be working on a local development plan to improve the area and draw more people into Lowestoft. There's talk of building a large waterside entertainment complex with eating places, a multi-screen cinema, fitness centre, and a nightclub. At least that's what I can gather.'

'Do you intend to sell?' I asked.

'Well. My father is the major shareholder. He's tempted as a way of realising some cash from the business. Mr Blacke owns some land near the fishing harbour and wants to develop expensive waterside housing and a marina. He would like us to run his marina and a smaller maintenance boatyard there. However, we'd lose our small dry-dock, and we'd have to move any manufacturing business elsewhere, possibly to an inland industrial site.'

'You would lose the sensory benefits of the sight, sound and smell of water when potential customers visit.' I offered.

'Absolutely. Personally, I'd rather stay put. We have invested in a modern factory unit and bought the dry-dock over the last ten years. Our reputation is spreading. We've recently achieved an order for four forty-five-foot launches for Her Majesty's Revenue and Customs. We've been doing annual maintenance on a number of large motor yachts since we bought the dry-dock. Gregor has a large boat, but he keeps her in Palma, Majorca.'

I had a flashback to the sixth formers and their survey of the abbey land. 'Strangely enough we had some sixth formers surveying the abbey grounds for a history project, a couple of weeks ago. They reported a chap in a Bentley stopping and asking whether they were surveying the land for sale purposes.'

'That sounds like him. The abbey land does look a bit wild and untidy in places, but it adds a sense of history and tranquillity. I'd be sorry to see it go.'

I walked back along Lakeside feeling threatened and low in spirit.

13

The rain had ceased late afternoon leaving thin higher clouds and a chilly wind. Jim was sweeping the floor under the tower as I made my way from the vestry to prepare the altar for our Tuesday evening service. June was assisting him with a dust pan and brush. I greeted them both.

'Has something been spilt, Jim.'

'No. Periodically I seem to find a little mortar or stone dust around here. It's probably wearing away from the floor slabs, or may be loose mortar between them.'

June was a regular participant now and used the opportunity to pray for others. Jim, for some time the sole churchwarden, had done much to keep the services of the abbey going during the interregnum, before I was inducted. I'd learnt that he had been the skipper of a large drifter until ten years ago when the shipping company nearby had closed down. After that he had worked as skipper of a boat servicing North Sea oil and gas rigs for the next six years until he retired. His wife, May, was a regular at our main Sunday service. They had a married daughter. When calling at their home I had commented on a photograph of a young man who looked like a younger version of Jim. He proved to be their son, Mark, who had drowned at sea, working on a trawler, whilst endeavouring to save the life of another crew member. Although this occurred some fifteen years ago, I doubted whether parents ever get over the loss of a child who dies before them.

So much of a parish's conversation with its priest tends to be general chitchat, making it difficult to get at the ways in which we may be able to help. I tried to seek out one-to-one occasions in which people can more easily raise concerns. At times I ached to put my arms around Jim, in compassion.

The lights were on under the tower and in the choir where we would sit. I walked to the Lady Chapel to spend five minutes in quiet prayer and meditation. Mostly I relaxed to endeavour to be a conduit for our Lord's love. I prayed for our hearts to be open and aware of God's presence and his healing grace of wholeness. Then I sat in my stall in the choir and waited.

The sound of women's voices, and the clicking of heels on the stone flags, broke my reverie. Alice Broad and Judy Pope greeted us cheerfully as they took their seats. Alice was the tall, lithe, retired matron of the Brandon Hospital. I had persuaded Alice to be a second churchwarden when our annual meeting approached last spring. Judy was a community nurse, although I still tended to think of her as the district nurse. She frequently contributed to our services giving the intercessions or in other ways. She was contemplating offering herself for ordination or reader training. We had talked about this a few times. Her two daughters were grown up. Rose, the elder one at twenty-seven, was a young G.P. in Ipswich, Sylvia was an Emergency Department nurse at the Brandon Hospital. As far as I could make out, Andrew, Judy's husband, was moderately supportive. He was a council manager in the Leisure Department.

After a brief chat, I moved to light the altar candles. As I then made my way towards the vestry a gaggle of five people entered the south door. I shook hands with each. Rex said a quick 'Hello' and disappeared into the vestry to robe. Next was Jodie, the historical geographer from the Endowed School. Much to my surprise and delight she was followed by Jane and Brian, the parents whose ill baby I had christened eleven days previously.

Jane was carrying her baby in one of those basket contraptions. Apparently, Mary Elizabeth had improved dramatically after her transfusion and was discharged four days later. Her parents wanted her participation in the healing service to optimise her future. I had a few words with them outlining the service. They were happy to have her specifically mentioned in our prayers.

The last person was new to me. She was tall and slim woman in black, who looked to be in her mid-thirties. Her fine-featured face with high cheek bones was topped with artistically arranged golden hair.

'Hello. Welcome to St. Mary's.' I said. 'I don't think we've met before. I'm John.'

'Hello. Lucy. I just wanted to see what your healing service was like.' She gave a smile, with a hint of strain.

'Perhaps we could have a brief word afterwards, if you have time? I could answer any questions and see how we best might help you. By the way, for this service we sit in the choir, where the monks sat many years ago.'

At six-thirty I walked in to the choir preceded by Paul, Rex, and Judy. Judy would act as assistant in the giving of Holy Communion, Paul and Rex would join me for the laying on of hands.

'Please kneel or sit. As we gather together to ask for Our Lord's healing love on others and ourselves, let us be silent for a few seconds to remember that he is with us now.'

After a few seconds I moved to the opening prayer:

'Christ taught his disciples to love one another. In his community of love, in praying together, in sharing all things and in caring for the sick, they recalled his words: "In so far as you did this to one of these, you did it to me." We gather today to witness to this teaching and to pray in the name of Jesus the healer, that the sick may be restored to health and that all among us may know his saving power.'

A little later, Jim led our intercessions 'Lord, grant your healing grace to all who are anxious, sick, injured, or disabled, and to those who are gathered here this evening, that we with them may be made whole and better able to serve You and our fellows.

'We thank you for the recovery of baby Mary Elizabeth and ask your continuing blessing on her and her parents, Jane and Brian.'

After further prayers for the wellbeing of the congregation, the parish, and the world at large, we moved to the Laying On Of Hands. Jane and Brian brought their infant forward. I was joined by Rex and Paul.

'In the name of God and trusting in his might alone, receive Christ's healing touch to make you whole. May Christ bring you wholeness of body, mind, and spirit, deliver you from evil, and give you his peace.'

After the service Lucy and I returned to sit quietly in the choir stalls. She confided her wish to participate further. She and her partner, Matthew, were about to start their third and final attempt at IVF. She had lost a baby at three month's pregnancy during their previous attempt. Experience in the health service had shown me the adverse effect that anxiety and stress can have on conception and pregnancy. I explained this and suggested prayer and separate counselling sessions. She agreed to meet me the next evening and to ask Matthew to meet me an hour later.

14

A little nose pushed under my hand which was resting on my knee. Moses didn't usually bark in the abbey. He was trying to tell me that he had heard the latch on the big south door. It was ten past nine and I had just finished saying morning office. Sixth formers were due in the building and its grounds until lunchtime. A group came in, said 'Hello', and made their way to the tomb at the southwest of the high altar. They arranged flash-lighting and photographed the text around the top of the tomb.

Somewhat later I met Ben with another group of students looking at an A3 aerial photograph of the abbey and grounds.

'It shows up the infirmary, two cloisters, and the fishpond depressions quite well, as it was taken in the early morning when the shadows were pronounced.'

He handed the photograph over to the group, had a few words with them, and then came over to me.

'There is a slightly darker rectangular patch just inside the infirmary cloister, opposite to where the door would probably be. It might be a grave, although the graveyard would usually be further out into the grounds.

'We had a very interesting visit to the county archives. They had a box of records that came from the diocese some time ago and had not received much attention to date. There was a grant of land at Queensholme and fishing rights to the Abbot of St. Benet's, from a Fitz Osbert family of Somerleyton dated 1243. St. Benet's was a Benedictine monastery adjacent to the River Bure, below Horning. It's in ruins now. The title of Abbot passed to the Bishop of Norwich in Henry VIII's time. It looks as if St. Mary's is a daughter foundation of St. Benet's.

'We also found records of baptisms, marriages, and burials at the abbey. They go back to about sixteen hundred. The county people are helping us trace the Brandon family lineage. The students are finding out what a lot of hard work historical research can be.'

Ben spoke quickly and with great enthusiasm. He kept moving from one foot to the other and looked at me frequently.

'Well, Ben, you have been busy. How very exciting.'

'It is. I've been to see my old tutor at Cambridge. He was excited too. He is a medieval specialist. He suggested that I should register for a PhD. I've spoken to our head at school, she was very encouraging and will try to get me a little time off during the week.

'Oh, I nearly forgot, John. One of the boys has a metal detector. Would it be OK to use it in the abbey grounds? I'd be particularly interested to see if we could pick up anything near the infirmary.'

'Ben, I don't see any problem using the detector. However, we wouldn't be able to do any digging without a faculty from the diocese. A faculty is a legal authorisation. It can take a couple of months to get. I suspect that we would have a better chance if your Cambridge tutor was involved as well.'

'That's great. Thanks a lot. Of course, we have to see whether we detect anything first.' He bustled off to a group of students near the fish hut remains.

15

Six-fifteen. The evening May sun brightly illuminated the small rose window in the west wall of the abbey as I made my way from the Lady chapel to the vestry. I had said evensong on my own and included Lucy and Matthew Baines in my intercessions. Lucy was due at the vestry at six-thirty, to be followed an hour later by Matthew, if he agreed. Clare Parkinson and her St. Cecilia Singers were due at seven, having started using the abbey a week earlier. They would hold their sessions in the choir. The vestry, off the south transept, was well insulated from the sounds inside the abbey by thick stone walls and a heavy wooden door.

Lucy arrived a fraction early, which I read as both courtesy and enthusiasm. We shared a short introductory prayer asking for awareness of our Lord's presence and for acceptance of his healing love. Then I shut up and let her begin.

'Matt and I have been married for seven years. We've been trying for a baby for five. We've had two shots at IVF, the last one seemed to be going all right, but I had a miscarriage at three months. That was about eighteen months ago. The doctor said we could have one more go. We're due to see the specialist in about four weeks' time. I, we, wanted to do all we could to help.'

'Has your doctor suggested any counselling?'

'No. I did ask about it as friend suggested it might help. Doctor Marshall gave me a month's supply of tablets. I think they were antidepressants. He said he thought counselling was a waste of time.'

'Hmm.'

I couldn't help grunting. This was the same doctor that June had found very unhelpful.

'May I ask how old you and Matt are?

'I'm thirty-six and Matt's forty-one.'

'Have you considered adopting?'

'Yes, but we got the impression we're too old, and we'd rather have our own, if possible.' She took a deep breath. 'Can you tell me how this healing thing works?'

'Well,' my turn to take a deep breath and then try to express a most wonderful phenomenon in a few words. 'In the healing service we say "Receive Christ's healing touch" as in His name we place our hands on you. You might like to regard this as a physical symbol as the Holy Spirit flows into you. With a deeper trust in God you can let go of anxiety and fear, and grow in confidence and a sense of wellbeing. It's a sort of tuning of body, mind, and spirit.'

'How does that help the body, which seems my biggest problem at the moment?'

'It's very easy to overlook the considerable interaction between body, mind, and spirit. There are studies that show that communities of the faithful, such as nuns, tend to have a longer average life. It's a fairly common experience that worry, anxiety, or perhaps we might say indigestible issues, can produce problems of the digestive system. That's the mind interacting adversely with the body. Equally, there have been several studies that show that reducing anxiety and maintaining a positive outlook can improve the immune system. Of course, there are ways that the health service and you yourself can help.'

'So, what can I do?'

'Regular Holy Communion and providing time to listen to and talk to God can make it easier for him to help you. You can, and should, develop your awareness and response to your own guidance system, your feelings, picking out those that seem right.'

I went through a number of areas of human experience that I have found helpful to explore in psychological and spiritual counselling. The list included friends, family, romance, finance, self-expression and fulfilment, exercise, hobbies, having fun, helping others, spiritual nourishment, and work.

Lucy wore a slight frown. I waited, having talked more than I wanted to.

'I don't know quite what to say.' She thought for a moment. 'I don't think we have any major problems. Matt had to have four new tyres for his van last week, he's an electrician, but he has a reserve fund for that sort of thing. My work's OK, I have a hairdressing business with a friend. Mum and Dad are well and waiting for a grandchild. I'm an only child. It seems as if everything has been the same for some time — when I think about my life — it is a bit grey. No real problems except getting pregnant, but no real excitement. Matt isn't as cheerful as he used to be. I suppose we both blame ourselves for me not getting pregnant, although they tell us it isn't anyone's fault. I suppose, now you make me take stock, life could be happier. Maybe we ought to do more to help other people in a way that isn't for money — I don't know what? I listen and talk to my customers and endeavour to help them be cheerful. I'm pretty sure Matt is similar although he isn't usually right next to his customers like I am. We do try to keep an eye on Mum and Dad.'

'What do you do to let your hair down, to have a bit of fun?'

'Watch TV, I suppose. We go out to eat once a week. I used to play hockey, but stopped three years ago when we started the IVF treatment. I don't really feel like going nightclubbing, although I used to like dancing. A bit boring isn't it.'

'So, the overall impression I pick up is that there is a sense of guilt about not getting pregnant, possibly increased by the odd comment from Mum or Dad. Then on top of that, there isn't anything that gives a real sense of fun, fulfilment or excitement.'

'So, what do I, we, do to help?'

'Well, at this stage it's about relaxing, listening to yourself and God, and exploring options for making life more fulfilling. Interestingly, you asked "What do I, we, do?" It's useful to have both the time and interests for individual fulfilment, and to have something that you both share. Now seems to be the time to explore ways of having more fun, possibly in the form of a hobby. Is there anything that springs to mind, something you'd really like to do?'

Lucy thought for a minute or so. Her face alternated between frowning and looking blank.

'Anything vigorous like hockey, which I used to enjoy, is out for quite a while. I'll have to think about it.'

I opened a drawer in the filing cabinet, pulled out two sheets, and gave them to Lucy.

'Take this away and see if it throws up any ideas. It's an alphabetical list of hobbies and activities which is there to help. It's not so easy to just think of something out of the blue. If you think of any which aren't on the list please let me know so that I can add them. If you can, try to find several which stimulate some interest, then give them a while before you pick a couple which seem the most interesting to explore further.'

She brightened up. We said a couple of prayers together and then she left. As Lucy went through the big oak door into the south transept, I caught the sounds of Clare rehearsing phrasing with her Singers.

16

After Lucy left, I sat in the south transept listening to Clare rehearsing her Singers in the Ave Maria often attributed to Giulio Caccini, a sixteenth century Italian musician. Some say it was actually composed in 1970 by a Russian lutenist called Vladimir Vavilov. The sparse text is set to a penetrating and beautiful melody with a romantic and gently progressing harmony. It is commonly arranged for solo instrument and string or organ accompaniment. Clare's arrangement was for soprano solo and choral accompaniment combined with a soft organ background, which she played on her keyboard. The abbey acoustics made the combination spellbinding. The only frustration was Clare's periodic halting to direct all or part of the Singers to repeat a phrase to improve diction or timing. She was incisive but encouraging.

I wondered what Archdeacon Imogen would make of a prayer to the Virgin Mary. Would she regard it as heresy and popish? Personally, it seemed an entirely reasonable action to request the spirit of a very special saint to add her prayers 'for us sinners, now, and at the hour of our death.'

'Sorry I'm a bit late.' Matt interrupted my reverie.

I'd waited fifteen minutes for him. This suggested a little reluctance on his part. It alerted me to the likelihood that he experienced a loss of self-esteem in seeking help. On average, men are less ready to accept help than women. We made our way into the vestry.

Lord, please give me humility and grace to help this my brother.

'I imagine you've been going through a difficult and challenging time?' I offered.

I felt that I must endeavour to frame my opening remarks in empathic and male terms.

Thank you, Lord, for the guidance.

'You can say that again.' Matt's face lost a little of its tautness. He moved perceptibly in his chair.

'To be honest, I wonder if we need to adjust to being childless. It's such a shame, as I know Lucy would make a lovely mum. Do you think you can help?'

'I do think that faith, the love of God, and the health service can help. No one can guarantee that Lucy will become pregnant, but really putting your trust in God will help you to get the best outcome either way. The fact that your doctors are happy to do another IVF procedure indicates that they rate a reasonable chance of it working.'

We went through much the same ground as Lucy and I had covered. Then I asked:

'What do you do to let your hair down?'

'That's a sore point really. We both have enjoyed sport. Lucy used to play hockey and I play rugby. I used to play county rugby, but my left knee is giving problems and I'm dropping down through the teams now. Getting old and frustrated. Most of the other players in our club third team have the physical ability but rather less skill. I have the skill but am losing the physical ability. I haven't played for a few weeks now and feel doubtful about next season.'

Matt struck me as more at ease in conversation than I'd expected, and perhaps more of a people person. Maybe a companionable hobby would suit him.

'Would you say that you are generally happier when in company, or do you prefer more time on your own?'

'A bit of both, but probably the former as I do enjoy good

company.'

I gave him the same list of potential hobbies as I'd given Lucy, and the same basic advice.

'Given what you've told me I wondered if you'd considered rugby coaching? Or, as a complete change you might enjoy amateur dramatics. Your electrical skills could be very useful backstage, or provide a gentle introduction before you stepped onto the boards. But do take time to explore the list and see what takes your fancy.'

We worked through similar spiritual ideas of time to relax, reflect, trust, listen, ask, praise, and give thanks in drawing closer to the source of infinite love.

'So, with all of God's love, do we really need a healing service?' Matt looked at me and smiled.

'Our Lord's love will be equally strong whether you choose to use a healing service or not. However, for many people, participation in a healing service helps them to more easily open their hearts to receive.'

We talked a little longer and then concluded with a prayer. Matt decided the healing service would probably help him. As he was leaving, he offered:

'Should you need any small electrical jobs done around the abbey, I would be happy to provide free labour.'

I thanked him, shook hands and followed him out into the south transept.

17

After Matthew left, I sat in the west aisle and listened to Clare and her Singers. This was their second meeting since Clare had approached me about using the abbey for their practices. The PCC had agreed the use of the abbey. When I rang to confirm this to Clare, she offered to do one or two concerts per year in the abbey, with any profits split with the PCC. I had also spoken to Marie last week. She was working away on a farm in south Suffolk whilst staying with her grandparents who lived near Ipswich. She was due back last night.

'Strange,' she remarked, 'the choral society I'm in are meeting in your abbey on Wednesday.'

It turned out that she had been a member of the Singers since her PhD days. I could just make her out at the end of the front row on the south side of the choir. I did not want to embarrass her and had chosen to sit well away. We had agreed to pop into the Brandon Arms after her meeting.

It seemed no time at all until Clare called a big 'thank you' to her Singers. The group made their way down from the choir. A man carried Clare's keyboard.

'Hi, Marie, Hi, Clare,' I called and shook hands with both. 'That sounded fantastic from down here.'

Both called back to me. Clare added 'Would it be OK to use the organ some nights? Mark Ransome will play for us on some occasions, when we are getting ready for a concert.'

'Certainly. There is also the old grand piano over there, which you are welcome to use. It is pretty well in tune.'

I locked the south door behind us and walked with Marie towards her Discovery.

'It's lovely to see you again. Can I hitch a lift to the pub? I usually walk to the abbey unless the weather is bad. If I don't have to meet anyone, Moses often comes with me.'

'It's good to see you too, John.' She smiled. 'I think it's your turn to have a ride in my car anyway.'

She paused and looked at me. 'Who is this Moses? Is he your guardian angel, a relative, or a boyfriend?'

I laughed.

'I suppose he's almost a relative now. He's a Labrador dog that I rescued from the lake at the end of the abbey grounds. Three youths were trying to drown him. Nobody claimed him, and I didn't want him put down, so he stayed with me.'

The bar was half full as we entered. I noticed Clare and a few members of the Singers at a table in the middle.

'Do you want to sit with your choral colleagues?' I looked at Marie.

'Not particularly' she smiled back. 'How about that table for two by the window?'

She went for the table whilst I collected the drinks, a small glass of Pinot Grigio and a pint. She was driving, and sensibly was being cautious. The window seats were amongst the most popular as they looked out over Lake Lothing. As I settled down, and pulled my chair a little nearer to Marie, I could see the lights on the far side where the land climbed to the highest point of north Lowestoft. Down below, the still water reflected some of the lights. I noticed the red and white lights of a small boat probably heading for a marina further up.

'An amateur fisherman heading home, do you think?'

Strange, but those words gave me reason to look directly at her face, without seeming to stare. It also meant she knew something about boats.

'I didn't know you were versed in nautical matters, Marie.'

Her eyes, filled with the bright blue of a summer sky, looked briefly upwards in remembrance. 'My Granddad used to be a ship's master with Shell. He's retired now. He used to take Gran and me sailing along the east coast. He keeps his boat at Suffolk Marina on the Orwell.'

We learnt a little about each other's backgrounds. Marie's work in South Suffolk was a follow-up to some work last year when the farm of fruit trees had a poor crop. There seemed to be a problem with an insufficiency of bees, and the poor health of those that were around. She had contacted the local association of farmers about the use of chemicals and had installed a number of her own hives at the fruit farm.

'I've been building up several colonies of bees at the farm near Beccles. Of course, it helps our farmer friend. We've also been hiring out bees and developing a honey farming cooperative in East Anglia. We sell or hire-out hives and market the honey.'

All too quickly time evaporated and we were walking back to the Discovery.

'I don't have any parochial commitments on Saturday and the weather promises to be good. I wondered whether you would fancy a trip to Southwold, a walk along the coast and lunch out? If you're free of course?'

'I'd like that. Thanks. Would you feel OK if I came to evensong on Sunday? I haven't been to church for some time.'

'That would be great too,' I smiled.

When we pulled onto the vicarage drive, I asked whether she would like a coffee before driving home.

'Just a quick one, thanks. It'll give me a chance to meet Moses. We always had a cat at home.'

I was very proud of Moses. He said a quick 'Hello' to me and then went straight to Marie and sat down looking up at her, wagging his tail, waiting to be invited to get closer. Fortunately, he did not give off a strong doggy smell.

'I hope you'll bring him on Saturday.'

'Are you sure you wouldn't mind?' I returned her gaze. 'It'll limit where we can eat.'

'Perhaps we can go a little posher some evening?'

Then the house 'phone rang.

'Would you excuse me if I answer this, Marie? It's one of the hazards of the job.'

'Hello, John. Sorry to bother you at this hour. It's Alistair.'

The Rev'd. Canon Alistair Stuart was our rural dean. One step below the archdeacon, he was in charge of our local group of parishes. An empathic man of generous and humble disposition, he was well-liked by all that knew him. His parish had a tradition of middle of the road in churchmanship. Alistair appeared equally at home in both high and low church practice.

'Good evening, Alistair. How can I help?'

'John, I've just had churchwarden Brian Hayes from St. Chad's on the blower. It seems that Arthur Oldfield has been rushed to hospital with a suspected heart attack. He's not been a well man for some time.'

The Rev'd. Arthur was vicar of the three adjacent parishes: St. Chad's, Fleetend, St. Olave's, Whitehill, and St Margaret's, Lowford. The shortage of clergy and the shrinkage of worshippers had resulted in the combination of care of parishes throughout the land. It seemed the workload had proved too much for Arthur.

'I expect you will want me to help out, Alistair?'

'Please. I really am sorry to overload you. I know you don't have an eight o'clock Sunday service, normally. Would you kindly take services at that time, starting at St. Chad's this coming Sunday, and then alternating with St. Olave's? I'll get someone else to cover St Margaret's.'

'Of course. I'm very sorry to hear about Arthur.' I groaned inwardly, and hoped it didn't show in my voice.

Lord, forgive me. In your mercy, please give me the strength to fulfil my calling and duty to these parishes.

Eight o'clock at one of the adjacent parishes, nine-thirty at St. Mary's, and eleven o'clock at St. Giles'; three services on a Sunday morning, in three different churches, required quite a lot of spiritual and emotional energy. It tended to thin the care and love that a priest could give to a parish.

'Thank you, John. I'll try to get you some relief. There is a reader about to come on stream at St. Chad's which should help.' I heard him take a deep breath.

'I've had to let our archdeacon know. She said she's been planning to visit you and will bring it forward to this coming Sunday evening. She's asked for a meeting with yourself, your churchwardens, and myself, after the service.' I heard another deep breath.

'Imogen has also asked me to have a word with you.'

I wondered what on earth could be coming.

'Apparently she was at university with a chap who is now a local GP. He lives and worships in Kessingland and is a member of the diocesan and national synods. He has complained about your interfering with his patients. I don't know what it's all about, but he apparently said: "Look after the spiritual matters and leave the healing to the professional medics."'

I felt anger building up. I noticed my right fist was clenching.

Forgive my anger, Lord. Please help me to know what is right and your will, and give me grace to perform the same.

'Alistair, I'm sorry you have been caught in the middle. I suspect this concerns a certain Dr. Ian Marshall. I've had two parishioners who have found him un-empathic, unwilling to refer for counselling, and in my estimation practising bad psychology. I think I have a lot more professional understanding of these matters than he has. I'm not sure whether you know but I trained in clinical psychology and practised it for two years before training for the ministry. I also have a PhD which researched the area of belief and healing.'

My turn to take a deep breath. Then I picked up where I had stopped.

'I don't know what the Venerable Imogen's view on healing is, but there must be tens of references in the New Testament to our Lord commissioning the apostles to go out and both preach and heal. We have a healing service weekly at St. Mary's which follows the rubric set out in the official Anglican Common Worship.'

'John, I don't disagree with anything you have said. You will have my full support, but please be careful. I've taken up enough of your time. See you on Sunday evening.'

Somehow, Marie and I only managed a few words before she had to leave. She gave me the post-code and drew me a map of the location of her flat in Beccles, and then I saw her to her Discovery.

'See you on Saturday then,' she said.

I lifted my hand to my mouth and blew her a kiss as she drove off.

18

After a confused night's sleep I was now showered, breakfasted, and involved in saying morning prayer at the abbey, accompanied solely by Moses. Haunting phrases from Clare's choir, still seemed to resonate around the marble pillars, combined with images of Marie sitting next to me at the Brandon Arms, suddenly dissolving into a phantom of a large red-faced man with a stethoscope around his neck, emanating anger. I fought to focus on prayers of praise and intercession. At last I reached the dismissal blessing, bent down, and gave Moses a stroke.

'Come on old chap. Let's have a cup of coffee whilst I do a little work on my Sunday morning sermon.'

He trotted behind me as I headed for the abbey kitchen. I half-filled the kettle, switched on, and took out my 'phone to re-activate it. There were three missed calls from the same number, and a message from my voice-mail. It was Don Coates, sounding distressed. I brought up the missed call number and pressed the 'call' key.

'Hello, Don. Were you trying to get me?'

'Thanks, John. I've taken the day off sick and been to see the doctor. He says I have a duodenal ulcer and that it's probably due to stress. Can I see you sometime soon? I must talk to you.'

'Don, if it suits, you could come to the vicarage where I can offer you a milky hot chocolate. I'm at the abbey at this moment, and there's only tea or coffee here.'

Ten minutes later I turned the Golf into my drive. Moses and I ran through the light drizzle to the front door. Don arrived soon after. My study held two old armchairs, three wooden upright chairs, a small padded office chair on casters, a tall bookcase, an old desk with two drawers on the left side, and an adjacent small table holding a multifunction printer. An open laptop rested on the desk near the printer. A photograph of Dad's boat graced the wall opposite the window which looked out over the garden. A photograph of Mum and Dad perched on one of the bookcase shelves. I looked at the photograph and thought that I must get one of Marie.

Complete with hot chocolate and coffee, Don and I settled into the two armchairs. In therapeutic training, one of the most basic learnings was to place oneself psychologically and physically on the same level as one's client. Don and Rose had come to our Sunday evensong services most weeks since my visit to them. Whilst Rose was always chatty, I thought Don had seemed a bit distant over the last few weeks. Usually he was tidily presented. Today he wore no tie, which was unlike him. He had taken off his waterproof to reveal an old grey pullover covering a blue shirt. He looked drawn, had dark patches under his eyes, and brushed back his damp hair with his right hand.

'How can I help, Don? You mentioned the doctor.'

'Yes,' he winced. 'My gut's been playing me up for a while. I've been putting off seeing the GP, but just had to go today. He's given me some medicine and a diet sheet. He offered me counselling, but I thought I'd come and see you as in a way it concerns you.'

My first reaction was that an offering of counselling meant Don had not been to see Dr. Marshall. Then I wondered if Don's daughter Rebecca had developed a problem.

'Are the family all right, Don?'

'Yes, thanks. I don't know what I'd do without them. No, it's about work and the abbey. I've been bound to confidentiality about work, but it's just about to become public. The Council want to make the town more attractive and draw in more visitors. We've been told to work up a scheme to make more of the Lake Lothing waterfront, with more entertainment there, and some expensive waterside property associated with a new marina around one of the outer harbours. There's a local developer who owns a fair bit of the waterside land. He's really the driving force behind this. He's offered the Council a share in the income — plus the obvious rates they would pick up — in return for planning permission.' Don paused for a drink.

'What you've said so far seems quite a good idea and beneficial for the locality.'

Don frowned, and continued.

'The problem is that there are three main sites which interrupt the continuity of the waterfront plan. The developer either has, or plans to make, what he calls reasonable offers for these sites. The rub is that if they are not accepted, he wants the Council to make compulsory purchase orders at a lower value.'

I was beginning to sense why Don was stressed. He continued,

'The three sites this chap wants to acquire are the Brandon Arms, Southshore Boatbuilders, and St. Mary's abbey.'

For a few seconds I was lost for words. What I'd heard felt like the worst form of commercialism. To my mind this was sacrilegious, threatening, and offering what amounted to bribery. And here was a man in distress; a form of confession. My calling was to be aware of issues and to help him. He picked up again.

'I've felt awful coming to evensong at St. Mary's knowing this, and not being able to say anything. I shouldn't be telling you this now, but most of it will become public knowledge very soon. It will need the support of the full Council, but that is likely to come with the recommendation of the Planning Subcommittee. I'm so sorry.'

He put his head in his hands and slumped.

'Don. I think you've been very brave coming to tell me this. What you've told me will have to stay confidential unless and until I learn this officially through another source. You will be legally contracted to confidentiality in your job. I guess you or others can represent upwards anything that has a suggestion of unethical or illegal practice.'

'I've tried to do that, but my boss and the Chair of Planning have had the Council's legal chaps keeping an eye on this area and it appears to be within the law so far. My boss is away on a spot of holiday in Majorca at present. The chair of planning is away too. In fact, they often seem to be away at the same time.'

'A significant factor in your planning job must be to look after the best interests of your local community,' I tried again.

'I've tussled with that one a lot,' he looked up. 'But, does the benefit of the larger community outweigh the interests of the parishioners and all that have worshipped at St. Mary's over nearly eight hundred years?'

'Don, in the end it will depend on the full Council, and of course any local or diocesan opposition. I suggest that we place it in our Lord's hands, and ask his guidance for all those that are involved.'

We talked a few minutes more and then said a prayer together before Don left.

19

Saturday dawned sunny with a few scattered clouds. Moses keenly jumped up into the Golf boot and we set off to pick up Marie from her Beccles flat. By ten-thirty we had parked the car near Southwold pier, I picked up my small rucksack and we set off. Leaving car parks, beach huts, and the boating pool behind, we headed north and gave Moses a good run along the beach. He ran down to the water's edge and barked at the waves breaking onto the shore. The loose sand was hard going so we left the beach and took to the coastal path.

Tension seemed to slip away as we left the built-up area behind and headed into the natural environment. My eyes took in the sun sparkling on the water towards the south-east. Out at sea, a rig dwarfed the tug it followed, making slow progress well out towards the sea horizon. Sand grains glistened on the beach. To our left the land alongside the path varied from cultivated field, to shallow pools, and then to woodland.

Thank you, Lord, for giving me the means to appreciate beauty and order in the colour, form, and function I see, and for my companions.

Moses dashed off after a seagull. I glanced ahead at Marie who was leading where the path narrowed. We were passing a stretch of heathland with patches of heather.

'Do you find you are viewing what you see in terms of your scientific background, its visual beauty, or what?'

She paused, turned, and smiled. 'I would have said its artistic beauty, but did you say you brought a pair of binoculars? May I borrow them, please?'

I dug into my rucksack and pulled out an old pair and passed them over. Marie turned and looked at the heather.

'Oh, that's very exciting! Thanks.'

She handed back the binoculars, took out her mobile 'phone and crept slowly towards a patch of heather that was bathed in sunshine. She just had time for a quick photograph before a butterfly with dark-edged blue wings took off.

'A silver-studded blue. Fairly rare, although I have seen one in the Sandlings north of Felixstowe.'

Stepping back, she tripped over a clump of heather and collapsed in front of me.

'Are you OK?'

I reached down to help her up. She grabbed my hand and gently I pulled her up.

'My ankle's a bit tender but all right, I think. I hung onto my 'phone.'

She rested the 'phone hand on my shoulder. I realised her other hand was still holding mine. This was to be the testing moment.

'I'm so glad you're all right,' I smiled.

Her lips curled as she smiled back. I drew her a little closer.

'May I?'

She nodded gently back. I pressed my lips lightly against hers and was aware of a strange combination of comfort and excitement. Letting go of her hand I slipped my arms under hers and gently pulled her against me. We held each other cheek against cheek. She felt cool. I caught a hint of her fragrance. Moses barked and I glanced down. He was looking up and wagging his tail.

I supported Marie as she took her first steps back, but the ankle proved to be satisfactory. As we retraced our steps, we exchanged background information.

Both her parents were dead. Her maternal grandfather had told her that her father worked for MI5. He had died at work when she was one. A heart attack they had been told, although her granddad was very suspicious. Her mother had worked as secretary for a business man in Lowestoft and had married him three years later. When Marie was five, the three of them and another man were in a car skid and crash at speed. Her mother had died in hospital and the post-mortem had shown that she was pregnant. So, Marie might have had a brother or sister had her mother survived. Her injured stepfather had been in hospital for some time, so she had gone to live with her mother's parents in Ipswich. Granddad reckoned her stepfather had been drunk, but no case had been brought by the police. Granddad and Gran had gone to court and obtained custody of Marie. They had not allowed her stepfather into the house for several years.

'I don't see him very often. Don't really like him, although he has always sent me something at birthdays and Christmas. Somehow, I think he is trying to overcome his guilt.'

Granddad, I had learnt before, had been a master mariner with Shell, and had been promoted to a shore job as a marine superintendent. He and Gran, an artist, still lived near Ipswich, which was where Marie had spent most of her life. Granddad still had a trawler-style motor-sailer which he kept in a marina near Felixstowe. Marie had frequently sailed up and down the east coast, and even over to Holland, with them.

After our walk we picked up the car and drove a mile south to a car park next to the lifeboat station. Marie had eaten near here before and advised:

'I've sailed in here to the riverside harbour a few times with Grandad and Gran. We tried to avoid the ebb tide as it can run out quite fast and then joins the strong northerly flow along the coast. It's best to enter a little before high water. There are a number of moorings a little way upriver from here, and there's a good pub near the water. It was a trip of around forty miles from Grandad's home marina.'

20

I suppose that it was around three when we finished our lunch at the Harbour Inn right next to the River Blythe, which provided the harbour for Southwold. Ahead of us lay a walk of three quarters of a mile back to the car park, providing the opportunity to look at a variety of moored boats. The harbour consisted of a few stronger looking landing stages and several flimsy-looking ones several feet from the bank. These were accessed by narrow boardwalks reaching out over what would be mud at low water. They were supported by wooden pilings of varying degrees of straightness and age. There were also a few newer-looking floating pontoons tethered to steel posts. Despite the overall look of insecurity and make-do, there were several places where boats were moored two abreast. The place was clearly popular.

Near to the pub, the sailing club building offered a welcome to visiting yachtsmen and a view from its raised veranda. We walked back along the road with the river and its moorings on our right. To our left were a number of boats on stands for storage or repair. Further along, level with moored fishing boats, were an array of black fishermen's sheds, some with felt roofing, some with corrugated iron with varying degrees of rust.

The river took a kink left then right as it lined up for its final run out to the North Sea. I looked over the quay side. The tide was ebbing now, an hour or so after high water I guessed, perhaps about a knot. I looked beyond the harbour entrance. Far out to sea, a large container ship was heading south, probably en route for Felixstowe.

As we approached the lifeboat station the door was open. A woman with her back towards us was preparing to take a photograph of a lifeboatman standing beside the offshore lifeboat on its trolley. Behind her, watching, was a girl who seemed familiar. I recognised her as Louise, one of the sixth-formers who had talked to me about their first investigations into the abbey grounds. The photograph taken, the girl turned,

'Hello, Mr Green.'

Louise introduced the photographer as her Mum, Jessica Ellerman, a journalist with our local weekly, the Suffolk Siren. Jessica was preparing an article on the Southwold lifeboat station and its nearby museum. They had spent the morning a little further south at the coastal village of Dunwich.

'It was very interesting,' Louise continued. 'Most of the village, well they say it used to be a town as important as London, was washed away in storms in the thirteenth century. We saw the ruins of a friary and a leper hospital. Mum wondered if there was anything there that would tie up with St Mary's. Unfortunately, nothing really did. There were several religious ruins which are covered by the sea now, but the museum said that none were Benedictine, like our abbey.'

We chatted a while, and Mum agreed to cover a school exhibition on the abbey when the projects were finished.

21

The sun cast long shadows on Sunday evening as I walked up to the south door of the abbey. Overhead a flock of starlings wheeled and then settled on the tower. After three morning services, I had settled for a ready-made lasagne and salad lunch. Churchwarden Brian Hayes at St. Chad's and the congregation were very appreciative at the eight o'clock service. It looked as if I would be a frequent visitor for some time. The latest news about their usual vicar was that he was a very sick man, and likely to be forced to retire if he made it out of hospital. Moses, who had been out in the garden for most of the afternoon, had some food, and then went out again. Thinking about it, I could not remember where Moses was when I left the house. However, I also could not remember locking the front door. I shook my head, concern that all went well for the evening must be giving me a touch of obsessive-compulsive disorder.

There were thirty minutes until evensong. I had made all the arrangements I could to ensure that the night was the best we could offer. Organist Mark emerged from the vestry. I had spoken to him late on Wednesday evening, after learning of the archdeacon's visit. Since the parish council had approved his appointment, Mark had built up the choir for evensong. Father Rex had breathed a sigh of relief, and now added his fine bass voice to the choir unless he was assisting with, or taking, the service. Five or so of the St. Cecilia Singers were now also regular choir members.

'There's a short anthem for you, John. We had planned another couple of week's practice but I think we're sufficiently on top of it. John Rutter's Gaelic Blessing. The St. Cecilia Singers and the abbey choir have been working on it in parallel. I spoke to Clare and she confirmed earlier that she's spoken to around another twenty or so Singers who will join us tonight, including Marie.' He smiled at that. 'Clare will conduct. I've also done a little research on the music the Archdeacon likes. Apparently, she is very English in her tastes.'

'Thanks a lot, Mark. That's a great help. Things are looking up.'

I moved to the back of the west end of the abbey and helped Jim set up a folding table and six chairs near to the kitchen area. Our post-evensong meeting would comprise the Archdeacon, Rural Dean, two churchwardens from the abbey, the only one from St. Giles, and myself. Marie arrived. I introduced her to Jim and explained her offer to make some tea and coffee.

'I'll be in the choir tonight. Clare and our choir have been working on the anthem.'

I put my hand on her arm and squeezed gently.

'Thanks for coming.'

Carrying a shopping bag, she went into the kitchen with Jim.

Marjorie and Trevor Banks were next to arrive. Marjorie, who was a member of the PCC, was on sides-person duty and began moving a number of hymn books and Books of Common Prayer onto the table near the south entrance, with Trevor helping. Then a group entered, including Don and Rose Coates, Danny Murray, Sasha, and baby Gemma. I had spoken with Don on Friday evening. He was feeling somewhat better, probably from talking about what was worrying him. He had returned to work. Danny and Sasha were now occasionally attending our Sunday evening service. Clare and some of her Singers arrived. She sat them temporarily in the pews near the vestry, which would have been too small to hold choir, Singers, and priests. Jim and Alice, the churchwardens, who had been sworn into office by the Archdeacon, were waiting near the south door to officially welcome her. Olwen Drinkwater, churchwarden at St. Giles had arrived perplexed and had taken a seat.

'Hello, John. I see you are well prepared and it looks like a very good turnout. Is there any incense tonight?'

With outstretched hand, the well-built figure of Rural Dean Alistair approached. Over his left arm he carried his vestments. His voice was warm, his face wore an engaging, generous smile.

'Hi, Alistair. Good to see you,' I shook his hand. 'No incense at night. Any idea what this meeting afterwards is about?'

The rural dean winced. 'Just as well about the incense. Our archdeacon isn't too keen on it. Yes, about the meeting. But I'm sworn to secrecy. A mixture of good news and bad, you will probably think.'

A slim woman in her fifties, in the white robes of a server, emerged from the vestry carrying a taper and a box of matches. She greeted me and went to light the altar candles. It was Judy, the community nurse who, now, was hoping to enter the ministry.

The latch on the south door clunked and the door swung open again. Archdeacon Imogen Rodgers strode purposefully in. Dressed in a dark business suit with a clerical collar, her brunette hair was piled up to counter her short stature. Her corporation strained to escape the waistband and flexed as she advanced, trundling a large flight case behind her. The churchwardens started towards her. I followed.

'Hello, Archdeacon.'

'Welcome, Archdeacon.'

The greetings rang out, and hands were shaken. My offer to take the case was declined. I opened the door to the vestry and stood aside to allow my superior to enter. In the abbey I heard Mark start Elgar's 'Chanson de Matin.' The Archdeacon paused,

'Sounds like you have acquired a decent organist with a good taste. Can you leave the vestry door open for a while?'

She glanced at the censer hanging in the corner of the vestry, and wrinkled her nose. 'I wish I could convince you out of your popish high church practices here, John.'

I managed a smile. 'It's a very longstanding tradition in this parish, Archdeacon.'

She was greeted by Canon Alistair. I introduced Rex and Paul, both of whom would be in the choir.

'We have a seventeenth century processional hymn this evening, with music by John Ireland.'

That drew a smile from the Archdeacon. I went on to explain the seating arrangements and to confirm the priestly contributions of both ordained visitors to the service. I turned back towards the Archdeacon as Judy entered the vestry.

'Archdeacon, may I introduce Judy Pope. As you may recall she is attending a Bishops' Selection Conference in a week's time.'

This was part of the selection process for people hoping to enter the ministry. As an ordination candidate, Judy was well known to one of the other archdeacons, who was the Diocesan Director of Ordinands. Casting an eye on my watch I noticed that the service start time was approaching.

'If everyone's ready, I'll speak to the congregation.'

22

Arranging my surplice and stole over my cassock, I checked that priests, choir, Singers, and churchwardens were ready, and made my way to the steps of the choir. Mark brought his music neatly to a conclusion. A quick count indicated a congregation of nearly thirty.

'Welcome to you all on this sunny Sunday evening. I hope that you are in good voice. We have a number of special guests this evening, whom I will introduce to you when you can see them, after our processional hymn. Today we look back on Easter, and Ascension Day which was earlier this week. We look forward to next Sunday when we celebrate God's gift of the Holy Spirit at Pentecost. Our processional hymn reminds us of our Lord's great love, '

Mark waited for me to walk back to the vestry and then played the first few bars. He played softly as the choir and congregation started on the first verse:

My song is love unknown,
My saviour's love for me…

The procession snaked around the outside of the seats in the west aisle and then up the centre of the abbey towards the east end. Led by Judy as crucifer, our small choir in purple cassocks and white surplices followed. They comprised a young boy and a girl, followed by two teenagers, three women and three men. Next came twenty of the St. Cecilia Singers, practically even in men and women, including Marie, all wearing deep red jackets and black trousers or skirts. After a small gap, Fathers Rex and Paul walked together, just ahead of me. Next came Rural Dean Alistair. Finally came the Archdeacon preceded by churchwardens Jim and Alice, each holding a wand of office. In inverted ecclesiastical protocol, or snobbery, depending on your point of view, the first or highest walks last.

Crossing the transept, I felt a slight draft. The south door must have been open. I hoped someone would be aware and close it. There was a slight titter from the congregation. Something pressed against my right leg so I looked down. It was Moses, keeping step just behind, and looking up to check all was OK. Somehow, he must have escaped and found the way, which he knew well, to the abbey. Looking back, I could see Alistair was smiling. Behind him so also were Jim and Alice. The Archdeacon wore a frown. Fortunately, Moses was now well trained, would walk to heel, and would sit and stay. No going back now. I crossed my fingers.

At the start of the choir I peeled off to the left to my usual stall, the first rear one on the north side of the choir. Moses sat obediently next to me. Marie was in the choir stall in front. Alistair peeled off to his right and sat in the south side end rear stall opposite. Jim and Alice led the Archdeacon to the bishop's chair inside the communion rails near the high altar, bowed gently, and then took seats in the choir.

As the reverberations of the final verse of the processional hymn died away, I turned to the congregation.

'I said that I would introduce our visitors. I must apologise that we had one more than I expected.' There was laughter from all around.

'This evening we welcome our Archdeacon, the Venerable Imogen Rodgers, who is nearest to the altar. Opposite to me is our Rural Dean, Canon Alistair Stuart. We also extend a welcome to the St. Cecilia Singers and their conductor, Clare Parkinson.

Together with our choir they will be singing an anthem a little later. Lastly, adjacent to me is Moses, whom many of you have met. Perhaps his unexpected presence is a sign that we should have a service of blessing of pets. I'll have to take that up with the PCC. Now, would you please sit or kneel.'

We moved on to the introductory and penitential part of the service, at the end of which the Archdeacon stood and pronounced the absolution. As we sang the appointed psalm, 147, I reflected on what, for me, were its essential elements.

Praise ye the Lord...

He healeth the broken in heart, and bindeth their wounds.

Great is our Lord, and of great power: his understanding is infinite.

The Lord lifteth up the meek: he casteth the wicked down to the ground.

The first lesson from the Old Testament was chapter 61 of the book of Isaiah. I listened particularly to the first two verses.

The spirit of the Lord God is upon me: because he has anointed me to preach good tidings unto the meek; he hath sent me to bind up the broken hearted, to proclaim liberty to the captives, and the opening of the prison to them that are bound.

To proclaim the acceptable year of the Lord and the day of vengeance of our God, to comfort all that mourn.

The service progressed and I thought about the second lesson from the fourth chapter of the gospel of Luke. I recalled that the reading picked up where, following the temptations in the wilderness, Jesus had returned in the power of the Spirit into Galilee and taught in the synagogues. In one, Christ had read out the first two verses of Isaiah chapter 61, which we had heard a little earlier.

Before I had learnt of the visit of the Archdeacon and Alistair, I had prepared my sermon for this service, based on the first verse from Isaiah, which had been echoed by our Lord in the Gospel reading, which in itself was an echo of the appointed psalm. The obvious theme was the love of God, expressed in the focus on care, healing, passing on the 'good news'', and reference to the Holy Spirit as a forerunner for Pentecost next Sunday.

It seemed no time at all before I had said the collects and it was time to announce the anthem. Clare moved into the choir carrying her stand and music. An expectant silence spread around the abbey. Mark played the introduction softly and accompanied sensitively as the combined choirs steadily developed John Rutter's 'A Gaelic Blessing.'

Deep peace of the running wave to you...

After the anthem, and following ancient ceremonial practice, I walked to opposite the Archdeacon, bowed slightly and preceded her to the pulpit, and then returned to my stall. Whilst I tended to preach standing at the steps to the choir, Imogen had made it clear that she preferred to use the pulpit.

23

The Venerable Imogen glanced around the Abbey, adjusted her spectacles, and began.

'Our gospel, this evening, takes us back to the beginning of our Lord's ministry, immediately after his temptations in the Wilderness. Luke, chapter 4, verse 14 gives us "And Jesus returned in the power of the Spirit into Galilee". This is especially relevant to us after the gift of eternal life that Easter brings, and as we look forward to our celebration of the coming of the Holy Spirit at Pentecost, next week. Our Lord visits a number of synagogues and in one He reads the passage from Isaiah which we heard. Although Luke only quotes the first two verses of that reading, I think we can be fairly certain our Lord read at least as far as the fourth verse: "And they shall build the old wastes, they shall raise the former desolations, and they shall repair the waste cities, the desolations of many generations."

'From the very beginning of his ministry, our Lord challenged his listeners and followers to deal with the problems they faced. He may have been speaking metaphorically. It may have been the spiritual desolation and wastes of a people who followed the detail of the law but not the spirit of morality. Remember also, His was an occupied country, subject to control by the Romans, so there may also have been physical desolations. Whichever He was referring to, He was encouraging His people, and us, to energetically tackle local problems and move forwards. What, I wonder, are some of our local problems?

'As we gather together and worship in large buildings that dwarf us, do we remember that they were built in the days when there was no TV, no cinemas, few schools and colleges? Church provided not only spiritual renewal but also companionship, social occasion, education, and entertainment. People were more alert to the fragility of life, health, and the next meal. This building, like our other churches, would have been full. There would have been no shortage of clergy. The building and maintenance of churches would have been readily supported by tithes, gifts, investments, and endowments.

'And what about now?' She paused and looked around.

'Now we have worthy but small congregations in vast buildings which are expensive to maintain, with a lack of a hall and social facilities. Your diocese has to provide substantial funds for our many under-used and under-financed parishes. We have to do this against a background of rising costs and falling income. Few parishes manage to raise the real cost of running and maintaining them. The diocesan investments are now severely depleted and, as I'm sure many will know, the stock market is being very unhelpful. We have a shortage of clergy, most of whom, like your vicar, have to work under the stress of covering several parishes. You may have heard that the vicar covering three parishes near to this one, is seriously ill in hospital after a heart attack.'

The Archdeacon took a deep breath and looked around. I wondered what was coming next. There seemed a threat of further economising steps. It wasn't the sermon I would have given or expected. Then she was off again.

'And what of the desolation around you, of your town? You suffered here from bomb damage during the Second World War. The quick rebuilds under the then hard times are now showing signs of age. This area was famous for its large fishing fleets and the supporting industries of ship-building and food processing. I drove along Lakeside before the service. The desolation and wastes left by the collapse of these industries and of the British merchant navy are all too clear to see.

'I know that your local council and business leaders are themselves working hard on your account to respond to a number of challenges. They are developing business parks to draw in industry and commerce which provide local jobs. They are seeking to improve pedestrian ways and provide more attractive friendly facilities and entertainment, both for yourselves and also to draw in visitors.

'You and I must do our parts to move with the times and seize the opportunities to develop economic church facilities matched to our current evangelistic and social needs.

'And they shall build the old wastes, they shall raise the former desolations, and they shall repair the waste cities, the desolations of many generations. Amen.'

She bowed her head. Then I led her back to her seat as is the custom.

Shortly we had the collection hymn. Alistair said the grace and gave the final blessing. We processed out to the final hymn.

24

The Archdeacon took the sole chair at the head of the table. I managed to guide Jim and Olwen to the chairs either side of her. Alice sat next to Jim. Alistair and I took the two chairs furthest from her, which seemed to give a little opportunity to reflect before responding to whatever was to come.

Following the sermon, Marie had spirited Moses away to the back of her four-by-four, and then disappeared to make pots of coffee and tea. Resplendent with chocolate biscuits these were soon on the table awaiting the meeting. I thanked her and gave her my house keys. She would take Moses back to the vicarage and wait until I returned. The Archdeacon, Stuart, and I, had stood by the south door to say farewells to the departing congregation. As I was thanking Clare, I noticed a well-dressed man with curly hair complimenting the Archdeacon on her sermon, and heard her respond addressing the man as Councillor Jackson. Mark had played Elgar for a few minutes.

'Right. Let's get down to business,' the Archdeacon consulted her organiser.

'The desolations which I referred to in my sermon are pressing in on us. This parish and St. Giles' keep you pretty busy, John. And it's not helped by lack of a decent church hall, Olwen, Jim, and Alice. Your next-door neighbours, so to speak, the parishes of St.

Chad's, Fleetend, St. Olave's, Whitehill, and St. Margaret's, Lowford, have sparse congregations, covered by a very sick priest who, we have learnt, cannot work again. And, as I mentioned, the diocesan funds are in a parlous condition.

'Your local council is contemplating a compulsory purchase order for one of the five churches that I've mentioned, to, I quote, "significantly reduce an eyesore and improve local facilities."' They are working with developers who have made an alternative proposal. If we agree to sell two of the churches involved, it would release desirable building land. The developers would then build a new small flexible church, with an incorporated hall, on land in one of the parishes, and pay a very useful cash amount to the diocese. In the process this would release local facilities, including St. Giles', to the council. If we do not accept the offer, the council seem likely to proceed with compulsory purchase of one church at an amount that would be rather less than the developer would offer. In the first scenario, five churches would be reduced to three, with enlarged joint parishes.

'John, the five parishes come within Alistair's rural deanery. He has a priest who is just finishing her first appointment and who needs to move. We are planning to make you responsible for the five parishes, which will reduce to three, and to give you the help of this curate.'

The Archdeacon smiled at me. A subtle play to get me on board, I mused, wondering what was coming next. Perhaps it was time to contribute to the discussion.

'Well, Archdeacon, we do get poor use of St. Giles, Coxton. Probably fifty per cent of the Anglican church-goers from that parish come here to the abbey. I've often thought we should hand the St. Giles building back to the Council and merge the two parishes centred on St. Mary's.'

'Yes, that would make a lot of sense, we have the room here,' offered Jim. Alice nodded in agreement.

The Archdeacon seized the reins back quickly.

'That's part of the problem. Here, we have a lot of untidy,

unused land stretching down to the Lake. A number of people think of it as an eyesore. This fine old building is in itself a potential problem; a time bomb of expensive repair and renovation just waiting to happen. The developers would keep the building with a change of use. It would be their cost to maintain it. The waterfront land would become integrated into a more scenic leisure development, the planners say.'

'So, does that mean we are to lose the abbey?' I asked, sharply.

'Yes. It would be a very useful injection of cash into the diocesan funds. And, as part of the deal if we don't get involved in the compulsory purchase, the developers would build a small modern church with an incorporated hall and kitchen, on the site of a disused petrol station which they own. That would be the church for the combined parishes of St. Mary's and St. Giles. The developers and their architect would consult you, John, about the layout and facilities in the new church buildings.'

'The founding monks will be turning in their graves.' Alice slumped into her chair.

'And which would be the other church to go?' Jim bristled.

'St. Chad's, Fleetend. Although, it seems likely that in due course we will have to close St. Margaret's, Lowford, due to an uneconomic congregation. St. Olave's, being in the middle of the three parishes, would be best placed to serve a larger combined parish.'

The Archdeacon appeared to have all the arguments on her side.

'I can see that would suit your developer very well, even though St. Chad's has the largest congregation.' Alice was red with anger.

'How do you mean?' The Archdeacon's eyebrows went up.

'St. Chad's, which has a large car park and a closed small graveyard, is in the middle of a development of very expensive houses. It would be an investment with a very good return for a developer.'

'The developers' view is that it all helps to provide funds to create a new church suite to serve your parish in an up-to-date and economic way. They see it as an opportunity to help the diocese. They are offering you, John, the chance to contribute to the design of the new church and hall. I hope you will seize the opportunity to move forwards in an all-embracing middle church way, and lose some of your high church practices. Perhaps you can then have a church that is likely to appeal more to women and offers them a greater chance to contribute.'

'I'm afraid that you don't know our parish at all well, Archdeacon.' Alice's back straightened as she stood up to her full height of just under six feet. She looked down at the dumpy Archdeacon with her best hospital matron's withering frown. With a tense face, steely eyes, and jutting chin, Alice continued.

'Since John arrived, our congregation on a Sunday morning has increased from four or five to between twenty and thirty. Probably two thirds are women, a slightly higher percentage than in most churches. Roughly half of the PCC are women. Women take their turn to assist at holy communion, and to lead the intercessions. One of our women members has offered herself for ordination, and has been invited to a selection conference. And in case you are worried, we also supported the move to have women bishops. So, don't claim that our moderate high-churchmanship has negatively impacted on women. It hasn't!'

The Archdeacon looked at her watch and pushed her chair back.

'Well. I think that will be all for now. This is a wonderful opportunity for you to help the church in this part of the diocese move forward economically. I have spoken to the churchwardens in the Reverend Holmes' three parishes. Canon Stuart and I will be firming up on an enlarged team of five churches initially, and setting the necessary measures in motion. John, you are authorised to speak to the respective churchwardens. Canon Stuart will speak to the Rev'd Anne Fox and ask her to get in touch with you. She should be able to start within the next three weeks. We shall have to find some way of clearing the Rev. Holmes' belongings from St.

Olave's vicarage, for the new team curate. Canon Stuart or I will do the licensing service. It will help the diocese if we have a resolution of support from the parishes concerned. So perhaps you can put this on the agenda for your next PCC meetings and let me know. Thank you for your hospitality. Now I must fly as I have an important diocesan meeting early tomorrow.'

She put her organiser away in an outer pocket of her flight case, stood up, and started for the door. I eased ahead, opened the south door, and saw the Archdeacon to her car.

'This a wonderful opportunity for you to step up and manage a team, John.' She gave a grey smile. 'Not everyone gets the opportunity. Think about it. Good night.'

'Good night, Archdeacon.'

25

Marie's 4x4 was on the vicarage drive when I arrived home and opened the front door. She was sitting in the lounge watching TV. Moses got up from his seat next to her and, wagging his tail, trotted over to welcome me.

'Thanks so much, for looking after Moses. I must have been too preoccupied thinking about this evening when I came out. I may have left him in the garden. I'll have to check it for escape holes. And thanks for the coffee, biscuits and the anthem. You looked fabulous in your outfit.'

I leant to give her a quick peck on the cheek. It turned into a longer embrace as she put her arms round me. We stayed close for a few seconds, our cheeks touching and eyes closed.

'Actually, I thought that Moses fitted in perfectly. He processed in, beautifully to heel, with the occasional glance up at you. He was probably more of a hit than the Archdeacon. Did your meeting go well?'

I frowned.

'To be honest, I'm rather confused. The Venerable Imogen strikes me as a very clever woman. She put her fingers on a number of actual and potential local problems and promoted a solution which seemed more financially based than spiritual. A lot of what she said made uncomfortably good sense, but —

something seems wrong and I can't put my finger on it.'

I thought about Don's comments and distress, but that was too confessional and confidential. A priest has to keep some sufferings and possible wrongdoings close to his chest.

'Effectively she wants to close St. Giles and a neighbouring church, and sell off the abbey. A local benefactor would then build a smaller modern church and hall for our combined two parishes. I need to think about it and get the reactions of our parishioners.'

'Wow! It would be very sad to lose that historic beautiful building, although I suppose the church hall would be an attraction.

'John, I'm sorry but I need to go now. I'm due back in the Ipswich area early tomorrow and have to pick up some kit at our lab tonight. I'll be back for the Singers' practice on Wednesday, if you're around?'

We had a long clinch, then Moses and I saw Marie to her car.

26

For most of Monday I felt foul. A night spent tossing and turning. Prayer did nothing to help, neither did self-hypnosis. There was a certain logic to Imogen's plan, and yet everything within me screamed 'No! No! No!'

Periodically through the day I was aware of a tautness in my body, and clenched fists. Moses seemed to sense this. After initially pressing his head into my legs, he kept his distance with his head hung low, taking an occasional furtive glance to see if my mood had changed.

We left the house at six a.m. for a lengthy run. Over the swing-bridge, and up the pedestrianised High Street, we then picked our way down one of the scores. Lowestoft's scores are narrow alleyways stretching from the High Street down-hill to the lower level of the fishing harbour. They are associated with past fishing and smuggling activities.

A few minutes later, standing on the outer harbour wall we looked out over a still grey sea. Above, a uniform layer of low stratus pressed down, denying access to the sun. Moses sniffed. It didn't need a dog's sensitive nose to pick up the smell of rotting fish. I glanced inland looking up at the town. There was certainly need for urban regeneration. A few buildings had their historic story tastefully maintained. Unfortunately, many displayed brash modern shop fronts below dilapidated tired reminders of past architectural styles, like old ladies with extra short skirts. Time to jog home for a shower and breakfast.

My 'phone rang every few minutes through the day, with parishioners from both St. Mary's and St. Giles' calling to ask if the gossip they had heard was true. Mostly, it was. Mostly, the caller felt resentment. I managed to catch our abbey PCC (Parish Church Council) secretary, Olivia, on her lunch break. She worked as a secretary for a local company that made electronic components. As it happened, our next PCC monthly meeting for St Mary's was scheduled for three weeks' time. Olivia would circulate the members with a few notes I promised to put together during the day. St. Giles' PCC secretary, Geraldine, would do the same for St. Giles' next meeting. This was scheduled to be held in the abbey, for lack of alternative facilities, the following week. We agreed to bring the meeting forward and have it follow on after St. Mary's.

The only light in the day was a call from schoolmaster Ben. He had now registered for a Ph.D. and his supervisor would be in the area late afternoon and wanted to look around the abbey. Ben wondered if I could be there. At four-thirty, I had said the evening office and was trying to relax, sat at the organ, playing a mournful, but simple piece of music by Purcell, 'When I am laid in earth.' Written in the latter part of the seventeenth century, I reflected, it was a little after the time when the abbey would have been most active. Somehow it prompted me to think of fighting to preserve the contribution of the building to the local community, whilst there was life.

I heard the clunk of the latch on the south door and drew the music to a conclusion. Closing the organ, I rose and made my way over the crossing. Ben was accompanied by a tall well-built man wearing a worn green Barbour jacket. Totally bald, his dark-framed spectacles and black bushy eyebrows gave a powerful finish to a round smiling face. He moved his man-bag onto his left shoulder and stretched out his hand,

'Robert Bedford.'

Ben added to the introduction, qualifying his tutor as Reader in Medieval History at the University of Cambridge.

'I've driven out of rain on the way here, so perhaps we could have a look outside first and then come in.'

There was not a lot I could add to Ben's knowledge about the outside, so by common agreement I went into the kitchen and put the kettle on. They returned inside just as the rain arrived with us. Armed with coffee and biscuits they went into the body of the church whilst I went to switch on all the lights.

'Most of the exterior looks to be thirteenth century, but your tower looks a little later,' Robert offered, 'that is apart from the west end of the nave, which is quite interesting and is probably mid-sixteenth century, as Ben suggests.'

He made his way to the chancel steps. 'That's a fine coat of arms, Henry VIII. There are not all that many of those, especially in that condition.'

Then he was off again moving around the nave. From his bag he took a pair of binoculars and surveyed the high wall paintings.

'Those are exquisite. They must have survived through being so high up. Probably fourteenth century, I would think.'

Moving towards the crossing he examined the paintings over the arch leading to the chancel. 'Once again, a beautiful example. This time a doom painting, a depiction of the last judgement. It would have been very obvious to those in the nave. A warning of the trouble they could expect if they did not behave themselves.'

The Brandon tombs and hatchments drew further comments and a suggestion that Ben spent some time in the county record offices, and scoured the National Archive, the Cambridge library, and the Bodleian at Oxford.

'This is a time for expansive thinking and exploration, Ben, before we focus in on a narrower, directive theme for your thesis. Thanks for the coffee and biscuits,' he turned towards me.

Before he left, I told him of the Archdeacon's proposal.

'Well, I can see the financial attractions of the Archdeacon's scheme, but,' he took a deep breath, 'I would think this must be a listed building. From what I can see it is of potentially great historic interest. You could almost certainly get a grant towards the preservation of those paintings. And those comments don't take any account of the spiritual potential of the place. Must be off. I've a lecture to give in Norwich, this evening. Let me know if I can be of any further help. Bye, Ben,' and off he strode.

27

Lowestoft's Brandon Hospital lay at the southern edge of the town in a pleasant green setting. Although I had visited many parishioners there, I had never had cause to enter the High Dependency Unit. Much of the light green wall space had electrical or flexible pipe connections to sophisticated looking medical equipment. Arthur Oldfield was in a small bay at one end. Looking frail, he was hooked up to a monitoring display, an intravenous drip, a catheter output, and wore an oxygen mask. The sister, or ward manager in modern parlance, advised that he was very ill and had been on assisted breathing, and would I please limit my visit to five minutes. She told me that his sister from Nottingham had been to see him and was staying in his vicarage.

Arthur's eyes were sunk deep in dark grey bags. He was too weak to converse but would weakly nod or shake his head gently to my questions and suggested answers, with an occasional word or short phrase. I held his hand for a while. It was one way of passing love and good will. I learnt that Alistair had visited him the day before. Arthur had been unable to respond as he was then on assisted breathing and struggling to retain sensible consciousness. Arthur felt his time was running out and wanted communion and anointing. After clearing a little more time with the ward manager, we shared the short service. He looked more at ease as I squeezed his hand gently and withdrew.

    Later that evening I received a call from the ward that Arthur had suffered another massive heart attack and died with his sister by his side. At the hospital again, after saying the last rites I took her back to his vicarage and stayed a while. Back home, with a cup of hot chocolate and Moses resting his chin on my knee I reflected. A sense of great sadness mingled with anger and pressure. I knew that Arthur had spent his whole working life as a priest. More scholarly than outgoing he had been a private man. Conscientious and concerned to do a good job, he had remained single-minded and lacking in companionship.

28

It was a little over three weeks since Arthur had died. Alistair conducted the funeral service at which I assisted. It was well attended, largely by people from his three parishes. His sister was the only family member present.

After the funeral I met with Alistair a couple of times. The first was privately. We talked over the intended new team, which was to be formalised at the deanery synod. I took the opportunity to tell him that I had a girlfriend. I think he had sussed that from Marie's help before the meeting with the archdeacon. Technically, this was probably not necessary, but the Bishop has to approve the marriage of a priest, and it seemed a prudent way to combat any possible tittle tattle.

'And what do you think of the archdeacon's building plans?' he asked.

'I am still thinking about it, Alistair. My licensing requires a vow of obedience to the bishop, and his delegated authority. However, I reckon that my duty of cure of the parishes is of higher moral priority. I wait to see the reactions of the various PCCs. I expect that St. Giles' will be quite happy with any new proposals. Only last Sunday evening when I arrived to take evensong, we found that the piano we use had been vandalised. Jackie, the primary school teacher who plays for us, popped home and fetched her keyboard.

It is a very unsatisfactory arrangement there. The abbey is a quite different matter.'

Alistair and I had met with the churchwardens of the five parishes to discuss the team arrangement. Most appeared glad to hear that an additional priest could be provided quickly. The patronage of all the parishes lay with the bishop, although I learnt that of the abbey's was historically unclear.

A few days later the deanery synod met. This was a committee of clergy and elected lay members from each parish in the deanery. They rubber-stamped the proposal for a team of two to initially cover the five parishes. The only real discussion was on what to call the team. We ended up with 'the South Lothing team', an unimaginative term and an unfortunate homonym.

Parish life went on as usual. A small group of ladies kept the abbey tidy and arranged flowers for Sundays and feast days. An anonymous person put an envelope containing a hundred pounds cash through the vicarage letter box. There was a brief note asking for this to be used for the benefit of the parish. With the agreement of the churchwardens we bought some play apparatus for the mums' and toddlers' group.

Sasha and Danny decided to have Gemma christened and announced that they planned to get married. Lucy and Matt Baines came to a healing service. Lucy started her IVF procedures. Judy came back from a Bishops' Advisory Council meeting spiritually moved and accepted for training for the ministry.

A previous PCC meeting had focused on how we might develop the parish. Our ways forward included promoting the engagement of the abbey in the local community and some fund raising. At an earlier meeting Judy had suggested that in the absence of a church hall, we should use the abbey building more for social secular purposes. After a little initial opposition, this was accepted. After all, that was exactly what was going on at St. Giles, although the church could rarely get a look in for social use, due to the regular demand by other organisations who paid a fee to the council. Since then we had grown our mother and toddler group, which was proving very successful.

All such activities in the life of a parish depend on good will and volunteers. Dear old Alice looked after the mums and toddlers. Most fortunately, she was fit and energetic. She had moved her Zumba class to the abbey on Monday evenings. The ladies who did the abbey flowers ran an arranging class. They planned to run a flower festival in late June to raise a little money to help our funds. When I mentioned this in passing to our organist Mark, he offered to organise a jazz festival over a weekend. The school started rehearsing for their end of term concert. Clare promised a late autumn concert in shared aid of abbey funds.

A week after the visit that Marie, Moses, and I had paid to Southwold, a newspaper article was drawn to my attention after our Sunday morning service. On its second page, the county weekly, the Suffolk Siren, carried a photograph of the Southwold lifeboat station, and an article by Jessica.

29

Clare's Singers finished their rehearsal and made their way down the chancel. As I walked over the crossing below the tower to meet Marie, I felt grit beneath my shoes. Probably we needed to get the stone slabs sealed in some way, another expense that we could ill afford. I recalled that Jim had swept up some mortar or stone dust several days ago. I locked the south door after all had departed.

Marie and I set off along Lakeside towards the Brandon Arms. The air was mild and twilight was just starting. We left her Discovery on the abbey car park. She slipped her hand into mine. Walking there and back was a small contribution to health. As we passed the derelict Waveney Shipping Company, a fox ran across the partially grass covered concrete yard and disappeared behind the dilapidated office building. I had to agree that the place was an eyesore and could benefit from development. At the far end of the yard, next to Southshore, was a bungalow with a small garden. I had learnt that it used to be accommodation provided by the shipping company for the yard foreman. When the company closed down the foreman, Max, had bought it at an attractive price. Max and his wife were occasional worshippers at the abbey on a Sunday evening. I knew he was now the caretaker at the Endowed School, and also a keen gardener.

There was a white van on the road. It bore the name of a plumbing company. As we drew nearer Max was at the border of his front garden talking to a man in an overall. An inspection cover lay on the small but immaculate front lawn.

'Problems, Max?'

He came to the roadside.

'I'll say! We thought we must have a blocked drain as the toilet was backing up. Unfortunately, the blockage is on our land and turns out to be our responsibility. Some bugger must have dropped a load of cement down the drain whilst we were out last night. The police have been, but we still have the problem of fixing it.'

'Max, you are welcome to use the abbey toilet in the daytime, if that would help.'

'Thanks. It's strange but I've just turned down an offer for the bungalow. Maybe I should have accepted it, but we've lived here for the last fifteen years and I thought it would see us out. I don't know whether the house insurance covers things like this.'

A few minutes later Marie and I were sitting at a patio table outside the rear of the Brandon Arms, looking out over Lake Lothing. It was one of those evenings in which a clear sky follows a sunny day, tempting one to sit out, although the temperature was starting to drop. Marie's fine features were in profile. She looked gorgeous. No, she was gorgeous, yet cuddly and very desirable. She looked at me, then leant over and squeezed my hand.

'You looked far away.'

'I was just thinking how much I enjoy your company, and how beautiful and desirable you look.'

As far as I could tell in the dusk, she blushed. I was surprised at my forwardness. She got up and came around to my chair, moved my arms, sat across my lap, put her arms around my neck and placed her lips gently against mine. I was aware of her left breast pushing against me. Just as spontaneously as she had approached me, she quickly stood up and went back to her seat.

'I wondered how vicars felt about these things?'

'I'm sure our feelings are just like anyone else's. It's just that we try to keep our intentions and actions honourable.'

The landlord came out from the inside dining area and cleared the empty glasses and plates from the table next to us.

'Hello, John. Have you had any vandalism at the abbey?'

'No. Why do you ask, Simon?'

'Well we've had the plate glass windows on the side of the dining room sprayed with red graffiti that won't clean off. Southshore, next door, had a boat cut loose from a mooring and get badly damaged. The mooring ropes were actually cut. That has to be deliberate vandalism.'

'Strange you should say that, Simon, but we've just been talking to Max who lives in the bungalow, the other side of Southshore. He's had a load of cement dropped down a drain access in his front garden. Oh, sorry. Marie, Simon. Simon meet Marie, a friend of mine.'

He smiled, 'Yes, I had noticed. Welcome, Marie.'

'Thanks for the warning,' I continued. 'We deliberately keep the abbey unlocked during the daytime, to make anybody who drops in welcome. We'll have to keep our eyes open.'

Marie and I stayed a little longer, then walked back to her car, hand in hand.

30

Churchwarden Jim arrived in the abbey whilst I was finishing the morning office. He ran a long extension lead to the raised Brandon tomb in the Lady chapel. The school history group were due for further work in and around the abbey.

'How do you think the future of the abbey will go, John? What's your guidance going to be?' He sounded despondent.

'Jim, I'm inclined to go with my feelings. The abbey has been a focal point and inspiration for the locality for so many years, I think we should continue with its use towards those ends. However, it could become too expensive to maintain.'

'Don't you have to do what the archdeacon wants?'

'I do have an obligation of obedience to the bishop, and therefore his lieutenants, but I also have a commitment to the cure or care of the parish. This cure I rate as of higher moral imperative. So, I think I have to wait to see how the PCC votes.'

There was a burst of chatter as a group of pupils entered, followed by Ben. I recognised two, a boy and a girl, who I had met on a previous visit. The girl was Louise Ellerman, daughter of the journalist. I remembered the boy was called Alan. He had seemed somewhat shy when we first met.

'So, what are you working on today, Alan?'

'Morning, Vicar. We've done some work on the photocopies we

received from the Norwich Archives and we've visited the Lowestoft Archives. The Brandon family are turning out to be very interesting through their wills and your church registers of births, deaths, and marriages.' He sounded a lot more confident.

Louise added 'I think it should be "baptisms" rather than "births", Alan.'

'Yes, of course. Anyway, we wondered whether we might find graves or memorials to any later Brandons. They are linked to our school.'

'Well, ladies and gentlemen, there is definitely a tablet set in the floor of the Lady chapel and also one in the chancel. They are rather worn, especially the one in the chancel. There is a large chest in the Lady chapel, just behind the organ. It's used for storing altar frontals. I'll move the frontals to the pews and then perhaps we can slide the chest to see if there is anything underneath.'

Somewhat later I joined the students and Ben. They showed me their notebooks and talked me through their researches and conclusions.

Alan started very logically.

'We have gathered information from the Norfolk County Archives at Norwich, from the Lowestoft branch of the Suffolk Archives, they're over the library, and online internet searches. Mr. Fillingham has added some of his findings from the National Archives, and we have looked at their online catalogue.

'If we start with the abbey, we know there was a family called Fitz Osbert who made a grant of land at Queensholme, together with fishing rights, to the abbot of St Benet's abbey at Horning in 1245. We also know that St Mary's is a daughter foundation of that abbey.

'From the parish registers at Norwich, after a lot of trolling we have identified a number of the Brandon family until the line appears to run out locally. From online searches we have details of Sir William Brandon and Charles Brandon his son. Charles was the first Duke of Sussex and Sir Richard's dad. Some details of the line have emerged from wills and trust papers at Lowestoft Archives.

Louise has the tidiest copy of the male line.'

Louise opened a double page spread in her notebook and took up the story, stopping from time to time to point to a table in her book.

'Sir William Brandon, 1456-1485, was standard bearer for King Henry VII at the battle of Bosworth Field. He was killed there by King Richard III, who himself died there, and whose body was discovered under a car park in Leicester.

'Charles Brandon, 1484-1545, was Sir William's son. He grew up with King Henry VIII. They were close friends, generally. Charles was made the first Duke of Sussex. He had a home at Westthorpe, near Stowmarket, and is buried in St George's Chapel, Windsor.

'Sir Richard Brandon, 1504-1570 was one of a number of illegitimate children of Charles Brandon. It seems likely that King Henry VIII would have at least known of Sir Richard as a child. Mr. Fillingham found in the National Archives a court order of 1535 appointing Sir Richard as full admiral with a fleet of five warships, orders to defend the east coast, and authority to build coastal forts. Mr. Fillingham also found a grant from King Henry VIII, dated 1537, giving to Sir Richard, the abbey church, its land, and the grange. The grange has gone but we still have a Grange Road in Coxton.'

'What exactly is a "grange"?'

'It comes from a French word which means 'grain store'. Sometimes they were developed into manor houses. Papers from Lowestoft Archives show that Sir Richard previously had a town house in Coxton. It seems that he gave this to the town in 1540 for a school, and moved into the Queensholme Grange. The town house was the origin our Endowed School.

'Mr. Fillingham also found some payment records in the National Archives which showed payments made for building forts at Lowestoft and Languard Point, Felixstowe. There were also payments for support of the infirmary at Queensholme following a number of injuries sustained in a tunnel collapse at one of the Lowestoft forts in 1539. There were three forts defending access to Lowestoft and the offshore roads. So, it confirms that the abbey infirmary continued its medical work. It would have been on land owned by Sir Richard.'

'Thank you, Louise. Alison, would you like to take over the story now?' Ben interjected.

Alison had a similar table in her notebook, although it was rather less tidy than that of Louise, so I was glad she talked as well as pointed.

'Right. We found papers of John Brandon, 1540-1603, who gifted the infirmary to the aldermen of Lowestoft in 1601.

'He was followed by Roger Brandon, 1570-1630. Roger appears to have been a farmer and landowner.

'His only son was a Charles Brandon, baptised in 1595. We haven't found any trace of him except his presumed heir. This was Sir Henry Brandon, 1618-1695. We think that one of the hatchments is his.

'We think the other hatchment is of his son, Sir Robert Brandon. We know he was an MP. He also endowed a new hospital in 1710 which is probably the forerunner of our Brandon Hospital. We haven't located his will, yet. He is the last that we can discover of the male line.'

'Josh, would you take over now?'

Ben looked at a tall lad with blond hair, who seemed to have been taking a lot of photographs during the morning. Josh laid down his camera and flashlight. He looked at me.

'Thanks for moving the chest in the chapel. We have photographs of three tablets now, plus the raised tomb. In the chancel, the tablet was for John Brandon. In the middle of the lady chapel was a tablet for Sir Henry Brandon. And under the chest was a tablet, in excellent condition, for Sir Robert Brandon, the MP. So, these were three Brandons who have either helped the abbey or the town or the parish.'

'April, will you tell the vicar about your special interest?'

April was a fine-featured girl with long blond hair.

'I'm interested in heraldry. I've been looking at the hatchments and how the two are related. There is a coat of arms on the tomb of

Sir Richard and his lady. We think she might be "Anne". The coat of arms is a bit indistinct. If we can clarify it and its colours, we want to suggest that it becomes our school coat of arms as Sir Richard endowed the school. At the moment our coat of arms is a plain shield with the capital letters from the name of the school. It's really boring and unimaginative.'

I had to agree. 'CES' might be an unpopular label to wear.

31

'Mr. Blacke will be free shortly. Would you take a seat? Can I get you a coffee?'
The shapely secretary/receptionist was business-like and polite. She wore a smart black jacket with snug-fitting skirt and a sparkling white blouse. Her hair looked to be long, but was in a plait arranged neatly on the top of her head. Her three-inch heels were topped by elegant legs in dark stockings. I accepted a coffee and made my way to the group of expensive leather chairs and settees. The second-floor room looked out across Waveney Way, over the derelict shipping company site, and thence to Lake Lothing. To my left I could see the Southshore boatyard and the Brandon Arms. Two low glass-topped coffee tables carried a small selection of pristine magazines. I noted a 'Country Life', the local advertisers' glossy magazine, 'Motorboat', and 'Yachting Monthly.' On an inside wall were photographs of office blocks, industrial units, a local primary school, and a fifty-foot motor cruiser, the type that my dad would call a gin palace. There were two doors nearby, one carried the designation 'Boardroom' in gold, the other was unmarked.

A few days earlier the archdeacon had telephoned and asked me to be ready to accept a call to visit a Mr. Blacke from the development company that were working in co-operation with the local authority. I explained that our PCC meetings had not yet taken place, and that my initial reaction was against the proposal. Apparently, the development company were keen to be ready to progress our possible new facilities as helpfully and quickly as they could. As a result, the PCC meetings were pushed back a week, so that I could better inform them as to what the alternatives were.

After ten minutes, the plain door opened and a smart curvaceous young woman emerged. She looked to be about thirty and well-endowed or else she sported breast implants. I find it difficult to tell. The telephone on the secretary's desk rang. She stood up and came over towards me.

'Would you care to follow me, Mr Green?' She led me through the plain door into a luxurious but efficient looking office which shared the view over towards Lake Lothing.

Gregor Blacke introduced himself and invited me to sit in a comfortable chair. He was tall, well-built, expensively dressed, and walked with a slight limp. I guessed he was a little under sixty. Once he would have been good-looking. Now his face held a strange mixture of aggression, pain, and sadness.

'The Lions have started well in their tour down under. Do you follow the rugby, John? Is it OK to call you "John"?' His eyebrows lifted slightly as he looked at me.

'"John" is my Christian name, so you are welcome to use it,' I smiled, slightly. 'Yes, I did hear the news this morning, although I am more into sailing, when I get the opportunity. My father has a boat. Did you play rugby?'

'Oh, yes! I played for a local club and Suffolk County — that is until I damaged my hip in a car accident. But that's another matter.' His eyes went up and to his left briefly and the sad look was more pronounced.

'When everything is settled, perhaps you might join me for a few days on my boat, "the Blacke Swan"? That's her.' He pointed to a photograph of the same cruiser I had seen in the reception area. 'I keep her in Majorca.'

I did not reply. He moved to the matter in hand.

'Thank you for coming in. I gather you have been in Lowestoft for around twelve months. They tell me you are well received and building an increasing congregation despite poor facilities. What do you think of this side of the town?'

'A vibrant school, a successful boatyard, an attractive restaurant, an historic abbey, but a number of areas of desolation due to the decline in fishing and its effects on the local economy. There has been some regeneration. The people themselves are much the same as those in other parishes. They have their joys and challenges as we all do.'

'Well, you see our local council have had a massive problem to contend with. They have been getting on with it slowly with a new supermarket, and our light industrial and commercial estate. There is a potentially attractive waterside area next to Lake Lothing. You can see the remnants of an old shipyard.' He pointed through the window. 'Then there's the wilderness at the end of the abbey grounds, an old quay, and a couple of slips that haven't been used for years.

'It requires quite an investment. That's where my company can help. If the council can proceed soon, we can put a lot of money into making this an attractive area that will draw people for pleasure and business, and create a lot of jobs. However, we have another opportunity for a development up in the north-east, where the desolation came from the loss of mining and steelworks. We can't do both. If we are unable to proceed here quickly, we don't want to miss the opportunity up north.'

He shrugged his shoulders and turned his palms upwards.

'I'd like the opportunity to help this area. I've spent most of my life around here. That's why I appreciate your coming in today. As soon as we can get a concerted agreement to go ahead with the waterside strip, we'll pull out all the stops. We want to be ready to roll. I'm going to hand you over to my chief architect who has a lot of experience. He wants to hear your views and advice on the facilities and layout for your possible new flexible church and centre. You'll find he has some good ideas as well.'

With that the man picked up his phone, 'Josie, will you ask Ed Beale to come along and meet the Reverend Green.'

After an introduction, I followed the architect out and along to his office. I noticed a suave chap with very curly hair was waiting in the reception area. I felt I had seen him before, but could not place where. I heard Gregor address him,

'Come in Bruce, back on dry land now.'

The days of drawing boards seemed to have gone. The architect's office had a desk with two computer screens and key boards. One screen was television size. Next to the desk unit were work surfaces with cupboards and draws. I noticed a bottle of white antacid medicine. A book rack contained suppliers' catalogues and files on building regulations. A couple of metres away from the computers were two printers, one of which had the width to print full-sized plans. The window down one side of the room looked out over the business park. Ed led me to a table with six chairs. Stretched out were two A3 sized plans. One was an enlarged plan of part of Coxton. The other was a building plan. Next to them lay an A4 pad of plain white paper.

Ed pulled over the Coxton plan. His movements were quick, as if nervous. He pointed:

'This is the location that Mr. Blacke has suggested for your new church complex. The company bought the site a few months ago. You may recognise that it was a good-sized petrol station. It is also virtually central to the parishes of Coxton and the abbey.'

He pulled over the other plan.

'I've researched a number of modern church designs and produced a basic layout. The altar area, here, can be screened off when the rest of the space is used for secular purposes, enabling a preservation of a sacred space. Over here there is a kitchen, and decently away are toilets. There is a meeting room here, and a vestry next to it.'

He looked at me hopefully. I felt he had been briefed that I might be unhelpful. Taking out a precision drawing pen, he pulled his pad towards him.

'What we have here is not fixed in stone, or should I say brick. We can alter the general shape somewhat, and considerably adapt the interior to suit you. There would be parking for around ten cars and there is no restriction in the adjacent roads. We thought that building space was more important than lots of on-site parking. We can select the interior surfaces to give good acoustics. It seemed best to have an initial outline with some of the factors that experience has shown to be important, but, I, we, would appreciate your comments.'

I felt very resistant but obliged to contribute. We talked for around an hour, considering seating capacity, musical provision and a host of other factors. Eventually I stood up to leave. On my way towards the door I walked past other plans laid out on a smaller table. I recognised the shape of Lake Lothing and reckoned it must be the overall development area plan. Ed endeavoured to shepherd me on, but I just had time to spot a multi-screen cinema in the area of the Brandon Arms and Southshore, and the shape of the abbey with the words 'Abbey Nightclub'.

32

As Clare announced the ending of practice for her St. Cecilia Singers, I walked slowly over the abbey crossing below the tower. The school concert was approaching and arrangements needed to be confirmed. We had agreed that any money raised would go to the school's music department, although it seemed likely they would make a small donation. Whilst the abbey funds were very low, I was keen for the building to become a focus for local life. It was part of our investment in, and care of, the community. As we walked through the crossing, I felt that wretched grit under foot again. I wondered if the ancient stone flags needed sealing, another expense we could do without.

Marie and I made our way to my car for a change. Hers had an electrical problem and was being repaired. Rather than have her miss her practice, and I would have lost a little while with her, I had picked her up from the farm. This evening we would try the Wherryman at Beccles for a change, before I ran her home. Moses was in charge of the vicarage. On the way to Beccles, Marie mentioned that Anne, with whom she shared a flat, was out for the night, staying over with boyfriend Jake. As we approached Beccles, we decided to go straight to her home. It would provide a little more intimate, or should I say private, time together?

Nearing the town, Marie guided me along the more direct route that I had missed previously. We turned off the Norwich road near a village called Worlingham. We drove along a one-way side-street near the church with the separate bell tower. This took us past the front of a white-washed three-storey house, for which the access was directly off the narrow pavement. Then we doubled back and onto a parking area just big enough for two cars, at the back.

A gate gave access to a tidy courtyard, partly paved and partly pebbled, with flower boxes and a couple of small crab apple trees in pots. As she opened the back door, Marie explained that the once larger house was mid nineteenth century. It had been renovated some time ago and divided into two homes. She gave me a quick tour. The top floor had two bedrooms, one of which with an en-suite shower and toilet was hers. It felt strange looking at her neat and tidy room with a double bed. I wondered who might have shared it with her, and felt jealous. The next floor down had a bedroom, Anne's, and a large bathroom. The ground floor had a good-sized kitchen, utility room, toilet, and a long living room that looked as if it had once been two rooms. A dining table graced one end, the other had TV, and the conventional couch and two recliners. There was something special about being shown around. It was as if I was invited into Marie's private world. She disappeared for a short time, whilst I looked at a bookcase with a metronome on top. Other people's books are interesting. Amongst others, I noticed a YRA book on navigation, a book on pen and ink sketching, some chick-lit and detective paperbacks, amongst cooking, soil science, and specialist ecology tomes. There was also a red light flashing on a telephone.

Marie had changed before she entered carrying two glasses of wine. She wore a blouse, jeans, and flip-flops. Cheerful little warm red toenails smiled up at me. She walked over to a CD player and put on an old Lionel Hampton album.

Spotting the flashing light, she pressed a button on her answer machine. It was the garage to say her car would be delayed as they were waiting for a part. I knew she had an appointment in Aldeburgh, the next afternoon.

'Why don't you borrow my car for a few days? Apart from Sunday I won't need to visit the further parishes as I went there earlier this week. The weather seems OK for a while and I can easily cover St. Mary's and Coxton by foot or bike. The car has a good-sized boot, and I can fold the back seats forward if you have much to carry. I'll just need to speak to the insurance company tomorrow morning.'

She came over and sat next to me on the couch, put her arms around me, and gave me a big kiss.

'Would you really do that for me? Thanks so much. It's an important appointment at Aldeburgh and I'd hate to risk losing a contract.'

So, it was agreed.

Marie lay against me and I wrapped my arms around her. After a while I felt myself to be both relaxing and getting aroused. I recalled sleeping with a previous girlfriend when I was doing my clinical psychology training. That seemed worlds away. She had felt unable to marry me when I started down the route to the ministry. Now surer of my ethics it seemed wrong to have intercourse before marriage, although I could understand and sympathise with those who differed. The psychologist in me had often reflected on the approach adopted by many societies in the past, though less so these days, that couples should abstain until married and then suddenly be expected to perform as experts. Marie looked around at me.

'Will you be having a holiday this summer?'

'With everything that has been happening this year I'd completely forgotten about holidays. Nothing planned. I'm entitled to four weeks but expected to ensure that services are covered. I have to tie it up with the Alistair, the rural dean. However, it shouldn't be a problem as I'm sure Rex and Paul would be happy to provide cover. Would you be happy to do something together?'

'Love to. Granddad and Gran are very keen to meet you. Granddad wondered if we would spend a few days cruising in his boat, with him? Gran will probably stay at home. But we'd have at least one night with them both.'

'Sounds great. I'd love that.' I gave her a gentle squeeze.

We were regularly spending Wednesday evenings together, after her choir practice, and also parts of Saturdays. A priest's time off tends not to match well with that of the conventional worker. We had talked little of Marie's spiritual life, nor mine for that matter. It's one of those areas that can be a minefield, or conversation killer, despite its basic fundamental importance. Aware that I was at least very fond of her, I wanted to give her all that I could. Marie had been to evensong on a few Sundays. I gathered that she was confirmed as a schoolgirl, although at St. Mary's the practice was to offer communion or a blessing to anyone who came forward, known confirmed or otherwise. Last week she came to our morning holy communion at the abbey. I had noticed a tear or two at the communion rail.

'It was lovely to see at the abbey on Sunday and to share communion with you.'

'I've not been a regular attender since I was at school, when I used to go with Grandpa and Gran. The last time I went, before meeting you, was Granddad Webb's funeral five years ago. Sunday took me back to then.'

'How did you feel about receiving communion from my hands?'

'Well, it was a little strange receiving it from the man whom I had kissed the night before.'

'Both are about love, to me. The greatest gifts one can receive are the love of God, and the good love of a person.'

'Did you mean "the love of a good person"?'

'No. I think you can get good love from a bad as well as a good person. At least I hope so. For me, it was an opportunity to pray for our Lord's love for you, and to be very close to you. For which I thank you.' I was aware of tears streaming from my eyes. 'Good heavens. Look at the time. I must be off to be able to be back around eight-forty-five tomorrow. I'll 'phone the insurance company from here to save time in the morning.'

She stood. I put my arms around her and kissed her gently but firmly.

'Thank you for a lovely evening.'

'You can stay the night if you want to.' She looked up at me and locked eyes.

I felt her body against mine, 'I want to, but I mustn't. Anyway, I've left Moses at home.' I gave her a quick peck and pulled away. 'Must go now!'

As I picked up my mobile, I felt it vibrate and then ring.

'Hi, John. It's Ben. Sorry to ring you so late. I've been looking at a photograph of the royal coat of arms in the abbey. I think you have a problem. It looks very insecure. Don't stand under it. Could I meet you after school to show you?'

'OK, Ben. Thanks. Is four o'clock tomorrow afternoon all right?'

I drove home with my mind crowded with thoughts about Marie and concern about the abbey.

33

The lights of the abbey crossing and choir were on. I left the nave lights off so that the west side of the crossing had darkness behind. Ben, Jim, Alice and I peered up at the coat of arms of Henry VIII. It was painted on a black background on a large board, secured, or so I thought, below the tower, and above the arch that led to the nave.

'Use these binoculars, John.'

Ben passed them over to me and shone a torch onto the lower edge of the board.

'Look at the pegs,' he pointed. 'We spotted the problem on a photograph we took.'

The coat of arms was held in place by two L-shaped pegs along the top edge, and a similar couple at the bottom, which would be carrying most of the weight. With the aid of the binoculars I could see that the lower peg on the right was inclined downwards somewhat, whilst that on the left must be hanging on by the skin of its teeth.

'That's where the grit on the floor must have come from,' Jim looked at me. 'And I thought it was because the floor slabs needed sealing.'

'And to think we had all those people a week ago, for the flower festival.' Alice shook her head at the thought.

'We'll have to get the board down and then re-secured. Meanwhile we must keep people from walking under it. I think the traffic cones that we use to reserve space for wedding cars and funeral hearses will do the job. I'll have to get some white ribbon to string between them.'

'We'll need scaffolding and two or three people to get that down. Should I have a word with Dan and ask him to organise it?'

Jim was helpful as ever. Dan Brookes was a builder who was a member of St. Mary's PCC. He always gave us the cheapest quote or did small jobs for nothing.

'That's a good idea, Jim. Do you think you could put out some cones whilst I pop into town to get some ribbon?'

Jim agreed. Alice suggested I tried a craft shop in the high street. Jim suggested a DIY store. 'I hope we don't need a faculty for this.'

Jim was referring to the permission that was required from one of the diocesan committees for works of alteration in a church or churchyard. Typically, it took two months to obtain, when acceptable to the committee. Sometimes the archdeacon through whom it was referred would grant it, if relatively minor.

'Jim, I'll inform the archdeacon out of courtesy, but ask Dan for a quote first. I don't see any problem in proceeding, since this is also a health and safety matter.'

34

Around the table set up in the abbey nave, a sea of concerned faces looked at me. The PCC were about to address the last planned item on the agenda, the future of the abbey. Previous items had dealt with the growth of the parent and baby meetings and we had learnt that the flower festival had raised £600. Treasurer George, giving his report, had smiled slightly covering the income from the flower festival, but looked his usual glum self when explaining the overall position. We had run out of oil for the heating and decided we could not afford to heat the building for services over the so-called summer. The fabric account, for general maintenance, had a mere £500. I looked at our secretary and started.

'Before we consider item six, I'd like to brief you on an urgent matter under "Any Other Business". Some of you may have noticed the grit underfoot below the tower. We wondered if the floor needed sealing. However, Ben Fillingham, the head of history at the Endowed School, who is running a project on the abbey with a group of six-formers, has taken a photograph of the coat of arms under the tower. He has drawn our attention to a problem. The churchwardens and I inspected the area last night. There are two pegs which support the coat of arms and they look to be in danger of dropping out. We've cordoned off the area and Dan is arranging scaffolding so that we can deal with the matter. How's that progressing, Dan?'

'The scaffolding will be here at eight on Monday morning. I couldn't get anything for tomorrow unless we paid a fortune, as it's Saturday. We'll take the board down and make good the peg holes. Leave things for a couple of days to harden off, and then remount the board. I'd like to use stainless steel brackets and screws to refit. They will be more expensive than iron, but we need them to last for another five hundred years. I can only estimate the overall job cost. I'll provide the labour free. We can fit it in between other jobs. Better budget for around two hundred pounds for scaffolding and fittings.'

The treasurer flinched.

'Thanks very much for your kind offer, Dan. We can still use the majority of the abbey.' I looked around. 'It's just the area around the crossing, under the tower. As I said it's now cordoned off. Shall we press on with the next item?'

I filled in the background. A number had heard the Archdeacon's sermon. I referred to our subsequent meeting with her, the direction to ask for a supporting resolution in favour of selling the abbey, and my meeting with the developer's managing director and architect.

'What's your view, Vicar?'

'Well, Stephanie, thanks for asking, but I don't want to influence the PCC, so I'd rather save my contribution until everyone else has had a chance. However, I can tell you that St. Giles' PCC were in favour of a new flexible modern church centre that belonged to the church.'

We worked around the table. With little exception most were against giving up the abbey. Jim and Alice spoke calmly but strongly citing historical and family connections. Then we came to George, our treasurer.

'Whilst I understand the emotional connections in favour of keeping the abbey, the committee ought to bear in mind our parlous financial position. We have a very small amount of money in our fabric account and had virtually nothing in our running expenses account until the flower festival money came in. We haven't the money to pay our parish share. We haven't been able to afford any oil for the heating system. It only needs another problem like the coat of arms and we won't then be able to afford communion wine. If we had a new building, we could reasonably expect a good period without any major expenses. We would have a modern heating system. What would also be very helpful is that we would have a source of income. We could let the building when we're not using it. I really think a lot of people have got it wrong. We shouldn't balk from this golden opportunity. The disciples didn't have large expensive buildings, and they seemed to grow a lot better than we do these days.'

He sat down rather red in the face.

'If the patronage is with the bishop as I suspect, we may not have much option.' That was Marjorie Banks, a solicitor.

Now it was my turn.

'Thank you all for your contributions. I would be very sorry if we lost the opportunity to continue worship where people have met for over seven hundred years. However, what George has said also makes very good sense. I understand that the council are concerned that a considerable area fronting Lake Lothing is unsightly, running wild, and underused. That includes a good stretch of the abbey land. We cannot afford to maintain it. None-the-less, I would make a distinction between the abbey building and the land running from it to the lake. I'm also concerned at the possible future use of the abbey. As I left the room of the architect, I couldn't help but notice a plan of the area which had the abbey building down as a nightclub. That seems wrong to me.'

'Excuse me, John.' It was churchwarden Jim, looking angry. 'I think these developers are just intent on lining their shareholders' pockets. Take for example their aim to get St. Chad's, in a prime expensive housing area!'

The conversation flowed back and forward for some time until I felt all had a reasonable say. It was time to move on.

'I think the best way forward may be a compromise. Suppose we propose the sale of the land between the abbey building and the water, but keep the building, the car park, and a small green area. I'm sure you would welcome the parishioners of St. Giles joining us. That ought to raise some money for us or the diocese. It would save the developers from having to build a new church, and would allow them to make money in building on that site.'

That produced a little more discussion. George was moderately happy, provided some of the money raised went into the abbey accounts. A slightly revised proposal was agreed.

'John,' solicitor Marjorie grinned at me. 'I suggest you speak to Jessica Ellerman, the journalist on the Suffolk Siren. She's been at a number of our services. See if we can drum up some local support to retain the abbey as a place of special local interest as well as a place of worship. Perhaps we could even start campaigning to raise money to build an extension to the abbey for social use, or to make it more flexible?'

I thought that was a very good idea. Why not use the likely current publicity and support as an opportunity to raise money. We would need to apply for a faculty to build an extension and possibly to alter the inside. But, let's get a fund first. So, we set up a development subcommittee recognising our previous ideas but charged with publicising our case, raising money for a social extension or separate building, and developing our revised parish as a caring Christian family. Marjorie agreed to be vice chairperson. She also agreed to write a letter to the Archdeacon on our behalf, setting out our proposal on her company's headed paper.

Somehow, despite the threat of losing the abbey, we felt invigorated and ready for a fight, if necessary. It reminded me of my psychology days; when a client operated in tune with their internal guidance system, they felt so much better, inspired.

35

The Archdeacon was furious when I rang her on Saturday morning about the St. Mary's PCC outcome. An amalgamation of St. Giles' into St Mary's would not release any money to the diocese. She was more pleased about Arthur Oldfield's parishes. To my surprise, the PCC at St. Chad's had agreed to the sale of their church and land and the combination with St. Olave's. One of the churchwardens, Joan Archibald, was an accountant and on both the diocesan and provincial synods and finance committees. She had strongly supported the principle.

'John,' she said, 'when you have to sell the family valuables, you don't sell the stainless steel and hang on to the solid silver. We don't have a very good attendance. If you look around the parish on a Sunday morning, people are either washing their cars or taking their kids to football or the riding stables. When they do turn up for a wedding or funeral you are lucky if they put more than a pound in the collection.'

I wondered. In a hundred years' time, would we be forced back to basics with meetings in homes, few religious buildings, and a much smaller number of believers? Possibly, unless there was a major challenge to the stability and comfort of people's lives, such as a war, terrorism, serious famine, or major disease out of control.

On Sunday, Paul and Rex took the evening service at the

abbey. I went to St. Olave's to take evensong. A grumpy Archdeacon Imogen came to perform the licensing of our new priest in charge, the Rev. Anne Fox. Anne was going to be missed at her last parish judging by the coach load who came to the service. A number of the parishioners of St. Chad's came to join us as a step towards their amalgamation into the planned extended parish. This still awaited confirmation from the bishop and the diocesan committee. In her address, the Archdeacon made a particular point of congratulating Joan Archibald and Brian Hayes, churchwardens of St. Chad's, and their PCC for their 'sensible and innovative step in joining with St. Olave's.' She gave me a very pointed look.

Monday morning came and went. No scaffolding. The delivery lorry had a clutch problem that had to be fixed. Dan reckoned it would be Wednesday at the earliest. With an early matins at eight, the mother and toddler group at ten-thirty, and our healing service at six-thirty in the evening, Tuesday would have been a bad day for the delivery. On Wednesday the abbey was devoid of planned activity until the St. Cecilia Singers in the evening.

On Wednesday morning there was still no scaffolding. When I arrived at the abbey to unlock it and say morning prayer, I found that our glass fronted notice board, which faced onto Waveney Way, had been defaced with red spray paint and carried the message 'Tidy up this area.' I notified the police who promised to send someone around to investigate, when they had a car free.

On Wednesday afternoon Jessica came to the abbey to interview me. Solicitor Marjorie had briefed her. She grinned as we met.

'Any more trips to Southwold recently, John?'

'Not recently. How's Louise getting on with her medieval project?'

'She's really enjoying it. Wants to do archaeology or history if she can get a university place in a year's time. Now, before we get down to the future of the abbey, I notice you've been done with red spray paint. I've been following up some enquiries along Lakeside after I went for a meal at the Brandon Arms. They had a plate glass window sprayed with the same colour, as far as I can remember, and, there seems to have been a spate of vandalism nearby. The strange thing is, it has all been on the Lake Lothing side of Lakeside. Nothing on the business park. The boatyard had the mooring ropes cut on one of their boats. It drifted off in the tide overnight and was damaged against an oil rig ship on the north quay. Max Archer in the bungalow had a load of cement dropped into a sewage access point on his property. I gather he can claim on his insurance, but he has a fairly heavy excess so it will still cost him most of the repair bill. And now they're having a go at the abbey.

'Louise reckons that a couple of boys in her class were returning from fishing late one evening about a week ago and thought it strange to see a small cement mixer at work near the bungalow. Nearby there were two foreign-looking men and a green van. I've spoken to Rupert Bishop at Southshore. He's going to check his CCTV.'

We spoke for some time longer. She was very thorough in questioning our intentions and reasons. She sounded angry and frustrated.

'I've been trying to get an appointment with your Archdeacon, but her secretary seems to be trying to put me off. I need to get her views, to be seen to do a fair coverage. The Bishop's office just keeps referring me to the Archdeacon. I couldn't get an appointment with the chief planning officer as he seems away on a second holiday in Majorca. I'm told that the councillor who is chair of the planning committee is away, and that the MD of the development company is off on business as well. From what you and Marjorie tell me about the diocesan plan it seems to me as if there is coercion and collusion. Do what they want and get a better financial outcome or they will use compulsory purchase at a much lower return? Well, this weekend's Siren has a copy deadline of Thursday evening and I shall go to press, subject to my editor, with coverage of the current state of affairs. I shall also invite readers to write in with their views.

'I believe our arts reporter will be out here over the weekend for your jazz festival. So, you'll probably get a double coverage in a week's time.'

'Oh, that's good news. We have run an advertisement in the Siren for the last two weeks. You probably know Mark Ransome, our organist and a music teacher at the Endowed School. He's organised the festival for Friday evening, and Saturday afternoon and evening. There are good groups coming from London and Newcastle. Mark's own group are on for the early part of Saturday evening. They are followed by a brilliant crossover trio, playing classical and religious music arranged in a jazz idiom: pianist, bass guitar, and percussion. They should sound fabulous with the abbey acoustics. Mark also got us a plug on Jazz fm. We've even got Simon, from the Brandon Arms, to lay on a bar in the abbey.'

'Won't that offend people?'

'Well, that's possible, but it was agreed by the PCC. After all we do use wine and food at holy communion. We have tea, coffee and biscuits after our main service. We provide similarly for mums and toddlers on a Tuesday morning. It's really about using the building as the centre of our activities and appreciating that God is always with us. Simon will also give us a share of his profit.'

Later that evening Marie and I made our customary visit to the Brandon Arms. It also gave a chance to check that Simon was set up for the jazz festival.

'Oh, yes. I've ordered some real ale as well as lager. Not to forget plenty of soft drinks. You might be surprised at the number of people who go for lemonade or cola, often as a step towards responsible driving.'

I asked about the defaced window.

'We'll have to get it replaced. Tried a firm that removes graffiti, but they used acid and you can't see through the glass where they've worked on it.'

I told him about Jessica and her comments.

'Yes. I remember her asking about the window. It's at the side where the security camera doesn't face. I might just check the camera on the car park in case they came in that way. Funny but that Counsellor Bruce Jackson was in a week ago trying to encourage me to sell. Pressurising really. A threat of compulsory purchase. He's a smarmy beggar. I wouldn't trust him further than I could throw him. Never liked him. In his fancy suits and posh Mercedes. Don't know how he can afford them. I remember when he was first made chair of the planning committee. Came in here. Said he might be able to help me some time and he expected that I would give him free meals any time he turned up. I soon set him right and he hadn't been back until a week ago.

'The rumour is that he used to be the purchasing manager for a local electronics manufacturer. But he was made redundant. Supposedly given the push for allegedly taking a bribe. The company didn't want any bad publicity so it was hushed up and he was given a sweetener. That's what I heard. The next thing is he's working as an employee and negotiator for a local major trade union office. Then he's into local politics. I think he's quite clever, but very devious.'

36

On Thursday morning at eight-thirty, Moses and I arrived to unlock the abbey and say matins. Dan, two of his men, and the scaffolding lorry were waiting.

'Sorry to keep you waiting chaps. You should have called me, Dan.'

'Well, I spotted you at the Brandon Arms last night, having a drink with that dolly of yours, so I thought you might be tired this morning.' He blushed and added 'From the drink I mean.'

At ten I was making coffees all round when Dan called 'Come and have a look at this, Vicar.'

The coat of arms was resting against a wall in the Lady chapel and Dan was looking at where the board had been. The stones were slightly paler. Over an area of around 60 cm square the stones were smaller and were resting one on top of another, with no mortar. Dan had already removed one and was peering into its recess. One of Dan's men returned from their pickup truck carrying a torch. I climbed up after him. Dan reached in.

'There's a gap at the back of the facing stones, John. Slightly further back I can feel a surface which doesn't seem like stone, it's softer and warmer. A different material. I think we'll remove a few of these loose smaller blocks. They don't seem to be doing anything structurally.'

Twenty minutes later six good sized stone blocks were resting on the abbey floor. In the space in the wall we could make out a chest with rusting metal on its corners. Like the removed stones, the wooden chest was extracted and lowered by block and tackle. I felt a pang of guilt as the hinges came away from the lower part of the chest when I lifted the top. Below layers of old cloth, we saw a tarnished but beautiful silver chalice encrusted with jewels around its stem. Next to it lay a tarnished silver paten. To one side of the silverware lay a collection of ancient looking books between leather covers.

'I think we'd better leave these until we have some rubber gloves, Dan. I'll have a word with Ben Fillingham, head of history at the Endowed School. But well done, lads.'

We put the chest in the vestry and locked the door. Dan's chaps filled the places where the securing pegs had been for the coat of arms. There was no sign of anything else in the cavity but we decided to leave it open so that it could be photographed.

It seemed a long wait but Ben turned up at lunch time in response to the text I had sent him. He was equipped with rubber gloves and camera. First, he climbed up onto the scaffolding platform and photographed the cavity. This was followed by photographs of the chest with its objects in their original positions. To my surprise he then went for the books first.

'These are in Latin, John. This one seems to be referring to herbs and sickness. It looks like the journal or chronicle of a frater medicus, a learned medical monk. There is a date in the fifteenth century. The book underneath looks older. I'd like to put things back in the trunk as they were and ring Robert Bedford. These could go back to the origin of the abbey in the thirteen hundreds. Would that be OK with you? Since these are religious items related to the place where they were found I don't think they could be called treasure trove, but it might be best to cover yourself and report the find to the coroner for the area. I think you have a fortnight, but I'd wait until Dr. Bedford gives his opinion. This is very much his specialist period.'

Robert Bedford arrived with Ben about six-thirty p.m. He was very excited. Once again, he went for photographs of the cavity and chest first. Then, after pulling on a pair of gloves he carefully lifted out the books, all five, and laid them down gently. After glancing through each book, he settled on one which looked a little the worse for wear.

'This looks like the chronicle of an early abbot of St. Mary's. Possibly it's the first abbot, one Ralph de Neatisheade, with an "e." That's a tiny village off Barton Broad in Norfolk. He writes about their arrival here and choosing to build on the site of an earlier wooden church. It'll take me some time to transcribe these books. We can probably do much of it digitally with character recognition software, although the transcriptions need to be checked with the originals. At times the software will jump to the wrong conclusion. I can get our Department of Antiquities to clean and assess this beautiful chalice and paten. I suggest that I take these back to Cambridge and keep them in a controlled humidity environment whilst we work on them. I'll give you a receipt. Would that be OK?'

'That's fine. Ben mentioned reporting the find to the coroner.'

'That would be a sensible thing to do. I'd also be inclined to tell the county museum people, and of course your diocesan authorities. I don't think there should be any problems with the ownership. Ben will be involved with the research. The school holidays start before long and I understand he hasn't planned any trips away.

'There is another side to your discovery, of course,' he looked around like a lecturer hoping for some good input from his students.

Ben jumped in quickly.

'My guess is that the monks in the fifteen-thirties decided to hide some of their most precious treasures from the plunderers of Henry VIII and Thomas Cromwell at the dissolution of the monasteries. What better place to hide them than behind the coat of arms of the king and head of the church?'

37

An interesting few days followed the chest discovery. I received lots of telephone calls of support and enquiry. The Suffolk Siren came out on Friday afternoon. The school concert had a half page spread on page five. Particular praise was showered on a fifteen-year old girl playing classical piano music, and on a sixth form jazz quartet.

Jessica had two reports side by side, taking up nearly half of the front page. The headline 'Save Saint Mary's?' topped a photograph of the abbey. The text below started boldly 'Diocese, developer, and local council threaten abbey parishioners: sell now or suffer a compulsory purchase pittance.' The article went on to outline the reported archdeacon's proposal and give the views of a number of the church council, churchwardens, and vicar.

'Strangely,' the article continued, 'diocesan official, developer, council chief planning officer, and chair of the planning committee are away on holiday or business. No one was available for comment.'

The article concluded with a request for the views of its readers, 'Write or email the Siren with your view. Should our famous and beautiful abbey be sold, possibly to become a nightclub?'

Jessica's second article, adjacent to the one covering the

abbey, had the headline: 'Vandals target potential development properties but ignore adjacent business park.' It went on to quote from interviews with Simon from the Brandon Arms, Rupert Bishop from Southshore Boatbuilders, Max Archer from the bungalow, and our churchwarden, Jim. The local police were reported to be investigating but having nothing to report.

On Wednesday after her choir practice, Marie and I wandered through the abbey grounds on our way to our usual drink at the Brandon Arms.

'It is quite a wilderness in places, but there are a multitude of wild flowers. Just look at that one.' She bent down to examine a small green flower stem. 'It's a frittilaria meleagris, fairly rare. It typically flowers in May and has a beautiful purple bell shape. Do you think I could leave a couple of beehives on here? I'm exploring for bee variants that may be more resistant to parasites.'

'I'd be delighted, if that doesn't sound too corny. This area between the abbey building and Lake Lothing has probably been wild since the time of Henry VIII.'

A little later we were sitting having our drinks on the Brandon Arms terrace, looking out over the Lake.

'Granddad asked if the second or third week in August would suit you to come sailing? He suggests that we go on a Saturday and return on a Friday. That would give you the following Saturday back in the parish to prepare for your Sunday services and catch up on parish matters. When we sail will depend on the weather, but a week should give us a reasonable chance to get away.'

'That sounds very interesting and very thoughtful. I did speak to Alistair, our rural dean, but I can tie up precise dates now. I'll also have to arrange things with Anne Fox, and Fathers Rex and Paul. We are very lucky at present, what with access to Rex, Paul, and Anne, and Anne has a reader at St. Olave's. We don't have a reader at the abbey or Coxton yet, but Sean Wells is interested and has started on the path. He's a young food technologist and a member of our PCC. Oh, I'm really looking forward to this holiday.' I squeezed her hand.

'Are you two at it again? I'll have to have a word with the parish council.' Landlord Simon had crept up unnoticed. 'That reporter Jessica has her head screwed on the right way, I reckon. Did you read her two articles in the Siren? And clever putting them side by side. Makes you think. Max in the bungalow says she even took away a sample of the cement they got out of his drain. That's more than the police could be bothered to do.'

'Jessica said that you were going to look at your CCTV recordings. Any luck there?' I asked.

'Possibly. We caught a glimpse of a green van on the road, with two chaps wearing hoodies returning. It's a scanning camera, rotates, so it can miss some moving things, although it covers a good area. It's meant for the car park. We got part of a number plate. It ended "5 JBA". Rupert Bishop next door at the boatyard didn't get the van on his cameras. They probably left it outside the Arms. But he did get two men coming off the pontoon where his boat was moored. One of them had his hood blown off by a gust of wind, looked to be east European, Rupert thought. Possibly early thirties. It was about ten minutes after my recording. Same night that Max Archer's drain was done.'

The next day, Thursday, my mobile rang at eight a.m., when I was out for a run with Moses. It was Councillor Bruce Jackson who wanted to meet me. We met at nine-thirty in the abbey. When I arrived, I noticed a smart new Mercedes sports just outside the south porch. Not even the disabled parked as close as that. Jim had unlocked the door and was inside. I heard raised voices as I entered and was passed by a red-faced Jim on his way out.

'Morning, John. You've got a very important visitor. At least, he thinks he is. Look where he's parked his car! Ring me if you need me. I'm off to try to develop some Christian charity.' He headed towards the wilderness and lake.

'Good morning, Vicar.'

The voice was plummy and cultured. I was greeted by a tall, muscular, almost handsome, man, wearing a smart white summer jacket over a purple shirt and gold coloured tie. His matching fine white trousers carried knife-sharp creases, breaking slightly on highly polished light brogues. A purple handkerchief corner peeped out from his breast pocket. His short brown hair was slicked back, with a straight parting on his left side. Somehow his face seemed small for his height, his nose was sharply pointed, and his eyes were too close together. A dark narrow moustache contributed to a weasel-like look. He stood feet astride with his hands behind his back as I approached.

'Mr. Jackson?' I held out a hand. 'How can I help?'

'Call me "Councillor"! It's more like how can I help you.' His hands stayed behind his back.

Lord Jesus, give me calm wisdom and help me to lead this man towards your love.

Two can play games. I elevated myself, mentally, to an imaginary position looking down on the pair of us, known as 'third position' in Neurolinguistic Programming. Additionally, I envisaged him as barely reaching my waist in height, dressed in grubby schoolboy shorts, and with a large red nose. And waited, looking directly at him with feigned patience and an attempt at a gentle smile. After a long pause he eventually shifted his balance and dropped his eyes for a second.

'Well, Vicar, I dare say we both aim to help the local people. But I have been elected by the people of this area. Together with other members of the elected council, I am endeavouring to give our people a more pleasant environment to live in and more jobs. Our council has been working to replace the dereliction left by the Second World War and the decline in the fishing industry. We have had the ideas and plans for some time, but not the money. Rather like the Church, when you think about it.' He paused to savour his humour.

'Now at last we have found a developer who will supply the finance, if we are able to progress soon. Additionally, the developer sees an opportunity to help the church financially, in return for taking into care a dilapidated building and waste land.

'I am told that if you have the foresight to share the vision of your diocesan colleagues and our local council, you could progress to considerable heights in the church. You just need to convince your church council of the many benefits and reduction in financial risks they would gain by accepting a very generous offer from a charitable benefactor. You need to act fast if you are not to lose this offer. Otherwise the council may employ compulsory purchase. You would then lose the abbey, and at a much-reduced valuation.'

My turn.

'Councillor, unlike you, I have not been elected by local people. I have been invited by them. I have been appointed by the bishop. You might say that I am Christ's representative in serving the members of this and a number of neighbouring parishes. After prayer, they have chosen to continue the work of our Lord over seven centuries in this great building. Local people protected it from destruction by a king five hundred years ago. I have little doubt that we will find ways to continue its contribution to local life. If there is anything that I can do to help you personally, please let me know.'

With some difficulty I restrained myself from replying to his threat.

'Well, I've done my best to help you,' he shrugged his shoulders. 'By the way, I thought I saw mouse droppings by your kitchen. I shall have to notify the council's environmental health department.' With that he turned and left.

I doubted the mouse droppings, but forewarned was forearmed. The kitchen and toilet areas were given an extra thorough wash down and treatment with disinfectant. A mousetrap produced no victim. An inspector did turn up a day or so later but gave us a clean bill of health.

38

The following week the Suffolk Siren again had plenty of coverage related to the abbey. Two jazz festival photographs on the front page showed sixth-former Beth Jones playing her oboe, and Alun Pryce-Thomas, whose crossover trio had rounded off Saturday evening's session. The photographs were linked through to fuller coverage on page five. The Friday afternoon session was well attended. Saturday afternoon and evening were sold out. Mark's group started Saturday afternoon with their dinner jazz style. Baker's Half-Dozen followed them. They were a sextet of sixth formers from the school, who had developed under Mark's tutelage. They were led by Ewan Baker and included Beth on oboe. They played a mix of music. As a tribute to the evening trio they played a haunting arrangement of an old Welsh tune, 'David of the White Rock.' The evening was rounded off by the very successful crossover group, the Alun Pryce-Thomas trio. The abbey acoustics and atmosphere particularly suited their music. Simon from the Brandon Arms ran a bar over the two days. Helpers from the abbey congregation sold sandwiches, cakes, tea, and coffee.

A front-page photograph of Councillor Bruce Jackson led a description and extolled the virtues of the Council's regeneration plan for the south side of Lake Lothing. A well-reasoned statement from Archdeacon Imogen Rodgers pointed out the need for the modern church to set an example of belt-tightening and financial prudence in these times of austerity. It ended with her expectation that local parochial issues could be resolved with prayer, goodwill, and common sense.

Jessica's earlier request for reader's views had produced a flood of responses. Past baptisms, marriages, history, heritage, and wild life were all cited as reasons for continuance of the abbey and its grounds. Jessica reported an interview with Dr. Marie Webb, a local ecologist, who commented on rare plants and insects in the grounds, and 'hoped that at least some of the abbey grounds would be preserved in their present condition.' On the other hand, the managing director of one of the firms on the business park wrote about the 'unsightly wilderness of the abbey grounds and the overgrown and unused wasteland of the late shipping company.' An 'unemployed father' welcomed the hope of more jobs in the locality. An 'irate parishioner', local GP, Dr. Ian Marshall, argued that since the abbey was now used for entertainment and the sale of food and alcohol it might just as well be turned into a nightclub. Jessica rated the responses as roughly sixty per cent in favour of preserving the abbey as a church.

We hit the front page a third time with a photograph of the chest and contents recovered from behind the coat of arms. There were brief comments from Ben and myself. Earlier, I had notified the coroner, the Suffolk Museum Head Curator, and our Archdeacon.

I rang Marie's mobile a little later that Friday afternoon.

'Thanks for the comment to Jessica about the abbey grounds. Do you fancy a meal out tonight, or will you take a chance on my cooking?'

'Hi. Jessica rang me on Thursday morning. I think Jim gave her my number and suggested she try me. I tried to be supportive whilst staying scientific.'

That rang a bell. I'd mentioned to Jim the wild flower Marie spotted. She continued,

'Thanks for the invitation but I'd better decline. I've an analysis I need to do tonight, or the specimen will have dried out too much. Our spectrometer is giving trouble and I'm waiting for a technician who's due any minute to see if he can fix it. Why don't you come and have an evening meal with me tomorrow night, say around seven? Anne is going out with Jake.'

Marie on her own. That sounded inviting. So that's what we agreed. Instead of anything special that night, Moses and I went for a brisk walk. Later after a shower, I prepared a ham salad and went to the cupboard for a tin of dog food for Moses. He was hot on my heels, endeavouring to help.

'Moses, I'm sorry. The cupboard's bare. I'll pop to the supermarket to get you some grub.' My mobile's battery was low so I put it on charge. The salad went into the 'fridge and I went out of the front door.

It was only a five-minute walk. The store was busy with early evening shoppers. I aimed straight for the pet food aisle, inevitably at the furthest corner from the entrance. *Dear, Mother,* I reflected, *you would start at the first aisle, fruit and veg', and trawl up and down. 'Looking for ideas,' you would say. 'When you do the cooking for everyone, a well set out display can be an inspiration.'* I was more of a list person. Do the job and then get out.

'Evening, John.' Supervisor June looked up from clearing a frozen till printer.

'Hi, June. You've drawn the short straw for the late shift tonight?'

'I have to set an example and take my turn.'

Thank you, Lord. It's good to see June feeling useful, cheerful, and looking well. She must be well past the demise date predicted by Dr. Marshall.

I made my way to the self-check-out with a bag of dog biscuits and a six-pack of tins of moist meaty chunks. As I walked out, the sun bathed the abbey tower in warm ochre. Near the car park exit I noticed the athletic figure of Rick Driver, the local footballer with the red Porsche. He was standing talking to someone the other side of him. Stepping sideways, he put an arm around what was now clearly a woman, and gave her a kiss. Waving her farewell, he got into his car and drove off. As I watched it dawned on me that the woman he kissed was Marie, carrying two bags of shopping. Her Discovery was parked nearby. She climbed in and drove off.

And I thought she was working late! I had felt sure our relationship was blossoming. After all we were going sailing together with her Granddad in a couple of weeks' time. But you don't just kiss anyone. Do you? And I recalled seeing her talking to the same chap before. His athletic figure and worldly goods, I could not compete with. After all, she was human. I made my way out by the pedestrian access to the service road and headed home.

Moses gave me a big welcome and devoured his food with a healthy appetite. I nibbled at my salad. My book failed to involve me. I watched the TV news repeat twice. The inevitable evening soaps didn't appeal. I couldn't motivate myself to play my keyboard. A few prayers for peace in the world, for others less fortunate than myself, and for Marie's well-being, helped a little. Best to do something more energetic to take my mind off myself. I changed into jogging kit, and then went out with Moses to pound the streets for an hour.

39

It was late twilight as I returned my pint glass to the bar of the Brandon Arms. Moses and I had set off on a slow jog. We had run to the shores of Oulton Broad and along by the marina. At Mutford lock, which connects the Broads to Lake Lothing and thence the North Sea, we had joined the road heading back towards south Lowestoft, before cutting through the business park towards Waveney Way and the pub.

Leaving the pub, I picked up a steady jog again. Each pad of the feet seemed to express anger. I don't like feeling angry. It's often due to misunderstanding, but I couldn't get away from that image of the footballer with an arm around Marie giving her a kiss. Maybe I'm old-fashioned but I couldn't feel comfortable sharing that degree of intimacy with another person. Was she managing two relationships in parallel? We reached the derelict shipyard.

'Come on, Moses, let's run through the abbey grounds to the old quay and then back home up Magdalene Lane.'

Picking our way around the odd clump of wild blackberry we passed the old fishpond depressions and approached the water's edge of Lake Lothing. I recalled that this was where I had first met Moses. He didn't look distressed with old memories. There was no sign of the mud we had both been covered in. It was clearly near high water. The subdued purr of a throttled back engine drew my attention to a motor cruiser proceeding in towards Mutford Lock or the marina just short of it. The red sidelight and white masthead light glowed brightly, although there was still enough light to make out the boat. I guessed that probably they had needed to lower the short mast to pass under Lowestoft's road bridge with its air draft of around seven feet.

We headed towards the old quay where Magdalene Lane ended. A car was parked by the hedge. I could make out someone sitting on the quay edge, dangling their legs over, probably another angler. I find it difficult to resist asking whether an angler has caught anything and headed over, breaking my run into a slow walk. I kept well back from the edge so as not to disturb any fish.

He heard us coming and turned.

'Please don't come any nearer.' His voiced sounded slurred.

I checked. I recognised the face as that of a man I had seen once at compline but who had left before I reached the south door after the service. He looked around forty. It was then that I noticed the half empty whisky bottle and a crushed cardboard pill packet. What I thought was a turned-up collar I could now see was a rope around his neck. It looked as if it led off to a short thick metal bar next to him. Moses ran over and licked his face and then came back to me.

'I'm John. Do you mind if I sit down here? We've just been for a run and my legs are tired.' I sat down near the edge about ten feet away from him.

'This is Moses.' Moses looked at me and I gave him a gentle pat.

'Strange name for a dog.'

'Well, I had to rescue him from the Lake, not far from here. Some boys were trying to drown him. I guess you must have been going through a bad time as well?'

He went quiet and reflective for a while.

'I'm just waiting to get more drowsy and fall in. I didn't have enough courage to jump straight in. But I'm nearly there. Don't you come any nearer or that'll push me over the edge, huh,' he grunted at his own gallows' humour.

'And what's brought you to this, Bill? Sorry, did you say that your name was Bill?'

'No. It's Rory.'

I cursed myself. My second question could have distracted him from answering the first. Try again.

'Life can be very hard at times.'

'Is it a sin to commit suicide?' He looked directly at me.

'Well, I don't think so, and I'm pretty sure that in his love, God, doesn't. But I think he'd feel pretty disappointed he hadn't been able to help you. Perhaps it's something you can talk about? He would listen.'

He took a deep breath and sighed heavily.

'Women!' His eyes looked up briefly and his head turned looking into the distance.

'They screw you up and spit in your face. I love my wife and kids, but she wants a divorce. Wants me out of the house. She's met some other chap. I try to get her to talk, to see if there's anything she wants me to do differently. All she says is "Go, I don't love you anymore."'

'I guess that can hurt a lot, and make you angry.'

Somehow Rory's predicament made me think of Marie. Rory and I both felt angry. He was turning his anger onto himself. Somehow, I needed to help him develop reasons to live.

'Rory. How old are your children?'

'Lewis is eleven, Margaret's eight.'

'You said you love them?'

'Of course, I do. But when she gets her divorce, they rarely let the father see the children.'

'Rory, unless you have been treating your children unkindly, I'm pretty sure you would get access. But think how Lewis and Margaret would feel, knowing that their father had chosen to kill himself, rather than to see and keep in touch with them, to be there to support them when they needed you, to be there when they married, or had your grandchildren. They would have a whole lifetime of sadness. You can do something about that.'

He grunted and slumped a little more.

'Rory, would it be all right if I moved a little nearer?'

'No. Stay there.'

'If you fall in, I'll have to come in after you, and I'm not a brilliant swimmer. But I'd like to be able to help you.'

I hoped I hadn't lied. I am a fairly good swimmer, but that is not the same as brilliant. If he fell in the iron bar would make it difficult to get him to the surface. I supposed that was why he had it. I was only wearing running clothes and didn't normally carry a knife any way. He yawned.

'Can you tell me what you've taken?'

'Some tablets the doctor gave me and some whisky.' He picked up the crumpled prescription box and threw it towards me. It landed five feet from him. That gave me a chance to shuffle a little nearer. If I could convince him that he had a future, he would fare better in recovery, rather than take the next opportunity to do the same or something worse again.

'Thanks.'

I picked up the packet and shuffled a bit further away to build trust.

'Are you going?' He looked across.

'No. I'd like to stay until you feel ready for me to get you to hospital. You see, I think you could have a good and useful life. You have things to do and challenges ahead.'

I didn't want to mention that he might find another woman in due course. That would remind him of the current one. I looked at the prescription packet. Amitriptyline! I hated that stuff. It was commonly prescribed for depression. One of its side effects was to make some people more suicidal. Why on earth doctors prescribed it, rather than use referral for some form of psychological help, I could never understand. It could also have very unpleasant withdrawal effects.

'You've been to see a doctor?'

'Yeh. Wasn't much help. Told me to pull myself together and

gave me those.'

'Who was the doctor?' But I had a good idea.

'Dr. Marshall.'

'You may not know it but these tablets can actually make some people feel worse. Did you go back?'

'Seemed a waste of time,' he was getting more slurred and looking very drowsy.

'Do you feel more nearly ready for me to help you away from the edge?'

'No. Not much point is there?'

That actually sounded as if we were making some progress. He was querying his actions. Maybe I could use his anger to help him by turning it outwards?

'What do you do for work, Rory?'

'I'm an accountant.'

'Do you own your house?'

'Well, with my wife. And we have a mortgage.'

'Have you made a will?'

He nodded.

'Who are the beneficiaries?'

'My wife. Oh, and the children if she were dead first.'

'Presumably, you have some life insurance?'

'Yes, of course.'

'Does it have a no-suicide clause?'

'Um. I don't think so.'

'So, if you kick the bucket, or jump in the water here, who's going to be well off?'

'My wife.'

'What do you think will happen to the other chap if you die?'

'He'll probably move in, and maybe marry her, I don't know.'

'So, he could end up with a share of your house and life insurance?'

'Probably.'

'And how would you feel about that?'

'Bloody angry. Oh shit!' He fell over sideways tightening the noose.

'Can I help you now, please?'

'If you put it that way.'

'Come on. We've got to get you on your feet and walking.'

I loosened the noose and removed it from around his neck. He started coughing. I remembered I had left my mobile at home for lightness when running. I managed to get him to his feet, walked him to his car, and lent him against it.

'Have you got a mobile?'

'In the car.'

'Keys?'

'In the water. Car's not locked. I wasn't driving home.'

As I leant him over the bonnet, I could feel him sobbing. The mobile was on the passenger seat. I brought the screen to life, only to find it wanted a security code. Try 1,2,3,4. It worked. I pressed the phone app and dialled the emergency number.

'Ambulance please, and hurry. Overdose. Lake end of Magdalene Lane, Lowestoft. Sorry, I don't know the number of this 'phone, it's not mine.'

I closed the mobile, put his arm round my neck, and made him stumble around until he couldn't manage any more. Then I lent him over the bonnet again.

It was probably only five minutes but felt a lifetime before I heard the ambulance, and picked up the flashing blue lights making their way down Magdalene Lane. I told the paramedics all I knew.

'Where are you taking him?'

'The Brandon Hospital.'

'I'm the vicar of the abbey. I'll pop home, shower, and go to see him.'

They closed the back doors and set off, one tending Rory and one driving, lights flashing and siren howling. Moses and I ran home.

40

I called back at the Brandon Hospital mid-morning on Saturday. Rory had been kept in overnight and looked very pale. The senior nurse on the ward advised me that he was likely to be sent home after the psychiatrist's round, some-time later in the afternoon. The previous evening, I had reached Accident and Emergency after changing into a clean track suit and dashing out of the house. Rory was waiting to be seen in a curtained-off cubicle, with a nurse trying to keep him awake. I was allowed in and able to provide a little more information. Before long, he was vomiting whilst having his stomach washed out. Fortunately, many tablets were largely intact, and he had not taken paracetamol. I reckoned that the experience would either dissuade him from repeating the overdose attempt, or else encourage him to make a better job of it. If I could help, it would be the former. I stayed an hour, during which time he was moved to a ward for overnight observation.

Now, in the cold light of day, Rory was facing picking up his life again.

'I want to see if Julie will have another go with me. If she won't, I'm not moving out until we sell the house. That'll put some responsibility on the other chap.'

'You might both find it helpful to have some help from outside your relationship, if Julie is prepared to reconsider her hopes for the future. You could try "Relate", although they often have long waiting times. Your GP would also have access to a counselling service. If you try that route, you might be best to see one of the other doctors in the practice. I think that Dr. Marshall is of the "pull yourself together brigade." Equally, if you feel like talking with me, either singly or together, I'd be happy to help.'

He sighed.

'I'd like to come and see you anyway. I've been feeling very lonely.'

Lord, please guide me in helping this man.

'What do you do to let your hair down when you're not working?'

'Not very much really. I take Lewis to a Norwich football academy coaching session on Monday nights, for an hour, and to a football team on Saturday mornings. Julie takes Margaret to riding on a Saturday morning.'

'OK, and do you and Julie have any hobbies or activities that you do for yourselves?'

'Julie goes to a Zumba class and then out with girl friends on a Wednesday night, at least that what she says. I used to play golf, until we had the children. I've been pretty busy at work for the last couple of years as we've expanded. With a partner, I run an accountancy practice. Maybe I've got the balance a little wrong recently.'

Experience shows that satisfaction in a number of areas of activity in a typical life contributed to a general sense of well-being and happiness: fulfilment at work, a loving relationship, sexual expression, physical activity, engaging leisure activity or hobby, family relationships, and friends. A lower level in one of these could be helped out by good levels in others. Rory didn't appear to have many positives going for him. I wondered whether any could be opened up. I put this to him and would follow up if he came to see me after discharge.

'It might be an idea to take a little time off work and pick up something you have enjoyed in the past. Perhaps you could offer to run the line when you take Lewis to football. If you still have your golf clubs perhaps you could spend a little while on a local golf course or at a driving range. Many people find that a hitting or kicking sport helps to express anger. The more you enjoy it, the better it will help.'

There are several ways of looking at suicidal tendencies. Sometimes it seems as if a sense of anger is turned inwards. Rory would most likely have felt anger at Julie and her lover. In frustration and self-blame, he could have been taking out redress against himself. We talked a little longer, then I gave him my visiting card and took my leave.

'Give me a call when you feel like a chat, and definitely if you feel suicidal, at any time.'

41

As I opened my car door on the hospital car park a blast of hot air hit me. It was like an oven inside. I put the air conditioning on and stood outside whilst the interior improved. Taking my mobile out of my pocket I switched off the silent mode and checked for missed calls. There were several from Marie. I realised I hadn't looked at my 'phone since the previous afternoon. I gave her a call. She didn't answer. I noticed a message from her.

'Tried to get you several times. Hope you're OK. Strawberries, tonight. Forgot the cream. Can you bring some, please? X. M.'

At six-thirty, I parked at the back of Marie's house, grabbed the cream and a bottle of wine and made my way through the short courtyard. A table with a flowered cloth and candle was laid near a graceful potted shrub.

I rang the back door bell and opened the door, somewhat unsure of my feelings after last night. 'Hello.'

I put the cream and wine in the 'fridge.

'Down in a minute,' came from upstairs.

Two minutes later, Marie breezed into the kitchen. She was wearing a pink blouse, a loose-fitting white skirt with a floral motif, and high heeled shoes. Her hair was arranged elegantly up, emphasising her fine features.

'You look absolutely gorgeous,' I just had to say it.
She came over and we hugged cheek to cheek.
'Save the lipstick for later. I've just done it.'
'The cream and —,
'I tried to get —.'
We were talking together. I shut up.

'I tried to get you several times last night and this morning,' she started again. 'Even called round. I could hear Moses. My technician couldn't fix the spectrometer yesterday and had to call back with a spare part this morning. I went to the supermarket to get some things for tonight, and called round to see if you were still free. I rang several times last night and this morning but you must have had your 'phone off, or else there was no signal. Is everything all right? You look a bit upset. You haven't got another woman on the sly, have you?'

My turn.

'I ran out of food for Moses and walked to the supermarket around tea time. I forgot my 'phone. I must have just missed you in the store. When I came out, I saw you in the distance snogging that footballer with the Porsche. He must be able to offer you a lot more of the things of this world than I can. I'm sorry but I felt very jealous and angry. I couldn't share you with another man. I didn't eat much. Moses and I went out for a run and I left my 'phone behind. We came back through the abbey grounds. By the old quay at the end of Magdalene Lane we found a chap trying to commit suicide and I ended up going to hospital with him. I followed up this morning and only noticed your message when I left the hospital.'

I felt a mixture of being a failure and angry, partly at myself, partly at Marie, partly at the footballer, and partly at the values of a society that gave a footballer an abundance of financial wealth and a priest very little. What did I have to offer other than love and an insight into what, to me, was the most precious thing in life, the love of God? How did that compare, in the eyes of a young woman possibly choosing a mate, with a fast car, a speed boat, designer clothes, and an expensive nest? I became more aware of how much I would miss her, how much I had come to enjoy and value her company, and how much I loved her. Was it all a dream that was about to evaporate?

'Wow!' She looked taken aback and a little confused. 'That was Rick. He was my last boyfriend. I wasn't snogging him, he grabbed me. He wanted to pick things up again. I don't. He was quite a good-natured chap, good fun, and very generous, but he kept his brain below his belt. I felt I needed someone more cerebral. I thought you and I were getting along fine.'

Should I feel guilty about doubting Marie, I wondered? The thoughts of losing or offending her, concerned me. Could I find a positive way forward? I held her hands and looked into her green eyes that looked about to shed a tear.

'I'm sorry if I doubted you. It must be a good thing for us to be able to talk openly about any concern. It makes me realise how important you are to me. I don't think that my Christian love extends to sharing you, except with relatives.'

She pulled her hands free of mine, put them around my neck, and pulled herself close to me. I slipped mine under her arms and around her waist, and held her tighter. Her lips were moist and open. I felt tears run down my face. They were a mixture of hers and mine.

'I would be furious if I saw you kissing another woman.'

'Oh, by the way, the cream and a bottle of white wine are in the 'fridge.' We let go and laughed at each other.

'It's slimmers' food tonight, apart from the first course. Would you care to pour a couple of glasses of your wine, for which thank you? I'll just toast the tomato bruschettas.'

We were soon sitting out and tucking in. My body and mind eased. There was something very special about Marie.

'To us!' I lifted my glass to her and waited for hers to touch mine.

She rose to fetch the next course. I followed with the empty plates. Two hours later the temperature dropped and we went inside. I started on the washing up despite her protestations. Marie made coffee.

'That was a very tasty meal. Thanks.'

Chicken Caesar salad had been followed by strawberries and cream. We decided to have coffee inside.

'My Mum and Dad thought you were very special. As I do, of course,' I turned to look at her. 'I'm looking forward to meeting your grandparents in a week's time.'

My parents had come down for a long weekend a couple of weeks previously. Rupert Bishop and I had been in contact a couple times over the vandalism and he was happy to give Dad a tour of his works. Dad's work was concerned with bigger vessels than Rupert's, but they still had a lot in common. I joined them for lunch at the Brandon Arms. Mum spent the day out with Marie.

'It's strange isn't it? Before the event I felt as if I would be up for inspection. But we seemed to get on very well. Your Mum and I had a lot in common. I think she must be a very good biology teacher. And your Dad. He's quite a leg puller, isn't he? With his boating background, he and Granddad would get on fine.'

I lifted the tray with the two cups of individual filter coffee and followed Marie into the main room downstairs. Marie collected a box of chocolate mints from the sideboard and made for the settee. I was aware of a sense of pleasant anticipation. Coffee and mints consumed, she shook off her shoes and rested against me, with her feet up. I realised that we were both looking at each other.

I caught a whisper of her fragrance and was aware of a deep longing to stay close to her. Ideas of marriage had been going around my head. But I had spent a night doubting her. Would she think I would never ask? We had a week together coming up, with one or both of her grandparents. Perhaps it would be better to wait until after that, just to make more certain that we were compatible.

'Is it OK to sample the lipstick now?' She sighed, nodded, and drew closer.

42

On Tuesday, Alistair rang to say that he would be in the area later that morning, and asked whether I would be free for a brief chat. He called at the vicarage just after lunch and received a well-behaved welcome from Moses and a cup of coffee from me.

'There are a couple of matters I needed to raise before you take to the high seas, John. First, and most important, do you need any input from the deanery to cover services?'

'Thanks for the offer, but Paul, Rex, and Anne, have everything covered.'

'Right, I won't beat about the bush, but I'm getting a lot of flak about the reluctance of St. Mary's PCC to support the sale of the abbey and acceptance of a brand new, more manageable church and centre. The chairman of the Diocesan Board of Finance rang me yesterday. Diocesan funds are in a very weak state in poor economic times and this is an opportunity to realise an asset at a helpful value. The sale of St. Chad's is useful, but it wouldn't compare with what we've been offered for the abbey. I did make a case for your PCC, but equally I feel obliged to put to you the diocesan point of view.'

'Alistair, thanks for being open, and for your offer of pastoral help. I understand the financial arguments, although I have a suspicion that they may be mistaken. I have been charged with the care of this parish and feel that the PCC have taken the right decision.'

We chatted a little longer and then he left. A couple of hours later I had a call from the Archdeacon. She wanted to see me before I went on holiday and made an appointment for me to call at her office on Thursday afternoon. I guessed that Alistair had probably been tasked to report the result of his visit. On Wednesday afternoon, I received another call.

'Good afternoon, Reverend Green?' It was the cultured, positive voice of an executive woman. She sounded imperious, if slightly concerned. She had an aura that projected down the telephone line. I doubted if many people would dare to disagree with her.

'Yes,' I answered somewhat cautiously.

'May I call you "John"?'

'Yes. That is my Christian name.'

'This is Faye Billingham, FCA.'

She articulated each letter clearly and precisely. I struggled for a minute to recall what the letters stood for, and then remembered that I had seen the same on Rory's business card. I believed that it stood for something like Fellow of the Chartered Accountants' Institute. She soon set me right.

'I am your Diocesan Director of Finance. I approve the bank transfers of your stipend. The Diocesan Board of Finance have asked me to have a word with you.' She paused briefly. I recalled feeling like this when standing before a headmaster for some infringement of school rules.

'It would help the diocese, and no doubt please the bishop, if you and St. Mary's PCC would support the diocesan intention to sell the abbey and build you a new church and church centre. We don't want a spat, do we. As I understand it, the ownership of the abbey is vested in the diocese. So, it is really a courtesy to ask for the support of the parish.

'Perhaps you don't understand the financial problems that the church as a whole, and the diocese in particular, has. There is a significant shortfall in the national pension fund for retired clergy. All dioceses are having to make that good. Two years ago, the diocesan excess of expenditure over income was £600,000, last year it was £900,000. Many parishes, including your own, are falling well short of contributing their parish share. Much against our wishes it is now necessary to raise money from the sale of assets. It looks like we shall have to reduce the clerical coverage and have fewer priests per deanery, which would release clergy housing for sale, and reduce our expenditure. It could be that the Reverend Anne Fox, whose support you have currently, might have to be moved to another part of the diocese, leaving you to cover more parishes. I hope that you see the problems we are attempting to solve. At present we have an offer for the abbey which is probably well over any market value. We don't want to prejudice that. If it would help, I am quite willing to come and explain the position to your parish.'

'Mrs. Billingham, —.'

'Ms or Faye, please.'

'Faye, we do understand the diocesan position, but we believe that the abbey is very important to our parish and locality. We have a development committee, which is looking at ways to increase our involvement with the local community, to offer more to it, to increase the number of worshippers, and to raise more income. I am quite happy to represent your comments to our PCC but doubt if they will change their view. As concerns the ownership of the abbey, there is a strong feeling that it is vested in the PCC. There is a parishioner solicitor who is looking into this.'

'Well, I hope you appreciate that if your parish has problems with the abbey roof, for example, we are unlikely to be in a position where the diocese is able to help. I have a call on the other line now, so I'll have to go. Good bye.'

43

Late on Wednesday afternoon, Ben Fillingham rang. He sounded excited.

'Hi, John. Will you be at the abbey any time this evening?'

I usually went towards the end of the St. Cecilia Singers practice, and then locked up and went to the Brandon Arms with Marie and a few of the other Singers. So, we agreed to meet around seven. I took the opportunity to say evensong at the abbey around six-fifteen then went to the vestry to wait. Spot on time, Ben and a pupil whom he introduced as Ian, knocked and entered. Ian was carrying a contraption which he explained was a metal detector. Ben carried a small haversack.

At their request I followed them out of the south door, around the west end and up to the old infirmary cloister just to the north of the abbey. It was little more than parallel lines of old stones in the form of a square, although there were slightly taller fragments of the adjacent infirmary walls. There was a clear gap in the infirmary's west wall where it joined the cloister. Presumably, this was where a door had been.

'Vicar, Dr. Redford and I have done a lot of work on the contents of the chest from behind the coat of arms. We would like to make an appointment to brief you and your churchwardens about our finds. If you wanted to ask Louise's mum, the journalist, to be there, you might get some good publicity.

'Quite separately from that, Ian here has explored a lot of the area around the abbey buildings and near to the abbey. He didn't get much response except for this area near the infirmary doorway.

'Show him, Ian.'

'I normally use earphones,' Ian looked at me, 'because I can tell more from the sound. But so that we can all hear I'll put it onto the loudspeaker.'

He flicked a switch and looked at a dial whilst adjusting a knob. Then he traced a rectangular path around the doorway and across the cloister.

'Nothing there, but if I use a smaller rectangle —'

He closed in towards the infirmary door and traced out a smaller rectangular path, inside the first. The detector whined. He ran several straight lines across the area and produced the most intense sounds on a line running east-west.

Ben pulled a clipboard out of his bag and opened it to show me. It was the photograph that his pilot friend had obtained when flying over the abbey.

'Notice, Vicar, that the area where we have that signal comes out a deeper colour on the photograph. Ian has surveyed this area and graphed his detector readings. The aerial photograph has faint indications of some other structure within the infirmary cloister. I've shown both the metal detector survey and the photograph to Dr. Redford and he agrees that we should ask for a faculty to excavate this area. He has also spoken to the county archaeologist and the county archivist, and they agree. It looks rather as if this inner structure may predate the abbey.'

It all sounded very exciting if somewhat hopeful. This was the time to start organising.

'Mr. Fillingham and Ian, thanks, that's very interesting. You have my support. Can I ask you, Ben, to get Dr. Redford to make a formal request and proposal? Can you also get letters of support from the county people, if they will agree? We need to move fairly quickly as the diocese are hell-bent on selling the abbey. Let's make a date for you and Dr. Redford to meet with our churchwardens and myself on Friday fortnight. I dare say that other members of the parish may like to come along. I'm afraid I'm away on a week's holiday from this weekend. Will that give you enough time? I am seeing the Archdeacon tomorrow, so I'll let her know to expect this.'

Ben said he thought that with a bit of arm twisting he could manage. He and Ian took their leave. Eventually I went to the Brandon Arms with Marie, very excited.

44

The various diocesan committees had acted quickly to close St. Chad's, in preparation for its sale. I was surprised and disappointed that there were not more objections from St. Chad's parishioners. The Archdeacon had directed that there should be a couple of parish meetings. They were poorly attended and the Venerable Imogen was very persuasive with her glib tongue, helped by an input from Joan Archibald, churchwarden and synod member. They sold the idea partly by claiming that it was a Christian duty.

After Anne Fox was licensed in St. Olave's, we had started the practice of holding a short Holy Communion Service on a Thursday morning at the abbey. The service was followed by a brief team meeting. Whilst this was technically for Anne and me, Fathers Paul and Rex often joined us. Whilst I was away on holiday, they would take a number of services at the abbey although Anne would take the main Sunday service at nine-fifteen and Paul would take the services in Anne's patch. Paul and Rex left our meeting diplomatically after a while, leaving Anne and me the opportunity to talk about potential personal issues, such as Anne adjusting to her new role. On the Thursday before my holiday, after the two men had left, Anne and I were sipping fresh cups of coffee.

'Looking forward to your holiday, John?'

By then we had pretty well tied up the organisational loose ends.

'I am. It's my first let-your-hair-down holiday since I was inducted. My sailing bag is packed, and the weather forecast is pretty good. I was worried about Moses, but Jim has kindly offered to look after him, and he gets on well with Jim. Are you all right about keeping an eye on the abbey? You'll find Rex, Paul, Jim, and Alice, all very helpful.'

I looked at her. She was fifty-two and had been in social work before entering the ministry. Her husband was a social worker in Norwich. She still had a good figure which drew the male eye. With none of that hearty back-slapping approach favoured by some, she had a gentler approach and was a good listener, creating an environment that encouraged one to talk to her. I liked her, but today I detected some seriousness in her expression.

'I'm fine about the people here, and looking forward to taking a service in this wonderful building. But I had a call from the Archdeacon a couple of days ago. She knew I was taking the main service here on Sunday. She talked about both of us having a promising future in the diocese which would be aided by modernising. She praised the parishioners at St. Chad's for their sensible approach.'

'Go on,' I had some idea of what might be coming.

'I feel quite uncomfortable about this. I have a loyalty and obedience to you and to the Archdeacon as the bishop's representative.'

'Mm.'

'Well, she asked me to use such opportunity as I had to encourage you and the people of St. Mary's to adopt a more realistic and helpful attitude to the sale of the abbey. A carefully phrased sermon might help, she said.'

'And how do you feel about the issue, Anne, deep inside?'

'I would be very sad to see the abbey go. I'm not aware of any major need for repair. So, there doesn't seem to be any pressing millstone for finance around the neck of the parish. If we followed the Archdeacon's so called "modernising" moves we ought to sell off all our large churches, cathedrals, and abbeys. In the process we would lose a lot of tradition, history, and connection to the worshippers and benefactors of the past.'

'And having sold off many of our major assets we are still left with the need for income,' I added. 'I'm sorry that you have been put in that position, and although I probably ought not to comment out deference or obedience to, and support for the Archdeacon, I feel that was rather naughty of her. You know there is now a growing commitment in the parish to keeping the abbey and making more use of it. I tried to keep an open mind for a while but am becoming more and more convinced that it would be wrong to sell it. Whilst I support the district council's aim to make the lakeside area more attractive, I have a growing feeling that there is some conspiracy. A number of things don't feel quite right.' I paused and put my hand briefly on her arm.

'In all these cases of uncertainty, I am sure the best approach is to pray for our Lord's guidance, give it a little while for this to occur, and then trust one's own gut feeling. Thank you, for sharing this with me. I have every faith that you will be guided, and have the strength to follow that direction. Shall we conclude with a few minutes' prayer? I'll contribute the first one, you do the next, and we'll end with the grace, together.'

45

Just after eleven on Thursday, Rory called at the vestry. He had been discharged from hospital later on Saturday and had attended our Sunday morning service. He called me on the Wednesday for an appointment, as he was planning to get back to work.

'I had a telephone call from the practice to say Dr. Marshall wanted to see me, but instead I made an appointment to see Dr. May, a lady doctor I've seen once or twice in the past. She offered to refer me for counselling and wanted to prescribe some more antidepressants. I accepted the counselling but declined the antidepressants. I think they were concerned to have an attempted suicide on their books. It doesn't reflect well on the practice. I don't really like having counselling on my medical records but I suppose it would show I'm trying to do something positive. However, there is a waiting list and I'm told there is a wait of around six weeks, so I would appreciate your help.'

'How are things going at home?'

'Not very well. Julie said I was just running away from trouble and using suicide to threaten her. She's not interested in trying to improve things except by divorce. I think I'm slowly facing up to it. We've got someone coming around to value the house. I dug out my old golf clubs; haven't played for six or seven years. It felt good to be hitting something. But now it's time to get back to work. I have a couple of clients with pressing problems. Some small businesses seem to think that they only need to get their accounts pulled together once a year, and then wonder why they have a problem they should have spotted ten months previously.'

It sounded as if Rory was cut off from support and companionship at home, not good news for someone who has attempted suicide and has that in their repertoire of behaviours. If there was little other support, it might help to engage in some activity where there was companionship.

'How have you been feeling in yourself for the last day or so, Rory?'

'I feel better when I'm busy doing something. That's why I'm keen to get back to work.'

'Are there other staff around?'

'Yes. We have a secretary/receptionist, and I have a partner.'

'Do you think that the companionship helps?'

'Oh, I'm sure it does. My colleagues have a good sense of humour. They know about my problems and have been very supportive. Obviously, I have had to speak to them to explain my absence. My partner has offered me a room, if I need somewhere for a while.'

'What do you think it will be like if you sell the house and have somewhere of your own, I mean for the time when you don't have the children with you?'

'I've been thinking about that. I guess I'll be pretty lonely after living with companionship for thirteen years or so. I suppose I ought to consider in advance what I might do.'

'Any hobbies that give companionship, or mixing with other people?'

It can take a while to help people to dig into their own resources and explore their own interests and ideas. One can offer a few aids or ideas, but it is essential that the way forward feels right for the person, rather than for the helper. 'If I were you —' is not empathic, and usually a recipe for disaster.

By the time we concluded, Rory had worked through a number of issues. He admitted that at times he felt a failure and still felt suicidal. He reckoned he would offer to help more with the football team that his son Lewis played in. He would endeavour to play golf more regularly and would apply to join a local club where two of his clients were members. He would also experiment with joining a choir or amateur dramatic society.

46

Archdeacon Imogen's office was in an old Tudor building near to the cathedral. A secretary opened the door and invited me to take a seat in a room which doubled as reception and office. Apparently, there was someone in with the Archdeacon. After a few minutes a door opened and a tall man emerged, followed by the Archdeacon. The man had a serious face and his black hair was tinged with grey. I put him at around sixty.

'Ah, John, this is Dr. Ian Marshall. We were at Leeds University at the same time. Ian, meet the Reverend John Green, Vicar of St. Mary's, Lowestoft.' I noticed her eyes look skywards.

'Good afternoon, Dr. Marshall.' I offered my hand, but he declined to put his forward in return.

'Oh. So, you're the young man who's interfering with the care of some of my patients' health. I've just been talking to the Archdeacon about you?'

I felt an instant and antagonistic reaction to this man. And yet he was another human being, a child of God. I had no idea where he lived but he may well have been a parishioner of St. Mary's. Either way, I had to rise above this level of invoked anger, disagreement, and dislike. I still found it hard to resist a retort.

'I'm sorry you should feel like that, Dr. Marshall. I imagine that we both have the best interests of other people at heart, and are working to help them live healthier, happier, more fulfilling lives. I couldn't possibly discuss any parishioner with you unless they had authorised me so to do. I dare say that the Archdeacon has explained that the bishop charged me with cure, or care, of the people of the parishes of St. Mary's and St. Giles.'

'Well, you should stick to the care of souls and leave the bodies to me.' He frowned and stuck his chin out.

I could not let that go, but at times it was hard work to be polite and caring.

'There are many illustrations in the bible and psychological research papers that reveal a substantial connection between spirit, mind, and body. My work is to do with spirit and mind, and therefore inevitably affects the body. And, incidentally, St. Matthew's gospel tells us that Jesus sent out his disciples to preach and heal. Although "heal" in this context is generally taken to mean make whole, involving the body's connection to the spirit.'

'You'd better make sure you're not sued for malpractice.'

'I'm sorry if you feel like that. We should be working together for the well-being of the people of our area.' I forced myself, 'If you would like to meet anytime to see what we can do to improve things, I'd be happy to do what I can.'

I wondered whether I was being nice just to goad him?

He scowled. 'Anyway, I must be off. Good to see you again, Imogen. Perhaps you can knock some sense into this chap?'

He shook hands with the Archdeacon, strode for the door, and let himself out.

'Right, John. Come in.'

Archdeacon Imogen led the way into her office and closed the door behind me. It was a large room furnished in a way that was a cross between a doctor's consulting room and a set for breakfast television. An antique desk abutted the windowed wall and sported a comfortable wide leather executive chair. It needed to be generous to accommodate the Archdeacon's venerable posterior. (*Sorry, Lord. That was unkind of me.*) Two upright armless dining room chairs sat primly at one end of the desk. In the centre of the room, arranged around a coffee table were two wooden, armed, waiting room chairs and a three-seater couch. In one corner of the room was a small table, with a white table cloth, bearing a plain cross between two plain candle sticks. No popish figure on the cross. (*Sorry, Lord, again.*) Two low bookcases carried an assortment of photographs. I noticed a wedding photograph of a slimmer Archdeacon beside a tall thin man, and a photograph of the Archdeacon dressed in army uniform, with a baton under one arm.

I was invited to sit in one of the two armchairs, whilst the Archdeacon sat in the other. So, she was going to try the softly-softly approach rather than that of headmistress and pupil.

'Shall we start with prayer, John?'

She closed her eyes and went into what used to be called the 'Methodist crouch,' sitting, leaning forwards, with hands clasped in prayer. It is a posture that seems to be used in more and more churches of all denominations. We are getting increasingly relaxed and less subservient to the Creator. I followed her example. She prayed for our Lord's blessing on bishops and leaders of the church, and then that we both might be guided and inspired in our work and deliberations.

'John, I asked you to come to see me in respect of the proposed future of the buildings and organisation of your parishes. However, as you may gather, I've also had complaints from Ian Marshall. I've known him since we were both students at Leeds. He is a good man at heart. Perhaps I should share with you in confidence that he has been frustrated in a couple of ways. He was hoping to be an orthopaedic surgeon but failed his fellowship exams, changed to general practice, and moved well away from Leeds. He got a physiotherapist pregnant and then married her, but they split up a few years ago. I think that these have been factors contributing to an apparent crustiness. His failure to make the grade medically has led him to resent any intrusion by people he sees as non-medics. I was pleased to see you endeavour to hold out an olive branch and not react angrily. It may have been difficult but it was certainly a Christian gesture.'

'Archdeacon, thank you for your confidence. I do try to be understanding and caring to all people, whilst not necessarily agreeing with their behaviour. In confidence, I have a number of parishioners who have consulted Dr. Marshall and who have been poorly treated by him, in my estimation. He seems to be of the "pull yourself together" brigade and eschews psychological therapies, preferring to prescribe medication, some of which have a suicidal side effect. Quite apart from the usual priestly spiritual resources, I do have a background in psychological therapy.'

'I know, but just be careful.' She took a deep breath. 'Now let's turn to the other matter in hand. The sale of the abbey is likely to be approved by the relevant diocesan committees in the next few weeks. The bishop is keen that there should not be a dispute with the parish. So, I ask you to do what you can to encourage the PCC to see the benefits of a new building and the sale of the old one. I believe —'

'Archdeacon, please excuse me interrupting you. I have had the Diocesan Director of Finance and Canon Stuart on the 'phone. I am aware of the arguments about clergy pension funds, the impecuniousness of the diocese, the shortage of clerics, and the need for rationalising. I've even been threatened that my future in the church could be at risk. We did pray together for our Lord's guidance at the beginning of this meeting. All the guidance that I am getting is that the PCC is right.

'The PCC want to be helpful. They suggest that we retain the abbey building and a reasonable area of land around it, but sell the rest of the land reaching down towards Lake Lothing. They would be happy to support this. There would be plenty of room in the abbey to accommodate the parishioners of St. Giles.

'Additionally, there will be an application coming through shortly for a faculty for an archaeological dig in part of the abbey grounds, in the old infirmary cloister. Our local school, the Endowed, have a group of sixth-formers who have been engaged in a history project at the abbey. The Head of History is also doing a PhD related to the abbey. An aerial photograph has highlighted an area of interest overlapping the infirmary cloister. One of the pupils has followed this up with a metal detector scan of part of the same area and has some significant indications of metal below. The application for a faculty relates to this find and is likely to be supported by a senior Oxford don, and the county archaeologist.

'You know of the find behind the coat of arms in the abbey. That appears to be quite old. I expect to hear more about it soon. Put together, these historical finds make the abbey an even more significant focus of local, and possibly national, interest.'

The Archdeacon sighed. 'Well, John. I'll raise your suggestions with the relevant people, diocesan committees, the developers, and the council, but the sale is still likely to go through in a few weeks' time. The archaeological aspects would only cause a delay in the development, not stop it.'

She drew our meeting quickly to a close and ushered me out.

47

On Friday morning I packed Moses off on his holiday with Jim. Anne had left for work by the time I picked up Marie. I had folded the back seats of the Golf to make plenty of room for our luggage. Mine was a good-sized navy holdall with a separate loose jacket and semi-formal trousers on a hanger. Hard cases don't go down very well on boats. Marie was similar, with a dress or skirt of some sort in a transparent plastic clothing cover, as well as a smart soft maroon holdall. As we settled into our seats, I felt very close to Marie. We were off on an adventure together and would be close for a whole week. I looked at her fine-featured face, so fresh and full of life. She turned towards me and smiled.

'What's the matter? Have I missed with my lipstick?'

'Not at all. I'm just looking forward to spending a week close to you. Would you mind if I smudged your lipstick?' I took her hand in mine.

'I think that would be OK, kind sir.'

As well as I could, with the gear stick between us, I leant over, slipped my hand around her back, and pulled us together for a long gentle kiss. I parted with a sigh.

Andy and Peta Boyle lived in a large bungalow down river from

Ipswich, in a village called Levington. Andy looked fit for a man that Marie had told me was eighty. He was around five foot seven, with a good head of white hair, and wore a light blue polo shirt and light chino trousers. His face was intelligent, with a firm and warm smile. He looked used to giving orders. Peta was slim, with shoulder length white hair. Her face looked a little on the thin side but was full of character.

'I can see from whom Marie has inherited her beauty,' I remarked looking at Peta, who smiled back at me.

Marie showed me round Ipswich during the afternoon. Back, and sitting in the bungalow living room, I was inspected by a substantial British Blue cat. Having sniffed me all over, George, as he was called, discarded me and curled up on Marie's lap. After a late supper, Peta showed us to our rooms which were adjacent.

'We have presumed that you wanted separate bedrooms,' called Andy, with a smile.

'That might not be what we want, but it is what seems appropriate,' I replied. I fell asleep dreaming of holding Marie in my arms.

On the Saturday, Andy had planned what he called a shake-down cruise. We took our belongings and drove to Suffolk Yacht Harbour, a marina just a couple of miles from the bungalow. We would be returning there for the night and sleeping on board, except for Peta. Andy's longer-term plan was to spend a couple of days sailing to Gillingham on the Medway in north Kent. His boat, the Wild Goose was a trawler style motor-sailer. At thirty-seven feet long she was a little bigger than my father's boat. Her hull was navy blue which contrasted with her teak deckhouse. She was ketch rigged, having a tall main mast and a shorter rear or mizzen mast. Her sails were tan coloured.

We motored out of the marina and into the River Orwell, hoisted sails and set off down river. Passing the container terminals of Felixstowe, we headed out to sea past Landguard point.

'I thought we'd go to Hamford Water in Walton Backwaters today,' Andy pointed it out on the chart. 'It's what Arthur Ransome based one of his books on. He called it "Secret Waters".'

I looked a bit blank.

'Oh, I suppose he must have been well before your time. He wrote a lot of children's books, largely in water settings, down here, based on Lowestoft, the Norfolk Broads, and the Lake District. He lived for a while on a farm quite near to our bungalow, almost opposite Pin Mill. He was probably responsible for my going to sea.'

We anchored in Hamford Water and had a salad lunch and then sailed back to the marina. In the tiny galley, Peta cooked a casserole which she had brought with us, for our evening meal. After we had dined, she took her leave and returned home. When we retired for the night, Marie slept in one of the bunks in the fore cabin. Andy and I slept, one on each side, in the main cabin. On Sunday we sailed down the coast to Brightlingsea, just off the River Colne, itself a tributary of the Blackwater, a trip of around thirty miles.

Up early on Monday morning, we left our Brightlingsea pontoon mooring at six, just after sunrise clutching mugs of coffee, as we motored out into the River Colne. We were going with the ebb tide almost straight into the light breeze for some distance. It was a misty start to the day. Somewhere behind us I could hear a regular swishing sound. It grew steadily louder. There was a sharp bird call and then a squadron of five swans just avoided us and swept past down river.

'That was close. Not much point sailing here, let's wait until we turn southwest, well out to sea,' Andy said, to the steady beat of our powerful diesel engine. 'After all, we are in a motor-sailer.' He was wearing his old merchant navy master's cap, with its scrambled egg oak leaves around the peak.

'Right. You two have both done a fair bit of sailing, so I suggest that we keep watches of four hours on, eight off, except for berthing, changing sail, or pressing situations. I'll be on call and take the twelve to four. You take the four to eight, Marie, and you take over for the eight to twelve, John. So, over to you, Marie. Call me when we're approaching the Whittaker buoy.'

The Wild Goose was well equipped with an array of electronic aids, as befitted the boat of a professional mariner. There was a small radar, GPS, and chart plotter with the facility to overlay the radar onto the chart-plotter screen, electric log, forward-looking echo-sounder, VHF radio, auto-pilot, and wind instruments. Despite all the aids, Andy still had a paper chart on the mahogany chart table, on which he had drawn a planned course. We plotted our position at frequent intervals. Leaving the beach huts and caravans of St. Osyth behind us, we slipped into mist and followed two fishing boats down the Colne to its confluence with the Blackwater.

We passed two buoys with strange sounding names, the Eagle and the Knoll, and headed in a south-easterly direction across the channel known as the Wallet which ran along the coast towards Felixstowe. The two fishing boats headed northeast, up the Wallet.

'Now, watch the echosounder as we move through the Spitway,' advised Andy, as we headed through a dip in the sandbank finger known as the Gunfleet Sand, setting course for the Swin Spitway buoy. The echosounder reading, which had shown eight or nine metres below us as we crossed the Wallet, dropped quite quickly to around three metres as we crossed the Spitway. Some ten miles from Brightlingsea we reached the Whitaker buoy, hoisted two fore sails, and the main and mizzen, and then bore away towards the south-west.

Most of my sailing had been done in the deeper waters of the North Sea, sailing up the Northumberland coast or down to Whitby, with a couple of North Sea crossings to Holland. My father had a slightly smaller boat which we kept on the Tyne. Up there, half a mile off land, the waters were deep. Here in the Thames estuary, I was intrigued to find that the situation was very different. The sea bed was like a hand, with long fingers of sandbanks stretching miles out north-east into the North Sea, the deeper channels lying between the fingers. At places, there were connecting channels where the sandbanks were less high. The various channels often bore intriguing names like 'Gat', 'Swin', and 'Deep'. We were then in West Swin, between one of the shallow fingers called West Barrow and the Maplin Sands which we could see exposed, a mile or so to our right, and stretching north-west to the distant Essex coast.

The chop of short sharp waves in the Colne and Blackwater were caused by the ebb tide moving into the breeze. They had definitely eased. A sign of low water, I guessed. The tide we had been pushing against would now be in our favour, flowing in towards the Thames. The 'Wild Goose' was rolling slightly but heeled over away from the wind. She exuded confidence. With the tide turned, the freshening south-easterly breeze was pushing us along at nearly six knots through the water.

Over to the East the estuary appeared empty of traffic. An endless expanse of water, largely blue with temporary flashes of white as the crests of waves broke in the strengthening wind. The sea stretched away to that strange and humbling line where the sea meets the sky. Despite the electronic chart and GPS which showed our position, we used binoculars to spot the occasional buoy, Maplin, Southwest Swin, and Southwest Barrow, noting the time and log reading on the paper chart as we passed them, or taking a hand compass bearing when the buoy was further away. Three blips on the horizon gradually grew as we approached the narrowing estuary funnel. Two ships were approaching from astern and to the east. The third, a sailing vessel, looked to be slipping in from the south-east, probably heading in from the English Channel.

'Those two large container ships will be heading down the deep-water channel en route for London Gateway, the new container port near Tilbury. I sailed many times to the oil refinery next door, when I was at sea. Shellhaven, it was called.' Andy borrowed the binoculars back from me. 'It's closed now. That sailing vessel is a rare survivor of the coasting trade, a Thames barge.'

She was a little over twice as long as the Wild Goose, with tan sails, including two sprit sails, one on a tall mainmast, the other on a much shorter mizzen. She had lee boards that reduced sideways drift, instead of a deep keel.

'When I was a cadet on the training ship HMS Worcester,

moored at Greenhithe, we used to see Thames barges quite frequently. They have flat bottoms and could dry out on a level seabed. They used to carry cargoes all around the coast and to the continent, sailed by just two men.' He sighed with memories and pride in fellow seafarers.

'Those two container ships are catching us up fast. The deep channel route has been dredged along the Black Deep and Knock John channel which is parallel to ours, only two channels over. We'll keep to the north side of the estuary until we get nearly level with the Medway buoyed route, then we'll carefully pick the opportunity to cross over to the south, more or less at right angles to the deep-water channel. Those big ships don't have a lot of room to manoeuvre with enough depth, so we need to keep well clear of them. There were so many corrections to the buoyed channel when they dredged the new deep-water route that I bought new charts, rather than make lots of corrections to the old ones.'

Later we approached Sea Reach No. 1 North buoy, which Andy said was part of the new Thames deep water route. By then the two container ships were well ahead of us and the other shipping was relatively quiet. Tightening in the sails close to the wind, we headed south and picked up the buoyed channel into the Medway. I handed over to Marie as we were off Sheerness, and popped down to the galley to make coffee and sandwiches for everyone. An hour later we pointed up into the wind and took in all our sails, then headed upriver under power. Andy took us through the open lock into Gillingham marina.

'Finished with engines. Well done, everyone,' Andy chuckled. Switching off the engine at two-thirty, he went to check our moorings along the finger jetty.

Later that evening we sat around a window table in the nearby yacht club, swapping tales of nautical experiences. Out on the river as dusk developed, flashing red, green, and white lights sparkled from buoys and pier heads. Steadily moving lights showed boats still travelling, there were street lights, and cars across on the other side of the river. The club commodore, Alex, proved to be a retired cruise liner master who had known Andy for some years. He had not long ago returned from a boating holiday, cruising in the Mediterranean. He welcomed us on arrival and pulled up a chair to join us as we finished our meal.

'No Peta, this trip, Andy?'

'No. I think she prefers the comfort of her own bed and a steady deck below her feet. She'll often come to keep me company, but as I had Marie and John to do all the hard work, she promised herself some time painting at Pin Mill.'

'She might have preferred the luxury of the semi-displacement powerboat I've been on, an Aquastar 42,' the commodore sighed at the memory. 'One of the directors of the company I used to work for usually asks Linda and I to join him and his missis for a couple of weeks in the summer. He keeps his boat at Palma marina. So, we generally get good weather.'

He went on to recount various seamanship exploits in their trip to Menorca and back, and the high quality of seafood dishes at the Palma marina restaurant. He must have been a good cruise ship captain as he soon involved Marie and myself in the conversation. He seemed interested in my father's work and reckoned my Dad must have contributed to the design of one of his company's ships which had been built on the Tyne.

'And did Andy say you ministered at a cathedral, John?'

'Not quite. It's the abbey church of St. Mary Magdalene, at Queensholme, Lowestoft.'

'Ah. I have a feeling there was something in the news about some old documents discovered near you.'

'That's quite right. They were in a small old chest behind a coat of arms of Henry VIII.'

'Strangely enough, I met a chap from Lowestoft who keeps a big cruiser at Palma. I've met him a couple of times in the past. He was dining at the marina with a couple of council chaps from Lowestoft, a young floozie, and a rather rotund woman. The chubby woman was pleasant enough, I have a feeling she was something of a church dignitary. But one of the men was rather nauseous and supercilious, an important councillor of some sort. Or so he thought.'

That hit me with a jolt. It sounded rather like Archdeacon Imogen, Councillor Jackson, and friends.

We chatted a while longer until Andy suggested that Marie and I returned to the boat as he and Alex might exchange a few old yarns. I suspected he was being very considerate and giving Marie and me a little while together, without him. We walked back under a clear sky, holding hands.

48

The upholstery in Wild Goose's saloon, or main cabin, was a deep red. It looked very smart against the teak woodwork. With the bedding cleared away, we sat around the table eating a light breakfast. I'd slept badly, and was still thinking about the yacht club commodore's disclosure. What were the prime movers of the sale of the abbey doing there? Was there some conspiracy, or collusion? Andy broke my thoughts, introducing the planning of our return journey.

'It took us a little over eight hours to get here from Brightlingsea. The trip back to the Orwell is about half the distance again. There has been a high-pressure system fairly static over Denmark for the last couple of days, so I reckon the wind will continue to be largely south-easterly for a while, which suits us for the return journey. I reckon we'll probably take well over twelve hours as we will get at least one tide against us. I suggest we do a night trip, which will be a good exercise for you both. It's high water at Sheerness at 18.16. Let's have a good meal at 17.00 and leave around six. That'll give us the ebb tide in our favour for around six hours. We'll be leaving before sunset and arriving after dawn, with daylight for undocking and docking. You two might like to explore Rochester.'

Marie agreed to come with me to have a look at Rochester

cathedral which was only a mile or so away. We caught a bus. All in all, it was a disappointment. The cathedral was locked and Rochester high street was very grubby and yet incongruously boasting many connections with Charles Dickens. We ended up by the river, looking at Rochester castle and having a sandwich in a waterside pub. On our return, Andy was getting up from napping whilst we were away, so that he would be fresher for our night passage.

Marie took the helm as Wild Goose made her way under power through the open lock into the River Medway. A mile downstream we headed up into the wind and hoisted all sail. By eight we had passed Sheerness, avoided a cross-Channel car ferry and reached the outer buoy for the Medway approach channel. I took coffee up to the deckhouse for all hands and started my watch as Andy guided us across the deep-water channel to the north side of the Thames estuary.

Our route back to the Orwell was planned using the channel which was one finger east of the route we used down to the Medway. We headed for the Barrow Deep and then the Kings Channel. After this we would aim towards the Northeast Gunfleet buoy which lay at the seaward end of the sandbank finger known as Gunfleet Sand. From there we would cross over the Wallet Channel to the evil sounding Medusa buoy, just off the Naze, then almost northerly up the Medusa Channel to pick up the yacht route on the west side of the River Orwell almost level with Landguard Point.

Most of the time we sailed with the Wild Goose on autopilot, leaving the person on watch free to keep a good lookout and plot regular observations onto the paper chart, recording time and the log reading. The latter was like a nautical milometer giving us the distance travelled through the water. Up until eleven-thirty we had the tide behind us. Then it slowly changed direction, flooding to the south-west. At midnight, when Andy took over, we had made good thirty miles and were well up the Barrow Deep. The wind was not quite as strong as on our journey to Gillingham. There was a slight swell from the south-east, which gave us a slow roll.

I went below and wriggled down inside my sleeping bag, quickly falling asleep to the regular slap of wavelets on the hull and the gentle rock of the swell.

When I took over from Marie at eight o'clock, we were well past the Medusa buoy and heading into the tide flowing out of the River Orwell. Marie helped Andy make coffee and bacon sandwiches all around. Rather than struggle against the ebb for the rest of the journey we headed up into the wind, dropped sail and then pressed on under the strong push of our diesel motor. En route we stowed the sails tidily and put on the covers. Secured alongside by ten-thirty, we cleaned ship, and waited for Peta to come and pick us up.

By twelve o'clock we were sitting in Andy and Peta's lounge.

'Soup and a sandwich, then off to bed for you lot,' Peta said, as she placed a laden tray on the low table.

Andy and Peta sat in their favourite armchairs around the coffee table, Marie and I sat on the long settee.

A little while later, 'Right, I'm off to bed. I'll set my alarm for six. That should give us plenty of time to all shower and get to Bella's Bistro. Oh, dear, excuse me,' Andy yawned and left, carrying the tray of plates, bowls, and mugs, closely followed by Peta.

I had booked a meal at the restaurant in Woodbridge that Marie recommended. Marie was insistent that we would share the bill for a 'thank you' treat for Andy and Peta. She moved closer to me and snuggled up with her head on my shoulder. I put my arm around her and held her closely. We just managed to get both our legs on the settee. I felt the warmth of her cheek against mine. I could faintly pick up the scent that I had smelled in the Brandon Arms when she first passed near me. That took me back. Fancy, several months had passed since we first met. I was aware of her breast pressing against mine. The week together had been both exciting and natural. I realised that she meant so much to me. I was vaguely aware of Peta, entering the room, seeing us together, and withdrawing, before I fell asleep in a relaxing yet inspiring cuddle.

I slept fitfully. My thoughts were obsessed with Marie who stirred occasionally. Had I been snoring, I wondered? What would it be like to be in bed together? I could feel the outline of her curves fitting closely to me. I felt a stiffening and then somehow felt guilty. Having studied human behaviour and thinking for several years, I had come to the conclusion that normal sexual thoughts were an integral part of human development. For me, now, the moral line was drawn at physical activity. My thoughts revolved around Marie. Whether it was hand to hand, or cheek to cheek, there was a sense of something, warmth, love, flowing both ways. How lucky I was to have a desirable person whom I respected giving me her care and love. I wouldn't want it to end.

Later we enjoyed a tasty meal at the Italian restaurant in Woodbridge, an interesting boating village on the River Deben. Just as we were getting out of the taxi on returning to Levington, my mobile rang. I saw that the caller was Jim. I had spoken to him on Sunday evening. All was well, then. Had something happened to Moses? That would hurt a lot. He had become an amusing and loving companion.

'Hi, Jim. Is everything OK? Is Moses all right?'

'I tried to get you this morning, John. Moses is fine, he's a great little chap. But no, everything isn't fine. We've dealt with the problem, but I thought I ought to let you know.'

I wondered if the vicarage had caught fire? Had I left the cooker on?

'We've had vandals at work again. The Brandon Arms has had red paint tipped all over its stone patio and outside tables and chairs. Southshore Boatbuilders have had two boats cut adrift and the rigging broken with a chain cutter so one of them has a buckled mast. And we've had a food waste bin from the Brandon Arms dragged along and emptied in the main abbey porch. The place stank when I went to open up yesterday morning. But we've dealt with it. Dan Brookes has been a great help again. He had a few conventional plastic dustbins he uses in his building work. We filled them and he took them to the council tip in his van. The area has been hosed down and washed with disinfectant. We had to throw away the large door mat from the porch, but Alice has kindly offered to get us a new one.'

'Oh, well done, Jim. Thanks for all your help. I'll give Dan and Alice a call when we finish. What about the police?'

'Hm! I rang the police and that reporter, Jessica. She was here with a photographer within the hour. The police turned up yesterday afternoon and told me off for destroying all the evidence. I showed them the wheelie bin from the pub, but they weren't very interested. Jessica, on the other hand noticed some red paint on the bin. Apparently, it matched the paint on the pub patio. Anyway, I didn't ring you earlier because we have dealt with it. There is nothing you can do. So, enjoy the rest of your holiday, and we'll see you on Friday night or Saturday morning. Oh, and Moses says to give you his love.'

He must have put the 'phone near to Moses because I heard a loud bark.

I rang Dan and Alice and thanked them for their help, and then Jessica. She was engaged but rang me back a little while later.

'It's all too much of a coincidence, John. Just the sites that are wanted for this Lakeside development.'

I told her about the meeting in Majorca.

'Now that is interesting. There is a Spanish newspaper office in Palma. I'll see if I can get some help there. I'll have to find out who owns that boat your nautical friend talked about. The commodore of the Gillingham yacht club wasn't it. It should be easy enough to get his details from their website and get in touch with him to see if he can help. I'll also check out whether it was Councillor Jackson. I can have a good guess who the reverend lady was.'

49

Back in my parish, I was soon in the thick of it, with funerals in Coxton and St. Olave's, Whitehill, as Anne Fox was away for a few days. We had two baptisms at the abbey, one of which was Gemma Murray, Sasha and Danny's little daughter. Sasha's and Danny's parents, her brother, and friend, Anne, were all there. I hoped for a reconciliation between Sasha and her father. Sasha and Danny had booked a wedding in a few weeks' time. Sasha's father turned out to be a rough diamond. Gemma was irritable in the arms of most of the grandparents, but, in the arms of Sasha's dad, she broke wind, giggled, and was then as good as gold. Of course, he had solved the problem, and he was proud of it. Seeing the happy family somehow made me recall how much I had enjoyed the closeness I had shared with Marie and her family during our week away.

On the Wednesday evening, after the St. Cecilia Singers' practice, Marie and I went for a late meal at the Brandon Arms. We sat inside, where the tables had table cloths and linen napkins. We both had lasagne, which landlord Simon brought over. A little later he came over to chat.

'Sorry to see the mess these beggars have made,' I commented. 'Can anything be recovered?'

'The tables, chairs, and most of the patio floor were covered in red paint,' Simon fumed. 'I've got the insurance company on the job. We'll need it all replaced. I thought we might save the stone work, but it's come out blotchy. Sorry about our food waste in your abbey doorway, but we didn't do it.'

He pulled up a chair and sat down. 'The Bishops, next door at Southshore, not your boss, they had damage running into several thousand pounds, with two boats cut adrift and a ruined mast on one. Rupert and I both caught a couple of chaps in hoodies on our CCTVs. Max from the bungalow came in here for a drink last night. He had seen two men in hoodies pushing a large wheelie bin as he came our way down Lakeside, taking his dog out for a walk. He noticed that the sleeve on one of the men had slipped up his arm revealing a sword tattoo just above his wrist. On his way back he saw the two men getting into a green van in one of the business park roads off Lakeside. And guess what? He saw the name on the van: "Beccles Builders". Interestingly, Max wasn't the subject of any vandalism, this time. He now has an offer on his property from the company that own the business park.

'He hadn't put two and two together, but I did. I 'phoned Jessica, who soon called round on the chase. I told her what I've just told you.

'She called back later and said she had found red paint with a fingerprint on the bin left at the abbey. She photographed it. She was intending to follow Councillor Bruce Jackson for a day or two, as she was rather suspicious of a meeting in Majorca. She also had a cub reporter on the job following up on the green van and researching Beccles Builders. We've told the police. They say they'll look into it, but they're rather busy at the moment.

'Sorry, I'll have to go now as they look hard pressed at the bar. Anyway, I gathered you'd been away together. Reasonable weather and a good time?'

'One of the happiest weeks of my life.' I squeezed Marie's hand.

We walked back, holding hands, along Lakeside to her car which we had left in the abbey car park. My parents had been down for a long weekend a few weeks ago and had met Marie. They had liked her. Who wouldn't? Now I had met her grandparents. I think they approved. I was aware that not all would approve of a union with a clergyman. My previous proper, no, perhaps a better word would be 'full', or 'cohabiting', girlfriend had decided that she couldn't face life with a priest. That was a few years ago when I was a clinical psychologist and felt moved to enter training for the priesthood. My views on cohabiting have changed, indeed they had to. I suppose I was now at that exciting and yet frightening stage of wanting to draw nearer to Marie, yet being awed, wanting the best for her, and not wanting to make a mistake that I, or she, would regret for the rest of our lives.

I also thought of the target the Archdeacon had set when I was first interviewed for the abbey incumbency, that of achieving an economic congregation regularly in one of the Sunday services. Would engagement and marriage impact adversely on that? Or was I wrong to even consider that as a factor? If I squandered the present possible opportunity, how long would it be until another turned up?

When I returned home there were two messages on my landline answer machine. The first was from Ben. He was very excited about the discoveries made by his supervisor and himself amongst the contents of the old chest from behind the coat of arms of Henry VIII.

'They are very significant, John. Dr. Bedford suggests that you call a parish meeting and invite the local press. We will come and make a presentation of our findings.' He went on to outline their findings.

The second message was from the Archdeacon's secretary summoning me to a meeting with her boss.

50

The evening September sun sparkled through the small rose window set high in the west end of the abbey. The area below it was filled with exhibition stands showing the project work of the Endowed School students. Dr. Bedford was due to give an illustrated talk on our recent finds. Over half the seats were already taken. Jessica approached me followed by two men and a woman carrying expensive looking bright metal cases and two tripods.

'Is it all right if we use the pulpit for video-recording, John?'

'Sure. No sermons, tonight. Anyway, I usually stand on the chancel steps.'

'It's all very exciting.' She stood to one side talking to me, 'We expect to syndicate this to BBC East. That's why we have the video cameras.'

One of her assistants arranged microphones adjacent to a folding table which was overlaid with an old deep-blue altar cloth. The table was more accustomed to church fairs and the children's messy church use. On the table Dr. Bedford was arranging the now restored and glowing silver paten and jewel encrusted chalice, and a collection of old documents, some of which looked fragile. Ben was adjusting a large portable screen and a projector linked to a laptop computer.

'Thanks for the promotion in the Siren, Jessica. It's obviously worked wonders.'

'It was a last-minute action by the editor. He was very supportive, felt it was good local news, and worthy of front-page space. We've taken a series of photographs of the school's exhibition and interviewed Ben and the Head. We'll probably have to spread tonight's coverage over two weekend issues, with the abbey finds in the first one next week, and the school's exhibition the following weekend.'

Near a heavy wooden desk-like unit behind the pulpit Jim was fitting Dr. Bedford with a radio microphone connected to the abbey sound system. I wandered over to the school exhibition. Head teacher Sally Foster was talking to a forty-ish enthusiastic man in a smart blue suit. They were discussing a timeline of the abbey history. Seeing my approach, Sally turned.

'John, do you know Josh King? He's Director of the County Archaeological Service, and also an ex-student of Dr. Bedford.'

'Hello, John. Yes, I was at Cambridge a year before Ben. Robert called me about his, er, your finds, which are of interest to us. They throw some additional light on a number of periods of local history. We would have an interest in the display, care, and security of these items. I guess you probably wouldn't want the cost of all that.'

'Hello, and welcome, Josh. I don't think we have given any thought to those matters yet. I only have a rough picture of the finds.'

I turned towards Sally Foster. 'Hello, Sally.' I hoped I wasn't being too familiar using the Christian name of a head teacher. 'Thanks for bringing forward your pupils' exhibition. I know we had talked of doing it in another three weeks' time.'

'Too good an opportunity to miss, John. It will be a valuable experience for our students, look good on their CVs, and be useful publicity for the school.'

A few minutes later Ben said they were ready to start, and Jim gave me a hand mike. I welcomed our visitors, introduced the speakers, and then passed the microphone to Ben, and went to sit next to Marie in the front row of seats. Ben outlined the school's project work, the discovery of the find behind the coat of arms, and handed over to Dr. Bedford. The history don advanced the first slide, which was a colour photograph of the old chest and its contents.

'The objects which you see before you on this table, and on the screen, shed light on the history of this beautiful abbey from its inception until, we think, around 1537. They have come to light as a result of history projects carried out by your local Endowed School. The sixth form pupils and their head of history, Ben Fillingham, have been studying the abbey and researching its local background. I hope that you have all taken time to view their exhibition at the rear of the abbey.'

He went on to relate the truncated west end and coat of arms to the dissolution of the monasteries.

'Research in the Norwich Archives by the sixth form pupils and Ben Fillingham, unearthed a grant in 1245 of land and fishing rights at Queensholme, by the Fitz Herberts of Somerleyton, to the abbot of St. Benet's abbey, near Horning. This fits the picture of your abbey being a daughter house of St. Benet's.

'Also, in the National Archives, Ben found a grant, in 1537, of the abbey church, land, and grange, from Henry VIII to Admiral Sir Richard Brandon, an illegitimate son of Charles Brandon, first Duke of Suffolk. In your local Lowestoft Archives, Ben found papers relating to the gift in 1540, of Sir Richard's house in Lowestoft to be used as a school, the origin of your Endowed School.

'We will reveal a history of medical excellence originating in the abbey, including in 1601, the grant of the abbey infirmary to the aldermen of Lowestoft by John Brandon, the eldest son of Sir Richard. This was the beginning of your Brandon Hospital, the deeds for which were in your Lowestoft Archives.'

He paused and advanced a slide showing a thick ancient book with a worn hide cover. After describing the exciting discovery of the chest, he continued:

'This fragile book is a cartulary. It's a collection of chronicles of the abbots of St. Mary's that have been bound together at a later date. It is mostly in Latin. Now let's look at the first page. It's very faded but careful examination shows it is written, or possibly dictated, by Ralph de Neatisheade, first abbot, in 1245. He refers to the arrival of his monks on the holme or island, and starting work on the abbey construction. The advantage of being near a major waterway, of course, was its convenience for transporting the heavy materials used in building the abbey. It appears that the abbey church, in which we sit tonight, was built next to a much earlier church, and that there was a local legend that this housed the remains of an early queen. Hence, the area was known as "Queensholme."

'Two of the other books are chronicles by the Infirmarer, or later, the Frater Medicus, who ran the abbey hospital or infirmary. As we shall see, the work of one particular infirmary leader led to the gift of this beautiful chalice and paten. However, before we get to that, I'd like to tell you about earlier references to the work of the infirmarer. In the infirmarers' chronicles, a Brother Paul writes about the Black Death that decimated Lowestoft in 1349. It appears that he and his fellow brothers did all they could to help the citizens and lost a third of the monks to this plague. We know from other records that only a tenth or so of the Lowestoft citizens survived the Black Death.

'Now back to the abbots' chronicles. In 1471, Abbot Hugh de Plumstede, records the death of his current infirmarer, and the lack of a suitable candidate to take his place. In 1472, he is more cheerful as he attends the enthronement of the new bishop of Norwich, James Goldwell. Abbot Hugh writes about meeting the new bishop and recruiting a young member of his entourage, a Brother Francis, who has recently arrived from Italy, where he had trained in medicine. This young man had helped the bishop through a serious illness. He joined the monks of St. Mary's as a frater medicus, and represents a new breed of more professional leaders of the infirmary.

'A year later, 1473, we read of a call from the bishop and from Thomas Whyte, a priest at St Julian's church in Norwich, for help in the care of a pious and respected anchorite who lived in a small cell at the church. This woman had been seriously ill and was thought to be near to death. It seems that brother Francis attended this woman whose name is not given, for several days, and also treated the bishop. The woman apparently made a miraculous recovery on the 13th May, as did the bishop. This is recorded in the chronicle of the frater medicus. Later that year the abbot records receiving a letter and a gift from the bishop of a beautiful cup and paten.'

Slipping on fine cotton gloves Dr Bedford raised the chalice which sparkled in the abbey lights. He advanced the slide to show two photographs of the chalice, one a side view, the other of an inscription on the base.

'The chalice and paten have been cleaned by our experts. There is a similar inscription on both, although that on the paten is less clear. You can probably just make out "Ecce Agnus Dei. James Norvic dedit." The first sentence is from the communion service: "Behold the Lamb of God." The second refers to the giver. "Norvic" is the old name for Norwich and is still used by the bishop. This is translated as "Given by James of Norwich." The chalice and paten together would be difficult to value, especially with their probable link to the healing of the anchorite. She and her writings are much respected and still quoted. Her real name is not known but we think she must be the person known as "the Lady Julian of Norwich." She has taken this name from the church where she lived, and which you can still visit and see her restored cell.

'I have just two more pieces of history to comment on. It seems that the infirmary at this abbey continued to operate after the Dissolution of the Monasteries. I have already told you about the grant of the infirmary to the Lowestoft aldermen in 1601. Ben has found a slightly earlier reference in the National Archives crown payments records, of payment made to the abbey in 1538 in respect of medical care. It was authorised by Admiral Sir Richard

Brandon. We know that he was responsible for the defence of the East Coast by ship and fort. We think he was involved in the construction of three forts protecting the sea roads outside Lowestoft. It seems that a number of men were injured when a tunnel in one of the forts collapsed and that your infirmary provided help.

'The final discovery, in your Lowestoft Archives, is rather more recent. Articles of the government and funding of a new hospital donated by Sir Robert Brandon of Queensholme Grange, in 1710. Sir Robert was an MP and was the last of the line of Brandons, as far as we know. I understand that there is a Grange Road in the area, but all signs of the grange have otherwise disappeared. As yet his will has not been found.

'So, there you are, abbey parishioners and people of Lowestoft. This beautiful building and those who have worshipped here, have been associated with good works in the service of the local community and county for nearly eight hundred years. It would be good if these documents and communion vessels could be kept and displayed locally, but they would need care in preservation and security. I understand that there is some question of the sale of the abbey and possible use as a nightclub. In my estimation that would be a terrible waste.'

I noticed the County Director of Archaeological Services nodding vigorously.

After thanking Dr. Bedford, Ben and Sally Foster for their work and contribution to local knowledge, I ended with a prayer of thanks and blessing. Dr Bedford kindly agreed to look after the chest and its contents until an appropriate home could be found.

51

St. Francis of Assisi is probably best known for his simple rules for a way of life of service and poverty and the development of an order of the religious devoted to such a life style. He is also the saint most associated with the care and respect of animals. There are three days in the autumn associated with remembering him. The first of these is in mid-September, the Stigmata of St. Francis, when people remember the discovery on the saint of a copy of the wounds suffered by Our Lord. With the enthusiastic involvement of the PCC we planned a service of the blessing of animals during a shortened version of evensong on the Sunday after this day.

Jim and Marie took charge of sorting the pets and their owners into groups, with the aim of separating likely combatants. Marie had brought a container of her bees, and put them on a reserved seat in the front row, next to some stick insects. Jim's wife, May, looked after their pet greyhound, Jack, and sat in one of the rows near the back on the South side. Nearby, were whippets, poodles, two Old English sheepdogs, an Alsatian, three Labradors, a Jack Russell, and two noisy West Highland Whites. A wide variety of cats and kittens sat on the North side near the back. These included ginger toms, silver tabbies, Bengals, a Norwegian Forest Cat, a number of blacks and black and whites, and a multitude of general tabbies. At the back of the nave, near to the School's exhibition, was a lone Shetland pony. Jim reckoned we had a record congregation of just over one hundred, plus the pets.

Organist Mark, selected a soft register for our music. Our choir, which had now grown to twelve, processed in to the hymn 'All things wise and wonderful.' Two of the choir had dogs on the lead, whilst two carried cat baskets. Following the choir, Father Rex carried a very fat sleepy tabby, whilst Father Paul had a black and white crossed collie on the lead. Moses, as good as gold, ambled along close to my heels.

Carrying his very relaxed silver tabby, Ben Fillingham read our first lesson from Genesis, of the flood, and of God telling Noah to gather the many different creatures into the ark, and how the dove and the raven were sent out to explore the surroundings, eventually bringing back good news. For our second lesson, Rose Coates left Don in charge of their Labrador, and read a short extract from the Sermon on the Mount. This included a reference to God's care for the 'fowls of the air.' Judy Pope lead the intercessions including thanks for the companionship of our pets, and a request that we might have a healthy respect for all the natural world.

I kept my sermon short, relating our Father's care of all his creatures and their value to mankind, and to the two readings. A little later we moved to the blessing of the pets. Fathers Rex and Paul joined me by the communion rails. I asked everyone to stay in their places as Jim and Marie brought their dog and bees up to be blessed. Jim and Marie then returned, one to each side of the church to direct pet owners with their pets to come forwards for blessings. We had the cats up and then returned to their seats before the dogs left their places. Towards the end the Shetland pony was led up to be blessed. I wondered whether it would manage the two steps up into the chancel. But it took them in its stride. As I watched it retire, I reflected that quite probably a number of horses may have entered the great abbey in the past. Finally, Fathers Rex and Paul gathered their pets as Moses joined me, for a group blessing. Rex's tabby looked aloofly down at the two dogs and seemed fearless.

We emptied the abbey a group at a time, to avoid conflict. As Rex, Paul, and I said farewells to the leavers it was clear that the service had been enjoyed and there were many requests for a repeat. Perhaps annually would suffice.

As she left, solicitor Marjorie Banks commented 'This sort of service would scarcely be possible if we were moved to a more compact new church centre, John. I understand that the sale is to be discussed at a diocesan meeting in around three weeks' time. I have written to the chair to express the dissenting views of the parishioners and PCC, and to question whether they have any proof of title.'

Marie followed Moses and me back to the vicarage. She gave him some biscuits and laid the table whilst I rustled up mushroom omelettes.

'Thanks so much, for your help tonight,' I said putting the hot plates on the kitchen table. Just a little thing, but it struck me that we were drawing closer in that she had prepared the kitchen table, where I often ate on my own, rather than the more formal dining room table.

'Oh, that's OK, I enjoyed it. It went very down well, judging by the comments I heard. Apart from a few understandable droppings from the pony, there was very little mess to clear up.'

Leaving the tidying up, we took our coffees into the lounge, drew the curtains and sat on the couch. I switched on the television. The latest American detective programme had just started. Perhaps we watched some of it. Certainly, I could not recall much. I enjoyed the closeness of Marie. I thought she felt similarly. My head was in a whirl. I recognised that I was high on euphoria after a moving service and expressions of appreciation from members of the congregation. *Please keep me humble, Lord.* I was on the cusp of deciding to propose. I didn't want to lose the opportunity, but I didn't want to be turned down. Perhaps it was not an ideal time? I felt low and confused after she left.

52

'Come in, John, and sit down.' The Archdeacon lowered herself into the other armchair. This time she dispensed with any preliminary prayers.

'So, have the PCC moved any nearer to the plan? The Diocesan Finance Committee gave support to the sale last week. The Diocesan Advisory Committee meet in a few days' time.' Her eyebrows, dark and substantial, rose like a pair of Roman arches as she looked at me.

I took a deep breath. 'Archdeacon, the PCC, the parish, a number of learned professionals, and I, are deeply committed to maintaining and growing the abbey's spiritual and historic service. Congregations are getting larger. Indeed, we recently had over a hundred at a Sunday evening service. I did advise you about the analysis of the find from behind the coat of arms. It was also well covered in the local press and on television.'

She smiled, confidently. 'Yes, the find will help draw people to the abbey. The chief planning officer from the council, and the developer, both felt the find could be showcased in suitable settings in the abbey and would provide a daytime attraction to the entertainment centre which the abbey will become. Our finance committee reckon that this will enhance the sale value. It would provide a boost to the diocese's contribution to the clergy pension fund. As for the large service, I have had complaints about the suitability of the event. Horse droppings don't go very well with worship.'

It was clear that she and the diocese were set firmly in their plans and unwilling to consider the alternative.

'The Diocesan Advisory Committee have approved the faculty request by Dr. Bedford and the County Archaeologist. They reckon that the sooner the investigation is completed, the sooner the planned development for the area can go ahead.'

I could see that I was wasting time. Perhaps there was one last avenue.

'Archdeacon, I have endeavoured to represent to you the sincere view of the parishioners of St. Mary Magdalene. The abbey is a historic and spiritual focal point, there is every wish and intention to continue with worship there. We have the support of a Cambridge academic and the county archaeologist. We would be quite happy to lose some of the abbey land stretching down to the waterfront. But the building and an appropriate space around it are not negotiable. We recognise that there is an impasse with yourself and certain diocesan committees. I had hoped to avoid this. A member of our PCC is a solicitor. She has drawn up a plea to the Bishop, requesting a meeting of our PCC with him. There is a copy for yourself.'

I laid two envelopes on the coffee table in front of us. The atmosphere felt stormy to say the least. She picked up the envelope addressed to her and scanned the contents.

'Right, John, I shall see that bishop Francis receives this when we meet tomorrow. It's a shame that a priest with your potential is doing his chances of advancement no good at all.' The eyebrow arches inverted and closed towards each other like a raptor moving in on its prey.

She showed me to the door.

As I walked towards the car park the dark squall above threw rain at my face. I pulled my coat tighter and ran. Approaching the entrance to the car park I crossed an incline, only to have my socks soaked by a torrent of flood water that overflowed my shoes.

53

Friday arrived. It promised to be a busy, but very special, day this week. I usually met with Marie for some time together over the weekend. I had to be flexible as there might be a funeral on a Friday, or a wedding on a Saturday. At last I had plucked up courage and decided to propose to Marie. An evening meal at the Bungay Manor Hotel, an old riverside country estate adjacent to the River Waveney and a few miles up-river from Beccles, were to be the time and place.

The morning sun was shining and there was a slight breeze off the sea as I drove to Southshore. Rupert Bishop had telephoned to donate an unwanted pc and printer. I planned to get these to Sasha. She had offered to compose the monthly magazine for the combined parishes in our team. She now worked on a Friday, so I would have to deliver the items, together with some paper, on another day. Her relationship with her father had improved since Emma's christening. Her mother now came over and stayed one night and the following day each week. This gave Grandma time with her granddaughter and allowed Sasha to return to a day's work at a bookshop in the town.

A little later, after a quick shop, I was sipping a cup of coffee in the supermarket cafe. June spotted me and soon came to join me. She looked bright, happy, and bursting to say something.

'Hello, June. You're looking very pleased with yourself.'

'Jack and I are going to be grandparents.' A big grin spread across her face. 'Our daughter in law, Penny, is three months pregnant. They rang up last night. And I thought I'd be dead before we had any grandchildren. According to Dr. Marshall, I should have died three months ago, and here I am, generally feeling pretty good, and still working, and soon to be a granny.'

'I'm so happy for you, June. Does Penny live near? Will you be able to get to see her easily?'

I knew that June and Jack had two children, both in mid to late twenties. I'd heard more about the younger one, a midwife who worked at the Brandon Hospital and lived somewhere in Lowestoft. The girl had been keeping an eye on her mother since she was diagnosed with cancer, and particularly when June was having chemotherapy.

'Yes, thank goodness. They live in Beccles. Brian is an estate agent. I shall have to start knitting now. I don't really agree with it, but they asked and were told it was a boy.'

After an early sandwich, I collected Moses' lead, picked up a parcel of altar candles, and then walked to the abbey with my canine companion. The professional exploration of the metal detection in the infirmary cloister was due to start. An area containing the cloister was roped off. There were a number of people, some of whom I recognised, engaged in various activities. Dr. Bedford introduced me to a bustling man with a grey beard and a cowboy hat, Peter Blizzard, Professor of Archaeology at Cambridge. There were three post-graduate students. Two technicians from Cambridge were carefully advancing a wheeled device in regular tracks across the cordoned area. I recognised Josh King, the county director of archaeological services, this time in a boiler suit rather than a business one. He and two of his staff were engaged with a laser theodolite surveying the area. He explained that the sophisticated looking device also contained a very accurate GPS system.

Ben arrived during the school lunch break looking very excited and carrying a camera.

'The head's given me the afternoon off, which was very generous of her.' He took a bite of a sandwich, swallowed and continued. 'Ian, the lad who made the discovery, is coming up after school. However, there probably won't be any digging for a few days as they are doing all sorts of surface surveying work first.'

I watched for a while. Ben was soon chatting to Dr Bedford and the archaeology prof. I wondered if the spiritual side of the abbey would one day pull Ben. He occasionally came to a Sunday morning service with his partner, Jean. Perhaps they might decide to marry at some stage.

Eventually, I headed for the interior of the abbey. Closing the heavy south door behind me, I walked to the middle of the crossing. The sunlight was shining through the south side windows giving a warm glow to the ancient frieze and stonework on the north side. Turning to look at the east end and the altar candles that needed replacing, I noticed a woman sitting in the choir stalls. Her head was bowed in prayer. The candles could wait. Quietly, I made my way to the communion kneelers in front of the altar, and offered my prayers for her. Then I turned and walked slowly down the chancel. She lifted her head, and I saw that it was Lucy. She had been crying.

'Hello, Lucy. May I join you?'

'Yes, please,' she sobbed.

I sat down next to her and waited.

At last she composed herself.

'I should be so happy, but I'm frightened that things could still go wrong. I'm a little over three months pregnant. I had a scan this morning, and they told me everything looks fine. I've never got this far before.'

'Are you still working, Lucy?' When we met previously, she told me she worked as legal secretary.

'Yes, but I've cut down to three days a week.'

'What does your consultant have to say?'

'Oh, he's pleased with my progress, said it's probably a good thing to do light work part-time at this stage, no lifting.'

We talked a little longer allowing her to express her concerns yet build a positive way forward. Then we both made our way to the communion kneelers near the high altar. Whilst I'm sure our Lord is equally present in the kitchen, the choir, and at the altar, somehow the atmosphere can help focus awareness. I felt this was what had drawn Lucy to the choir stalls in the first place. Together, we said the Lord's Prayer. Then I offered a prayer.

'Ever present Lord Jesus, help us to open our hearts to your love. We thank you for the conception of this child. We pray for your blessing on Matt, Lucy, and their unborn baby. May they grow in health, happiness, and in your ways. Send your Holy Spirit upon them. Caring Father, we ask it in the name of your Son.'

We said the grace together, and then I left Lucy to say her own prayers in quietness.

As I walked down the aisle, I noticed an older lady leave the school exhibition and gaze around the abbey interior. She was carrying a child who looked a little under one. The woman seemed vaguely familiar but I couldn't place her. I wished I had a better memory. I greeted her.

'Hello. Welcome to our ancient abbey.'

'Oh, hello. I have been here once before, for a christening. My daughter is to be married here and I thought we'd look around whilst I was over for baby-sitting.'

Then I put two and two together.

'Ah, you're Sasha's mum, and this is Emma. We met at Emma's christening.'

'Yes. Sasha's so much happier now she is doing a little work. And Danny seems to be getting along fine and enjoying his. We heard that there was talk of selling the abbey. Will we still be able to hold the wedding here?'

'Yes, of course. If the sale goes ahead, we wouldn't move out until a new smaller church was built. I guess that would be at least a year away. The diocesan authorities want to sell the abbey, but most people associated with the place are opposing the sale. If you would care to add your name to our petition, I have part of it in the vestry, or you could write to the bishop, there are some forms on the table by the south door.'

She said she would write to the bishop. We talked a little longer and then I left her browsing.

54

The drive approaching the Bungay Manor Hotel threaded its way through pasture land with the occasional tall oak. The warm sandstone front glowed in the light of the setting sun. The restaurant to the rear of the house was light and elegant. At one end, near to a pocket-sized dance square a dinner-jacketed pianist played nineteen-forties' dance music, accompanied by a bass player and drummer. Marie walked in front of me, looking trim and desirable in a navy-blue skirt, jacket, and white blouse as the Maître D' led us to our table. He manoeuvred the chair for Marie whilst she sat, and then opened her napkin with a flourish before presenting it. It looked like being an expensive evening. Our window looked out over the croquet lawn to a ha-ha and then a meadow sloping down to the River Waveney.

I stretched my hand across the table towards Marie and she placed hers in mine.

'You look absolutely beautiful. I do love you.'

She squeezed my hand and blushed.

The starters came and went. Marie had Thai fish cakes, mine was chicken strips, a little salad and a tasty dip. We settled for a glass of wine each, as one of us would have to drive. Marie followed her fishy start with trout, for me the roast beef. Neither of us wanted a sweet. Perhaps, a little exercise before coffee? We joined two other couples on the tiny dance floor. It was an opportunity to hold each other. Not much room to progress, but enough to embrace. I put my arms around her waist, she eventually moved hers to round my neck. I suppose I was two or three inches taller than her. She rested her face against mine and I kissed her forehead.

That fragrance was there again. I was aware of inhaling. Her high cheekbones had a touch of rose colour. Her nose, retroussé.

Another couple bumped into us and the moment was broken. We made our way back to our table and ordered coffees. Outside, the sky was clear. I could see Jupiter glowing jewel-like. This had to be the time to propose. Should I go down on one knee?

A waitress arrived carrying two coffees. I was aware of a couple behind me, waiting for the waitress to leave. A vaguely familiar voice sounded out.

'Hello, Marie. How lovely to see you. I thought I spotted you earlier.'

The suave man limped nearer to Marie and gave her a kiss on the cheek. She frowned but said: 'Hello.'

The man turned towards me, 'Oh, it's the Rev John, isn't it?'

He glanced away at the young woman accompanying him. She had exaggerated eyelashes and heavy red lipstick on a childlike mouth. 'This is Susie.'

'Evening.' She looked embarrassed.

Gregor, for that's who it was, looked back at the pair of us.

'Has Marie been able to persuade you and your parish to support the diocese in the abbey sale, yet? She's a clever girl with a good brain, you know.'

Marie looked dumbstruck. Dark thoughts hit me. Was Marie a plant of some sort to convert me to the sale.

'Got to go.' Gregor ushered Susie away in front of him, revealing her sensual, figure-hugging dress. 'We've some unfinished business at home.'

He waved his hand and left.

My heart sank as I looked at Marie, 'I didn't realise you knew him.'

'Is he "the developer" you've mentioned a number of times?' She looked at me with sad eyes. 'I don't think you have ever referred to him by name. I didn't think he would have that much money, having invested in the business park. He's my stepfather. My father, who died when I was one, was a "Webb". Gregor Blacke married my mother when I was about three. He was driving with my mother and someone else in the car when they crashed and my pregnant mother was killed. I'm told Gregor spent some weeks in hospital with leg and pelvic injuries. I went to live with Andy and Peta and they obtained custody of me. Granddad reckons Gregor was drunk and would never let him in the house after that.

'I don't think he is really a bad man. He has always sent me Christmas and birthday presents. He came to my graduation, but Granddad had a big argument with him. He has had a succession of young escorts in the time I have been aware of those sorts of things. But he doesn't seem to be able to sustain a relationship. He doesn't have any family. He was an only child and his father, who was a builder turned timber importer, built up the investment business, or so Granddad says.'

I reckon I'm a reasonably good judge of character. No, that doesn't sound right, I don't like to judge people. Rather, I'm reasonably aware of people and what might be going on for them. I doubted that Marie was trying to turn me to support Gregor or the diocese. She had always seemed very open and supportive but ready to consider alternatives. I put that down to a good analytical scientific brain, one that didn't jump to quick, ill-founded conclusions. Then an image of Marie and the footballer crept into my mind. Was it just a peck from him, or a joint snog? I felt a confusing mixture of sadness, anger, and numbness. Somehow, the time no longer felt right for a proposal.

Marie picked up on it quickly. We paid the bill and left. I dropped her off at her flat. I didn't go in. We put our arms around each other in the car and tears intermingled. I think she didn't want to seem to be making excuses. I didn't want to be false or rash, or to hurt her, or to lose something that was precious. We agreed to meet for supper after her choir practice next week.

55

Light rain arrived on Wednesday morning. Leaving Moses looking hopefully out of a window, I drove to the abbey to drop off six bottles of communion wine and to say morning prayer. After the service I switched my mobile back from silent and noticed two missed calls and two voicemails.

The first voicemail was from Marie. She sounded very flat, 'Hello, John. Tried to get you. Sorry, can't make supper tonight, called away to a fruit farm in Essex. Staying with Andy and Peta for a few days. See you in a week's time, after choir. Love you. Marie.'

My stomach knotted. I wouldn't have seen her for a week and a half by then. Did that mean things were over? Was she cooling down, or drawing away after being discovered? I did recall she had done some work down that way earlier in our relationship, and she had stayed with her grandparents then. I'm sure they loved having her with them. And from what she had told me, they must have been like parents for her. They had all appeared such genuine and decent people.

The second message was from the director of the county archaeological services. 'Hi, John, Josh King here. We've finished and interpreted the surface surveys, and we're planning to start two trenches just after lunch. One of the trenches will go through the metal detector discovery area. If you happen to be around, I could talk to you about our interpretations so far. Oh, we've been in contact with the British Museum to try to raise some financial help. They're interested and coming in with us and Cambridge.'

As I walked out of the abbey a marked police forensic van pulled onto our car park. It was followed by an unmarked car. Two men in civvies emerged from the unmarked car. I recognised one as Jack Bills, June's husband.

'Hello, John. I'd better show you my warrant card. This is my colleague, Detective Constable Amiss,' he showed me his card: Detective Sergeant J. Bills.

'We've had a number of complaints about poor response to the vandalism around here, not least from my wife. My inspector has put me on the job. I'm keen to follow up any forensic evidence.'

'Right, Jack. Better late than never. If you look at our main external notice board, you'll see the woodwork has some red paint on it. We had to replace the glass. Over there we still have the food wheelie bin from the Brandon Arms. It has some red paint on it. Jessica, from the Sussex Siren, reckoned there was a finger print and photographed it. In fact, she has done a lot of following up, perhaps you might have a word with her?'

'Yes, I have heard about her. She's given us quite a lot of bad press over this. We have lifted some prints from a buckled mast at Southshore, and taken samples of the red paint at the Arms. Let me give you a card. If you get any more trouble give me a call, or dial 999 if you think it appropriate. We did hear reference to a green van belonging to some builders, but it seems they were doing some legitimate work on the business park.'

I left them to it as I had a couple of jobs to do before coming back to meet the county archaeologist.

I was back on the north-east side of the abbey just after one. Ben, Josh King, and Professor Blizzard, the Cambridge archaeologist were chatting as some technicians and postgraduate students were setting up two parallel lines of cord to mark out a trench for excavation. A small claw digger was waiting to remove the turf top layer.

Ben was recounting to the county archaeologist, the archives he had searched for records of the abbey and local notables.

'I've spent quite a bit of time in Ipswich, Lowestoft, Cambridge, and online at the National Archives.'

'You might find it worth a visit to Bury St. Edmunds and the Bodleian. The Lowestoft archives facility is fairly recent. Most of the Suffolk records were at Bury and Ipswich,' Josh offered.

Ben took his leave shortly as he had a class. Josh turned to me and opened a clipboard he was carrying.

'Here, John, have a look at these computer print-offs. We've done magnetometry and surface radar. Perhaps this is the best one to show you, a composite of one on top of the other. We can't get really fine detail of the spot Ben's pupil located. There is a strong magnetic response there. It possibly could be a grave, it's around that sort of size. There may have been a settlement of some sort here on the holme, well before the time of the abbey. There are indications of two buildings surrounding the strong magnetic response region. There is a good indication of a rectangular shape extending from just inside the infirmary towards the west, across the infirmary cloister. If you look carefully there is a weak indication of a smaller rectangular shape inside the stronger one, with both sharing the same east side.'

'So, what do you think these are? Earlier parts of the abbey?' I asked.

Professor Blizzard took up the analysis, 'We are hoping that excavation will reveal more clues, but,' he looked up at me, 'the first abbot, Ralph de Neatisheade, in his chronicle, refers to earlier worship on this site. So, it seems quite possible that these rectangles may be earlier churches. Possibly, the strong magnetic response may be from an important grave, which has something metallic in it.'

Josh King took up the thread, 'Our first trench will be a north-south one, through the potential grave, but also extending through the possible walls of the earlier buildings.'

'It all sounds very exciting. When do you expect to excavate the possible grave?'

'About the middle of next week. Security is a problem and expensive, so we want to know what we are dealing with and protect it before it can be robbed. First, we'll expose the top of the trench all the way along, then focus on the metallic area. Finally, we'll lower the rest of the trench'

I stayed a little longer watching the digger get to work skimming the top few inches off the north-south trench and then left. I had a sermon to prepare for the weekend. My normal work had to go on. Perhaps I would do some visiting during the evening. I didn't fancy going to the Brandon Arms without my usual Wednesday companion, Marie. She would be far away in Ipswich. I would give her a call that evening.

56

Tuesday came and I hadn't seen Marie for over a week. Her mobile seemed to be playing up. I'd managed a few words on her grandparents' landline at the weekend. After a quick walk with Moses and saying matins at home, I was waiting in for Jessica. She wanted more details of the ancient chest contents and especially about the Lady Julian. After that I planned to take a box of altar candles to the abbey.

Jessica impressed me as a very lively woman. I got the feeling she never sat still for long. I told her all I could about the cartularies, communion vessels, and early history of the abbey. In turn she gave me a USB stick with photographs of the paten, chalice and ancient books. I was able to tell her more about the Lady Julian and to point her in the direction of St. Julian's church in Norwich, where the anchorite's cell had been restored. I lent her a book of the writings of the Lady Julian of Norwich. After a second cup of coffee she turned to the problems in our area.

'Have you had anymore troubles with vandals, John?'

'Not that I've noticed. The police seem to be getting a little more active and I've seen more police cars down Lakeside in the last week than we've had in the last six months. Oh, and one of our congregation, a detective sergeant, is apparently on the job. I did point him in your direction.'

'Yes, I've shared some information with him. I took a sample of the cement poured down Max Archer's drain and had it analysed. Apparently, the green van we've identified in Lakeside a couple of times has a legitimate reason to be there. They are builders, and they're working on one of the industrial units in the business park. However, I don't trust them. We found a pile of sand on the building site and took a sample, and guess what?'

'It matches the sand in the cement?'

'Spot on. I've had one of our cub reporters, Mike Adams, following the builders' van. He sneaked up when the van doors were open. Guess again?'

'I've no idea.'

'There was a ring of red paint on the floor of the van, near the doors. Looked like where a can of paint had been put down. Mike photographed it with his smart 'phone and managed to get a scraping before the men came back. He's following Councillor Jackson at present. Apparently, the councillor is visiting Gregor Blacke's offices on the business estate at present, not too far from where the builders are working.'

The mention of Gregor triggered a memory of dancing with Marie, and of preparing to propose. I still struggled with his comment of Marie persuading me to support his venture.

'Right, I must press on. Thanks for your help,' she snapped her notebook shut.

'You're welcome. Thanks for the exposure of the abbey and our aim to keep it in the hands of the parish, although by all accounts the diocese are pressing on with the sale.'

'Don't be too sure about that. I have had confirmation from our colleagues in the Spanish press in Majorca that our councillor friend and the chief planning officer accepted the hospitality of Gregor on his boat and in the yacht club. Your archdeacon had her hotel bill paid by him as well. None of these individuals have declared a conflict of interests in the sale of the abbey as far as we can determine. That is certainly contrary to the practices required by our local authority and by the Local Government Act. When the time is right, and that'll be fairly soon, I'll be passing this on to Detective Sergeant Bills.'

I walked Jessica to the door, picking up my coat and the box of altar candles.

'Can I drop you off anywhere?' She asked.

'Well, if you are going near the abbey?'

So, I put the box of altar candles in her boot, and jumped into the passenger seat. As we turned off Waveney Way into Magdalene Lane, Jessica's mobile rang. She pulled to a stop looking excited.

'Hello, Mike. OK, well done. Don't get too near. See you there,' she turned towards me.

'Belt up again, John. My colleague walked past the builders with the green van as Councillor Jackson pulled up in his swanky Mercedes. Mike heard them agree to meet at the Woodman pub near Somerleyton, in half an hour's time. The councillor also told one of the men to bring the usual envelope with him and it sounded as if they were meeting someone else.

'You'd better come with me as a further witness. We haven't got very long.'

By this time, she had turned and pulled back out into Waveney Way and was speeding towards the bridge over the lock between Lake Lothing and Oulton Broad. We drove north and then turned west. As we approached Somerleyton, I noticed a sign to Somerleyton Hall. I recalled that a noble land owner from Somerleyton had given to the abbot of St. Benet's, the land at Queensholme on which our abbey was built.

The Woodman pub was half-timbered and looked inviting in the sunlight. There was no Mercedes in the rear car park. We ordered ham sandwiches and drinks and made our way to a table in a dark corner at the back of the pub. Jessica suggested that I sat with my back to the bar, partly as a screen, but also because the councillor might recognise me. Jessica put her smart 'phone on the table and switched it to vibrate only.

I took a quick look round. Three locals near the bar were

chatting with the barman. An elderly couple with walking boots and light anoraks were examining a map on a window table. Two east-European-looking men were talking over sandwiches three tables away from us.

'Action, I think,' Jessica muttered. 'Don't look round, but it looks like the two builders have arrived. They're buying drinks. One has walked over to those foreign looking chaps. They're all Bulgarian or Romanian I'd guess.'

I could hear them talking quietly but they weren't talking English.

Ten minutes later, I heard chairs scrape. Jessica picked up her whispered commentary, 'Here's Mr. Councillor. He's gone straight to join them. Surprise, surprise. One of the builders has jumped up to buy him a drink and food.'

All went quiet for a while. Jessica commented that she had spoken to the councillor over the 'phone but had never met him face to face. Her mobile vibrated and she answered it quietly.

'Yes, Mike. They're all here. We're in the far corner. Get a drink and stay roughly near the door. They're meeting with another two foreign chaps. Can you follow them when they leave? Get the number of their transport and see if you can find out anything about them. Have your mobile ready for a shot, especially of the two we don't know.'

She looked up at me, 'I might have to pretend you're my date, John. So that I can look as if I'm taking your photograph.'

Picking up her mobile she adjusted it to photo mode and made as if she was taking a shot of me.

'Here we go. One from each pair of men has drawn out an envelope —.'

She moved to one side for a better look with her 'phone to her eye. A few seconds later she pointed her phone at me again.

'Got him! Our dear councillor checked the contents of both envelopes before putting them in his jacket. It looked like money to me. The photos will enlarge. Oh, good. I think Mike got him from the other side as well.'

Her mobile vibrated again.

'That was Mike. He used the video on his 'phone, I should have thought of that.'

'Mike's leaving now. He says it's shadowing from in front.'

A few minutes later Jessica informed me that the councillor and friends were leaving. We gave it a couple of minutes before we left. Twenty minutes later, I carried the box of altar candles into the abbey vestry whilst Jessica continued on to her office.

57

Another Wednesday turned up and Marie was still working away in Essex. We had spoken for quite a while on Saturday, but I was missing her more and more. It appeared that she was missing me as well. She reckoned she would be back for choir the following week.

When I arrived at the abbey to say matins, the weather was dry but cold. Afterwards, I went out to the dig. The north-south trench was generally about two feet deep but down to five feet in the central part. A gazebo style tent covered the lowest area, presumably to reduce problems with rain.

'Morning, John.' Holding a trowel, Professor Blizzard walked over from the tent area. 'We're getting to the interesting part today. Nothing much in the trench so far. We've gone deeper around the metal-detector area first, so that any rain has somewhere else to pool.'

'OK. I'll look back later.'

I returned three quarters of an hour later, to find an excited group of researchers photographing the middle area of the trench. With deeper excavation all around, it was like a plinth. As the group parted I caught a glimpse of the top of a skeleton partially exposed and lying on top. The Professor came over.

'There you are, John. The pelvic bones indicate a woman, quite a tall one. The coroner will have to be informed, but I'd say she was buried well before the abbey was built.'

'Professor, Professor!' One of the researchers with a brush in her hand was calling. 'I've exposed a silver coin.'

The camera went to work again and then the coin was removed and carefully cleaned. The Professor took out a hand magnifying glass and carefully examined the coin.

'There's an embossed horse on one side and a head on the other. It appears to carry a name that ends "PRASTUS." That's very probably part of "ESUPRASTUS" and means we're talking about, say, around the middle of the first century AD. Iceni times. Let's go very gently.'

I waited whilst two researchers worked away very carefully with trowel and brush. The broken top of a small pot was exposed. Then the group stopped for lunch. I called Jessica to tell her what was happening and then went for my own lunch.

Back at about five, in addition to a number of other cars, there was a police car, a euphemistically named "private ambulance", a large security van, Jessica's car, and a Suffolk Siren van, on the abbey car park. A woman in a white overall was helped out of the trench by a policeman. A forensic pathologist I guessed. Arrangements were made for the removal of the skeleton to a mortuary.

'There are a few scars on the arm bones, but nothing to indicate how she died. We may know more after an analysis of her bone chemistry.' The pathologist picked up her case and left.

The County Archaeologist and his technicians were packing up small pieces of pottery into a box. 'We're taking these for safe keeping, John. Together with a number of silver coins and a gold necklace, a torc."

The Professor walked over, 'We at Cambridge are more humble, John. We are taking away, a collection of rust and the remains of a large sword. Josh also has a simple, but elegant, small gold crown. We guess this was the "Queen" of Queensholme. We wonder if she was the respected, and treasured, Boudica, or

Boudicea. Whoever she was, she looks to have been treated as a saint and had two churches built around her.'

I walked back towards the car park with Jessica. Over the last few weeks I had seen quite a lot of her.

'What an exciting life you've been leading, Jessica.'

'That's been very true recently, John, thanks to you and the abbey. By the way, Mike followed those two men, after their meeting with Councillor Jackson. He had quite a long trip, to the outskirts of King's Lynn. They had a mini-bus carrying the name "Anglian Horticultural Contractors." One of them turns out to be a gang-master who supplies immigrant cheap labour to horticultural farms in North Norfolk and Lincolnshire. Mike's also discovered that one of the Beccles Builders' men runs a large immigrant labour force. We wonder if any are illegal.'

She looked at me.

'How's Marie? Don't seem to have seen much of her recently. Is she all right?'

I took my time in replying. There had been no one that I felt able to talk to about Marie. Somehow, as a priest, it seemed wrong to discuss one's own concerns with a parishioner. I was a dispenser of help and solace, rather than a receiver. I had considered talking to Anne with whom Marie shared a house, but she seemed too close to Marie. I felt at ease with Jessica, she was probably ten years older than me. She had doubtless observed Marie and me together after services and at abbey events, let alone the meeting at Southwold. Perhaps she reminded me of my older sister.

'The truth is that I don't know. I'm confused. Ten days ago, we went to the Bungay Manor Hotel. I had arranged it as somewhere special to propose. And then Gregor Blacke came up and everything went wrong. I doubted Marie, and she withdrew. Things haven't been the same recently, and deliberately or otherwise, she's been working away since.'

I explained the rest of the background: Gregor's comment, Marie's explanation, and my probable over-reaction to seeing her previous boyfriend kiss her, plus all the deviousness that seemed to have surrounded the sale of the abbey.

'I miss her terribly. Life has turned so flat since then. It's just left a massive hole. I can't stop thinking about her.'

She let me talk.

'John, it sounds as if deep inside you have considered all the factors and have faith in Marie's integrity, or love her, despite everything. She has always seemed a genuine and caring young woman to me, intelligent and sensitive. Perhaps you need to tell her what you've told me.'

We chatted a little longer and then went our own ways.

The next day I went to a florist in Lowestoft High Street and sent a bouquet of flowers to Marie at Ipswich, with a simple note: 'I love you. Forgive me if I have hurt or doubted you.'

58

'Bye, John. Thank you,' Rupert Bishop offered his hand as he left after our eight a.m. Tuesday business service.

We used a version of Common Worship Prayer for the Day. Numbers fluctuated, particularly depending on the weather. One tries various ways to serve the local community. Since there were a significant number of business premises in St. Mary's parish, I hoped they would find benefit from an appropriately oriented service. Associated with this, I made brief visits to local firms. We had moved through the period of no congregation, when I had felt like the monks of old in offering prayer for my absent neighbours. Our service included inspirational elements aimed to help with creativity and innovation, as well as intercessions for employment, business growth, and ethical practices. The service today was attended by four who worked in local companies

As I walked home for breakfast, the world seemed a better place. I had spoken to Marie at the weekend and offered to travel to Ipswich to meet her for a meal. She had declined as her business commitment had mushroomed. She would be staying with Andy and Peta for at least another week but was intending to travel back for choir on Wednesday and would have a meal with me at the Brandon Arms afterwards. She had appreciated the flowers and sounded brighter.

I sat down to the aroma of filter coffee, an occasional treat, and hot toast, then applied the spreadable butter and marmalade. The taste was delicious. The 'phone rang. I let it go through to the answer machine. When I recognised the voice as Ben's, I picked up the hand piece and answered.

'Hi, John. Just a quickie. I've got a free period. Have you checked your emails today?'

No, I haven't.'

'I've been working through the Bury archives after school, for a couple of days. Made a massive discovery last night. They had the last will and testament of Sir Robert Brandon, MP, and a copy of a trust deed. He died in 1723 and was the last of the local Brandons. In his will he bequeathed the abbey building, land, and patronage to the parish of St. Mary's. So, the diocese does not have the right to sell it. I've emailed copies to you and Marjorie Banks.'

I thanked him for his diligence and for the good news. I would have to tell the archdeacon. But first, my breakfast.

I had made a point of keeping the Rural Dean, Alistair, and the archdeacon briefed on our various discoveries. Imogen's response to each new highlight was consistently a monetary one,

'Thank you, John. That is good news. It'll enhance the sale value.'

When I rang to advise her of the will, she was slower, but still had a ready answer.

'John, the Patronage Benefits Measure 1986 required all interested parties to advise their diocesan registrars of any claims to patronage. There was a limited time for registration claims. After that elapsed the registrars were empowered to assign patronage to the diocese. The registrars' decisions are final. I did make a point of exploring this in respect of the abbey, before there was any progress on the sale. There has never been another claim so the patronage is vested in the diocese.'

'But this will has only just come to light, Archdeacon.'

'Well as I explained, John, our registrar at the time was required to take a decision. The law provides for his decision to be final.'

I could see that discussion on this point with the Archdeacon had as much chance of success as that of a gnat fighting a rhinoceros. After I finished my call to the Archdeacon, I rang Marjorie Banks, the solicitor on our PCC. She was out, so I left her a voicemail.

Later that afternoon I visited the abbey grounds to see the dig progress. I knew that the first trench was finished and some soil had been taken away for analysis. The east-west trench was now well advanced. Professor Blizzard and Josh King had agreed to meet for a progress assessment. There was a light drizzle, so the two archaeologists accepted my invitation to come into the abbey for a coffee.

'We have pretty well finished, Vicar,' the professor accepted another chocolate biscuit. 'Thanks. You must be a pretty wealthy parish to afford chocolate biscuits. We only get digestives at mine. Let's deal with the bones first.' He looked at the county man who took up the story.

'We've had the pathologist's report. The dating processes put the bones as middle of the first century. There was no obvious cause of death. There were signs of ageing: arthritis of the right shoulder and signs of increasing curvature of the spine. The right humerus was noticeably stronger than the left, which goes with that substantial sword. The sword, crown, gold torc, and Iceni coins do suggest a warrior queen, which of course ties in with the name of the district. We are inclined to think she may be Boudica, the most notable Iceni queen. Her DNA has been determined, but as far as we can tell there are no known descendants with whom to compare. From a county point of view, we think there is sufficient of a case for an appropriate tomb. The abbey would clearly be the obvious place, provided that it isn't sold. If it is sold then probably Norwich would be the next choice. It really is a most important find; it's a national treasure that would draw many visitors. Over to you, Peter,'

'We've had the less glamorous jobs. The rusty steel is a long sword of about the first century. The coins were Iceni, almost certainly before AD 60. The gold necklace or torc, is definitely an Iceni trademark. The crown fits that period and is rare. The finds were registered with the local coroner and will probably be ruled as treasure trove, to use an old term. The value of these would probably be split between the finder and the landowner. I wouldn't know whether the landowner is the diocese or the parish.'

I jumped in: 'We probably have a dispute over ownership. Ben, the history master and researcher has just found the will of Sir Robert Brandon MP. This bequeaths the abbey, land, and patronage to the parish. Our Archdeacon is arguing that the patronage is vested in the diocese.'

'I can't advise you on that,' the professor picked up the thread. 'Returning to the dig, we have pretty well finished. The outer rectangle that we showed you in the survey analysis has come up as a less substantial stone, and tends to suggest an early church, probably around the six hundreds. There was little to see physically of the inner rectangle but we took soil away for analysis and it is very rich in the remains of wood. That leads us to think that there was an earlier wooden church, possibly of the third or fourth century. There is a substantial history of worship on this land. Further to the west we found a few remains of pottery, suggesting there may have been habitation here once.

'John, we are now about to tidy up the site and leave Health and Safety notices.

59

Wednesday came around at last. Marie was due back for one night for choir practice. I was both looking forward to this, as well as being aware of uncertainty in how she would react. My guide was the loneliness and hole that her absence had left in me. I also planned to map out next Sunday's sermon and to make some parish visits. In practice I found it very difficult to concentrate.

First, I took Moses out for a walk, ending up at the abbey to say matins. It didn't feel selfish to include Marie and myself in the intercessions. Switching my mobile back on after saying the office I noticed a voicemail and missed call from Marjorie. She was free when I followed up.

'Hi, John,' she was very cheerful. 'I don't think your Archdeacon is exactly a legal expert, although church or canon law is a speciality in itself. The Patronage Benefits Measure, to which the Archdeacon referred, does provide for correction. The measure provides for the Diocesan Register of Patronage to be rectified where previously supplied information is incorrect. That's only common sense, really. Additionally, if it got as far as disposing of the abbey, the Mission and Pastoral Measure 2011 Code of Recommended Procedure requires that a Scheme of Disposal be drawn up and that written objections can be submitted. However, all this legal arguing could cost both the parish and the diocese a lot of money. I doubt whether the proposal for sale will get very far now we have a copy of Sir Robert Brandon's will.

'If you agree, I'll suggest to Jessica Ellerman that she runs an article mentioning the will. When I spoke to her at evensong last Sunday, she inferred that she was about to expose the criminal practice of a councillor, local authority employee, local builder, local developer, and a member of the clergy. I'm presuming the last person is not yourself? She was just waiting for the article to be cleared by the Sussex Siren's legal advisors.'

'Yes, Marjorie. I'm happy for you to pass on details of the will. It ought to be common local knowledge. Oh, and no, I don't think I'm the member of the clergy to whom she referred.'

After our conversation, I wandered outside with Moses to see what was happening with the dig. The trenches were being back filled. I noticed that paving stones had been laid to mark the grave and the corners of the ancient churches. There were no signs of academics.

Back at home, I managed a few rough notes for a sermon. Following a light lunch, I set off to make a couple of visits. The first was to a retired woman from outside the abbey and Coxton parishes and on the north side of Lowestoft. Knowing there was little parking, I walked. At the swing-bridge, I had to wait. The bridge was closed to road traffic, to allow a rig support vessel to enter port. I watched as the red and white painted ship manoeuvred cautiously through the narrow bridge area. A little way into Lake Lothing there were sideways ripples near her bow and stern as she engaged bow and stern thrusters which pushed her gently alongside the north quay. From the stern of the ship a light line hurtled through the air to men on the quayside. They hauled a more substantial mooring rope from the ship and dropped the end loop over a bollard. As the winch on the ship took up the slack in the rope, I made my way over the now open bridge and up the main shopping street. London Road, now pedestrianised, looked middle to late twentieth century. It had wide pavements with no curb stones with a central narrow roadway of setts.

As the road gave way to High Street, it narrowed and bore signs of an older Lowestoft, steadily climbing to a higher area. Periodic narrow passageways called 'scores', led off downhill to the lower area nearer to the water and the fishing harbours. Above the shop fronts many of the buildings showed an older architecture. The red Victorian council offices on my left, stamped their authority on the surrounding area, being topped by a dominant central tower. Linda Jackson lived a little further along on the seaward side of the street, in a terraced house that showed signs of changes of use. It looked to have been a fine merchant's house originally. The ground floor front, however, bore a square projecting window revealing a period as a shop.

'Come in, John. How kind of you to take the trouble to come all the way out here to see an old lady.' She showed me into her lounge at the back of the house, and bustled off to get tea and cakes.

From the window I could just make out the sea. She explained that her husband was a recently retired chief officer with P & O. He had wanted a sea view. He spent a lot of time at the local yacht club and was contemplating buying a boat.

'He misses the sea, and he's not very churchy.' She poured me a cup of tea and offered the cakes. 'I tried the local church for a while, but the vicar's a strange man. If you greet him in the street, you're lucky if you get a grunt out of him. Our daughter and family came to stay last Christmas. She came to midnight mass with me. When we walked out after the service the vicar just stood by the vestry talking to the choir, couldn't even be bothered to say "Happy Christmas", or to receive the thanks of the people leaving. In the end I found it too distracting and decided to look elsewhere. You have a lovely old building and the people there have made me very welcome.'

'You are one of us now, Linda. Please don't see yourself as someone from outside the parish. You are now on the electoral roll. I appreciate the help you give with the coffee and tea after the service, and the readings you regularly contribute to.' I had a feeling that she wanted to talk about something deeper. Eventually she came around to it.

'Apart from when the children were young, I've worked in ladies' fashion retail, mostly in one of the large stores in Norwich. I finished up as a departmental manager. But somehow, I've always felt guilty that I didn't take up a more caring career. I had good A levels and thought about being a nurse. I seem to regret it more as time slips away.'

'Linda, this is something that a lot of people experience as they get older, especially as they become more aware of the spiritual side of life. We need good Christians in all walks of life. You might like to consider helping at our mums' and toddlers' group, or our good neighbours' group. The latter is a group of parishioners who call on the sick, elderly, or disabled, to help in a variety of ways. In many cases it's just listening, talking, and being a friend. In some cases, it's doing some shopping. One or two fitter people do a little gardening, but that's not everyone's cup of tea. As a way forward consider just opening your heart to our Lord and asking his guidance as to how you can best help.'

I stayed a little longer. Then we said a couple of prayers and I took my leave. The next two people on whom I called were out, so returning home I did some work on our next month's team magazine. Moses reminded me that it was his tea time. Before long it was time to set off for the abbey to say evensong and to catch the end of the Saint Cecilia Singers' practice.

60

'That's it, ladies and gentlemen. Thank you.' Clare Parkinson snapped her music folder closed and her choir started making their way out of the abbey. 'Are you back with us now, Marie? We've missed you,' she put her hand on Marie's shoulder.

'Well I'm back to Essex first thing tomorrow morning, but I expect to be finished by the end of the week.'

I'd been in the abbey since six-thirty, saying evensong and waiting to welcome Marie back. She'd walked in with a group of choir members. We'd only had the opportunity to exchange a quick peck with a hand on an arm. After that I'd largely kept out of the way, not wanting to appear to be snooping, nor to be invited to join in. Mark Ransome was playing the accompaniment, some on organ, and some on piano.

'See you in the Brandon Arms, if you're going there, John,' he said as he headed out.

We climbed into Marie's Discovery and looked at each other. I put my hand out and she put hers in it. A gentle squeeze.

'I've missed you terribly.' I looked at her.

'Me, too.'

The handbrake and gear lever presented a physical obstacle between us, but we lent across, closed cheeks, and wrapped arms around each other. I felt my own tears mingling with Marie's.

'I am sorry that for a minute I doubted you, when Gregor made his comment. I also had a jealous flash back to when I saw that footballer kiss you. I wanted you all for myself. Somehow, I've come to realise that even if you were there on Gregor's behalf, I still love you.'

'I should have realised that when you spoke of a developer, that it might have been him,' she looked up at me. 'He must have a lot more money than I realised, or else he plans to borrow it. He has built a lot of units on the Lakeside estate, and still has unused land there.'

When we pulled onto the Brandon Arms car park, it was nearly full. Marie parked next to some laurel bushes separating the car park from the adjoining Southshore premises. Mark Ransome and some of the choir were gathered around the bar as I went to order a meal and pick up some drinks.

'Excuse me if I don't stay to chat, chaps. I haven't seen her ladyship for a couple of weeks.' I nodded at them and made my way to Marie clutching a glass of wine, and a pint of beer.

She explained that she had been working at a fruit farm. They had experienced a poor harvest which she put down to problems with bees. This in turn appeared to be due to a nationwide problem that had decimated bee populations. Additionally, she had traced local issues to nearby farms using old-fashioned insecticides.

'We're working on improving the farm for both bumble and honey bees and planning to move in some of my own bees for a period next year. We've also got some promotional activity through the local farmers' association regarding alternative fertilisers and approaches to unwanted insects.'

Our meal came and was quickly demolished. As the coffee came, Marie's 'phone rang.

'Hello, Anne,' she frowned. 'What about the outside key?' There was a pause and in a resigned tone: 'OK, I'll run John home, then I'll be on my way.'

My heart sank. I'd been looking forwards to a few minutes'

privacy at home with Marie, before she left for her flat. She looked at me.

'Sorry, I'll have to go straight home. Anne's locked herself out. She can't find the hidden outside key. It's probably in the house from the last time she used it. I'll run you home first.'

'I can walk if it'll help?'

'No. It's more or less en route, and I'll have to say a quick "Hello" to Moses.'

We just had time for a quick standing-up clinch at the vicarage, before she climbed back into her car. She started looking through her small handbag.

'If you don't make it back at the weekend, I'll pop down to Ipswich on Sunday night. What's wrong?'

'Can't find my mobile. I used it at the pub.'

'Hang on. I'll ring them to see if it's been handed in.'

A few seconds later, landlord Simon assured me they had her mobile safe. A waitress had just found it on the floor under our table.

'See you at the weekend,' Marie swung the Discovery out of the drive and went off at speed.

'OK, Moses. I guess there's time for a walk.' I grabbed his lead and we set out for some unexpected exercise.

61

I put my book down around twelve-thirty. Moses was in his bed, shut in the kitchen. As I turned over to switch off the bedside light my mobile rang. It was charging at a nearby power socket.

'Hello, John. Has anyone rung you about Marie? It's Simon.'

'No. Is everything all right?' I recalled her tyre puncture. 'Has her car broken down?'

'No, she's been taken to the Brandon Hospital. The ambulance left an hour ago. The place has been swarming with police. She called to collect her 'phone some time ago. Mark Ransome and a group of the Singers found her collapsed and unconscious by her car when they left. He heard her 'phone ringing, found it in the bushes, and then spotted her on the ground next to her car. He wonders if she may have been mugged. Oh, the call was from her flat mate wondering where she was. Apparently, the police have taken her mobile away. We've got the police here at the moment looking at our front video tape, so I'll have to go.'

'OK. Thanks, Simon. I'd better get around to the hospital.'

I was dressed in a flash and quickly on my way to the hospital. At that time of night, the roads were clear. I was soon parked and making my way to Accident and Emergency. Detective Sergeant Jack Bills was there.

'Hello, John. Apparently, she came around in the ambulance,

which is a good sign. I'm waiting to interview her, when they let me.'

I made myself known and a nurse came to see me.

'Are you family?'

'No. I'm her boyfriend. Her only family are her grandparents near Ipswich. Can I see her? Is she all right?'

The nurse put her hand gently on my arm, 'I suggest you get a coffee for now. We've sent her for a scan. She's had a nasty blow on the head, not surprisingly she has a headache. She'll have a bad black eye tomorrow. Since she was unconscious, we'll be keeping her in at least overnight. Will you telephone her grandparents? I'll let you know when she's back.'

'Yes. OK. Thanks.'

Jack led me away to a coffee machine and generously bought me a cappuccino.

'Could be a little while, John.'

'Jack, do you know what happened to Marie? Or is that confidential police information?'

'Not at all. Frank Amiss and I were just writing up some burglary notes before going off watch when the emergency call came in. We were tasked, and it wasn't far from the station. Since it was near pub closing time there were a number of uniforms working as well. There were two uniforms and a squad car at the Arms when we left. Apparently, Marie called at the pub to collect her telephone and left immediately. About half an hour later, your organist and a couple of choir members also left. They heard a mobile ring but couldn't see anyone so followed the sound. There was a mobile in the bushes at the edge of the car park. Mark Ransome picked it up and answered it and then noticed Marie lying nearby, in shadow next to her car. He called the emergency services. One of the choir reportedly heard a vehicle driving off in a hurry, reckoned it was a van but couldn't get the number. I've got someone checking the front car park CCTV at the pub.'

His radio went. 'Excuse me, John.' He walked away to answer. A few seconds later he was back.

'That was my inspector, who is now involved. Frank's run the pub video and spotted the incident. Marie goes to her car, is about to get in, stops, then walks out onto the road and disappears behind the hedge towards the boatyard. A few seconds later she comes running back clutching something in her hand, with a man chasing her. He hits her and knocks her down and something goes flying from her hand. Then Mark Ransome comes out with others and the assailant runs off. They've examined the 'phone and found a photograph of a man coming out of the boatyard with what looks like a bolt cropper. They're blowing up the photograph to try to get a better picture of the man. The chap from the boatyard has come in to check his video and the yard security. As you know we've had a number of incidents there. Could be Marie discovered the vandal who's been messing with the pub and boatyard, he saw her and assaulted her. On her photo he's wearing a hoody. On the pub video the hood has fallen back so we may get something there.

'I think I'll have to come back and see Marie in the morning. Will you be all right?'

'Very angry, but OK. Thanks, Jack. Take care. I hope you get this chap soon.'

Half an hour later, through open double doors, I caught sight of a trolley entering the main emergency room. A porter was pushing and a nurse was walking beside the trolley. I suppose these little snippets of information keep one going. I realised I was worried and yet tired. At last the nurse I'd seen earlier, emerged.

'Mr. Green, you can see Marie very shortly. The doctor wants a word with you first.'

I followed her up a short corridor to an inner reception area. A fifty-year-old bald doctor was writing notes, and another nurse stood looking at a computer screen, both behind a waist-high bench. A second younger doctor was telephoning. The bald doctor looked up at me and stopped writing.

'Mr. Green? Your fiancée has suffered a hard blow to the temple.'

'Doctor, I hope she will be my fiancée but at present I'm just her adoring boyfriend.'

'Well, as a precaution we sent her for a scan. She doesn't have any sign of a fracture, I'm glad to say, although she will have extensive bruising to her head and her side where she fell. However, —.'

I flinched, wondering what was coming next. He continued.

'There is sign of a little internal bleeding. We can't be sure what that's from but it's near the blow area. It may well heal itself. I've arranged for a follow-up scan tomorrow morning. Meanwhile, we'll move her to the ICU, Intensive Care Unit, under a neuro-surgeon, so we can keep a good watch on her, in case pressure builds up inside her skull. We are waiting to be told when a bed is available, but it should be soon. You are welcome to go in to see her, in fact a familiar and caring face is probably the best thing for her at present. She needs rest and time to heal. Please keep her quiet and relaxed, she will be trying to make sense of all that has and is happening to her. The less stress the better.'

I thanked him for his care and followed the nurse into a large room where Marie lay, blanketed, within the raised sides of a trolley. A drip was attached to the trolley head.

Oh, Lord of all healing, please send your Holy Spirit to restore this my most precious love to health of body and soul.

She lay very still and with her eyes closed. The right side of her face was pale as snow except for a bloody graze on her temple, possibly where she had hit the ground. The left side was swollen from below her eye up to her front hairline. A puffy bulge hid her eye. A substantial dark bruise had started to develop.

'That bruise will probably grow out over the next few days as the colour works up from below,' the nurse offered. 'Then it will begin to fade. I'll leave you now.'

She came back a second later with a chair.

Marie's breathing was shallow and light. Her hands at her sides, rested on the cellular hospital blanket. Gently, I took her left hand in mine, in the process noticing a plaster on her arm. She stirred and opened her right eye. A gentle smile commenced, and ended in a wince. She pulled me closer, and I bent down to kiss her. But where? There was only one place, gently on her lips.

'I can't remember a thing between leaving you, John, and waking up with a paramedic talking to me in the ambulance. Oh, dear, Anne was waiting for me.'

'I expect it provided a good excuse to stay with Jake. I'll ring her, and Andy and Peta, in the morning.'

'I think she ought to rest now. The porter has come to move her to ICU.' The nurse was back. 'I'm going with her. You can come if you wish.'

The Intensive Care Unit was nearby to two pairs of doors, each with an inscription: 'Theatre', and 'Sterile Area' .

62

Marie was kept in hospital for a week. After a day in intensive care she was moved to the neurology ward. Anne Fox covered the Thursday morning team service for me. I rang Andy and Peta and they were up on Thursday afternoon. They were horrified at the massive bruising that had developed on the right side of Marie's face. I offered them the use of the vicarage, but they chose to travel up and back each day, staying at home to look after their cat at night. It was agreed that Marie would stay with them for a number of days after she was discharged. I also called her flat mate and business partner. Anne visited frequently.

On the Friday afternoon the Sussex Siren was published. Marie's bruised face stared out from the front page. Jessica and her photographer had visited the hospital. 'VICIOUS ATTACK ON BEE EXPERT,' the headline read. A smaller photograph of the exposed hooded attacker carried a request for readers to contact the police if they saw the man. Jessica had also spoken to Rupert Bishop from the boatyard and determined that more boat damage had occurred and what looked to be the same man had been caught on a new security camera. In her article she raised the question as to whether the attacks on the abbey, the Brandon Arms, Southshore's boatyard, the bungalow drain, and Marie, were all linked to the proposed redevelopment between Lakeside and Lake Lothing.

Adjacent to the photograph of Marie was one of Councillor Bruce Jackson receiving an envelope from the builder, with a headline 'CORRUPTION IN HIGH PLACES?' The article went on to cover the meetings in Majorca of the several parties with an interest in the redevelopment. Our diocese and the Archdeacon were included.

On the Saturday I received a call from the bishop's secretary. His grace wanted to see me urgently. An appointment was made for nine-thirty on Monday morning.

The Bishop's House oozed antiquity and was tucked away near a beautiful garden, at one corner of the cathedral grounds. A priest with blonde hair ushered me into a waiting room. He must have been about my age. Tall and good looking, dark rimmed glasses lent him a studious look. Destined for higher office, I thought. Unlike myself, after my opposition to the diocesan will. Probably doomed to obscurity on some remote island, unless I found a diocese who had never heard of me.

'Have a seat, John. I'm Hugo, the bishop's chaplain. The bishop will see you shortly. We are very concerned about the press coverage of the affairs in your parish, John. The bishop is quite upset about the damage this may do to the diocese.'

'I'm dare say that bishop Francis is also concerned about the young woman with a bleeding brain who has been lying in bed in an Intensive Care Unit, the local businesses who have been vandalised, the apparent corruption in our local council, and my many parishioners who pray for him regularly!'

'Quite.'

Ten minutes later I was shown into the bishop's office. It was a pleasant light room with French windows leading out to a lawn with croquet hoops. To one side of the room was a conference table seating around twelve. Under a window next to the garden access was an antique desk, clear except for one manila folder which lay open and what looked like a copy of the Sussex Siren. At the far end near a large stone fireplace was a circle of chairs and a settee. Tucked away at the opposite end was a small table bearing a decorated cross and two candlesticks. Two kneelers lay in front of the table. Bishop Francis rose from the office chair by his desk, and came towards me with an extended hand. He was a tall man, around sixty, with white hair, and a benign expression. Height seemed to be a distinct advantage for ecclesiastical progression.

'John. Good to meet you at last. Come and have a seat,' he led me to the chairs.

Let's get off to an appropriate start, I thought.

'May our Lord's guidance, grace, and love be with you, father in God.'

'Thank you. You have had a lot of challenges in your parish. How is the young lady who was injured? Was she your fiancée?'

'Well, she has just been moved out of intensive care, but there was bleeding at the edge of her brain and we wait to see how she progresses. In answer to your second question, I very much hope that she will become my fiancée, with your kind approval.'

'I hope so too, but I must take the advice of your rural dean, Alistair, who speaks well of you. I sense that there is perhaps some difficulty in your relationship with archdeacon Imogen?

He looked at me with penetrating eyes.

'I have the impression that the archdeacon is an able person with the best financial interests of the diocese at heart.'

'But not the most empathic?'

'I try not to judge, bishop Francis.'

'But I understand that you were a psychologist before ordination?'

'That's correct.'

'The Archdeacon had a plan to amalgamate the parishes of St. Mary Magdalene and Coxton St. Giles, and to provide a brand-new adaptable church and centre. You don't agree with that?'

'I agree that was the archdeacon's plan. Whether she was the originator, I doubt. When I was licensed by the archdeacon, I was charged with obedience to you and my superiors. I was also charged with the cure of the two parishes. I delayed hardening my own opinion until the proposal was considered by my parishioners. St. Mary's parishioners were very substantially against any sale of the abbey. It appears to be in reasonable repair, has considerable historic local connections, and recent finds of historic national interest. It is at the heart of our local community. I couldn't conceivably recommend to you that it be sold. As abbot of St. Benet's Abbey, Horning, you also have a very special connection to St. Mary's. The land on which our abbey was built was granted to one of your predecessors, and it was from St. Benet's that the original monks set out to build and develop St. Mary's. A recent discovery of the will of Sir Robert Brandon MP shows that the building, land, and patronage of St. Mary's was bequeathed to the parishioners. A letter to you requesting a meeting between yourself and the parishioners was sent around two weeks ago.'

He looked blank. 'Excuse me a second.'

The Bishop examined the contents of the folder on his desk and then walked to the room outside. I heard him speaking and heard the name, Hugo.

'I don't appear to have received this letter. How was it posted?' He took his seat again.

'It wasn't posted. Out of respect, I gave it to archdeacon Imogen, together with a copy for herself. She was intending to give the letter to you when you met the next day. It must have somehow gone astray.'

'John, being aware of the local facts how would you suggest we proceed?'

'Often the best way out of a dispute, Bishop Francis, is a compromise. The PCC did in fact suggest one. I think that the two parishes of St. Mary Magdalene and Coxton St. Giles should be merged and share the abbey building. That would release the mixed-use premises of St. Giles back to the council. I would agree that some of the abbey land, in fact from near the abbey up to the waterside of Lake Lothing, should be sold to the developer or the council. I am not sure that the developer will still be in business after the recent exposé. That land is in fact rather uncared for. We should keep an area near to the abbey. It contains visible remnants of the old monastic buildings. That route would, I'm sure, be acceptable to the PCC and would save us all from lots of legal expenses.

'In due course, I would expect that the remains of Queen Boudica would be interred in a suitable grave within the abbey. It would be entirely appropriate for that service to be conducted by yourself. I think that Boudica is very much more of a venerated national symbol than Richard III.'

Bishop Francis sighed and smiled.

'That sounds eminently sensible. You can take it that I will communicate my thoughts to the appropriate committees. I am left with a venerable problem that I must deal with.'

'If I might say, I believe that the venerable lady was well intentioned but misled.'

'That is charitable. Keep up your good work, John, and let me know when your fiancée is well enough for you both to come and have tea with me. Let us say a couple prayers.'

We did, and he gave me his blessing.

63

It was a worrying several days with Marie. She slept a lot. A number of tests were carried out on her and there was a chance she might need brain surgery. Fortunately, wherever the bleeding had originated, it healed itself. The liquid revealed on the first scan had disappeared, absorbed, after five days. It was around about then that she perked up and became bored. On the Tuesday after I had visited the bishop, I collected a few of her belongings from the Discovery, which was still on the pub car park. Then I made my way to the hospital. She was in a side room off a main ward. Whilst I was sitting beside her, in walked Gregor carrying some flowers. He looked a very worried man and was nearly in tears as he gave her the flowers.

'I'm so sorry this has happened to you, dear Marie. I hadn't expected anything like this when that wretched councillor Bruce said he was going to provide some inducement for the locals to fall in with his development plan. You are all that I have left of your dear mother. Bruce was in the car with us that night. He threatened to reveal that I'd had three pints before the journey. As a strong rugby player, I thought that would have been well inside my limit. When we were taken to hospital, I was unconscious and had a smashed-up leg as well. The police had no opportunity for a blood test. Bruce has blackmailed me on that ever since.'

Shortly after, Andy and Peta arrived and Gregor left quickly.

The business of the parish had to go on. Fathers Rex and Paul, and Anne Fox had been a great help for several days. On Thursday evening we were all present for compline. Somehow things were returning to normal. I had felt more at ease since Marie had improved without any operation. Jack and June Bills were present at the service. Afterwards I asked Jack how his investigations were going.

'Well, and not so well. We have arrested councillor Jackson and the council head of planning and charged them under the Local Government Act. We've also arrested Gregor Blacke in connection with our investigations, but I'm not sure he has knowingly done anything we could prosecute him for. As for the two builders, they've disappeared off the face of the earth. They may have slipped home to Romania or wherever they came from, or they could still be in this country. We haven't found any clear immigration records for them, but knowing the mess that service is in, it doesn't necessarily mean anything. We have a number of search warrants out in connection with the proposed development plan, including your Archdeacon's premises. We have questioned her, but there seems little likelihood of any prosecution. All are released on police bail at present. If we get those two builders, they'll be a different matter.'

A week after her injury, Marie was discharged with instructions to take it easy, no work or intense physical activity for several days. She was given a follow-up appointment with her neurologist for a week later. I collected her from hospital and drove her to Levington. George, the cat, made her very welcome and was soon rubbing his head against her and purring, very therapeutic I thought. I arranged to go down on Friday afternoon and return home on Saturday afternoon.

Marie looked so much better when I arrived on Friday, just in time for a late lunch.

'Do you feel well enough for a very short walk at Southwold?'

'Oh, yes. I have very happy memories of the place.'

'Well you take it very gently and don't overtax her, John,' Peta looked concerned.

'I promise to take extra care of her. She's very special to me.'

And so, an hour later we had parked the car and were walking gently northwards from Southwold along the coastal path.

'It seems strange without Moses,' Marie looked at me.

'Yes, I did consider bringing him and leaving him in the car overnight. I didn't want to risk him upsetting George. Jim is looking after him again.'

To our right the sea sparkled with back reflections of the south-westerly sun.

'Not many butterflies around today,' I observed.

'No. It's not their time of the year, although you might see the occasional one or two as the weather has been warm.'

We came to the area where Marie had stumbled and hurt herself last time. I recalled that this had been the memorable place of our first kiss. This had to be our very special place. I looked at her as we walked along holding hands.

'Would you ever consider living with a vicar?' There! I'd done it at last, or had I?

'What, in sin?'

'Of course not. In marriage.'

'I don't really know,' she replied smiling. 'I've never been asked by one, by anyone, come to that.'

I knelt down on one knee. 'Dearest Marie, will you marry me? I love you very much.'

'Of course, I will, my sweet. I thought you'd never ask.'

I rose and wrapped her in my arms, 'I love you, I love you, I love you. I thought I might even lose you a week ago.'

A few minutes later we relaxed and eased apart in a warm glow, as an elderly couple with a dog walked past.

'I think I'd better ask Andy's agreement, out of courtesy and affection. Oh, and I have to get the bishop's permission, via our rural dean Alistair.

'I think Andy would appreciate that.'

Back in Levington, I approached Marie's grandfather. 'Andy, I'd like your permission to marry Marie.'

He beamed and gave me a hug. 'Oh, I think that'll be all right. She's very special. Peta, where's the sherry, we haven't got any champagne? Come in here. Marie and John are getting engaged.'

He went to a cabinet and selected four glasses. Peta came over, gave us both a hug, and disappeared into the dining room to retrieve a bottle of Amontillado.

A little later we celebrated in the Crown, a recently refurbished Tudor pub and restaurant in Woodbridge. Andy insisted on hiring a taxi, so no one had to worry about driving. Before we dined, I rang South Shields and we both spoke to Mum and Dad. Later, I gave Marie a hug before we both retired to our bedrooms. I felt in a daze of emotional warmth, relaxation, and excitement.

Thank you, Lord, for the love that you have, and are, giving me through my dear Marie.

64

Marie seemed to look even more beautiful as we planned our more immediate future. I advised our rural dean, Alistair, of my wish to get married.

'I'll have to interview the young lady, for the bishop, you know,' he said. 'Wasn't she the one who brought us coffee and chocolate biscuits when the archdeacon visited? That should stand in her favour.'

The positive answer came back quickly. Marie and I spent a happy Saturday in Norwich choosing an engagement ring. We went to Ralph Hughes, churchwarden at St Olave's, as he was a jeweller. My name would have been mud if we hadn't. He had a very classy jeweller's with a wonderful range to choose from. Not that I'm mean, but he gave us a substantial discount. Marie chose an antique ring with a tourmaline stone, and bought me a bloodstone signet ring. To celebrate, that evening we booked a table in the posher interior dining area at the Brandon Arms. Landlord Simon treated us to a bottle of champagne. We semi-formally slipped the rings onto each other's fingers. Simon came over to check that the food was to our liking and to share a glass of champagne.

'Where's the wedding going to be?'

'In the abbey,' Marie replied.

'Well, you couldn't have a much more beautiful setting.'

Marie had moved around in recent years and didn't have a special relationship with any parish, although technically she lived in one of those in Beccles. It was a long time since she had been to church in Levington. So, with Andy's agreement and Marie's choice, we settled on the abbey for our wedding. Alistair agreed to officiate.

65

At six in the morning the sky was beginning to lighten. A light mist, condensed during the cool night, partly from the effects of the Great Ouse to the North and partly due to evaporation from the rainfall the previous day, covered the road that cut through the wooded area, a few miles south-east of Kings Lynn. Jessica's grey Vauxhall was parked in a short lay-by. She and junior reporter Mike ate their sausage sandwiches and drank cups of coffee from a flask. The car heater just about overcame the effects of leaving the front windows open. Hopefully that gave a better chance of hearing the approach of vehicles from the farm. A little way along on the other side of the road lay a gated farm track. On the gate a discoloured notice warned of 'Private Property' and 'Dangerous Dogs.' Similar notices appeared periodically along the verge of the wood, either side of the gate. Next to the gate was a locked box for post and a notice reading 'Worthington Farm.'

'I think you're right, Mike. Not many farm tracks have locked gates and warning notices.'

'I can hear a vehicle approaching and I think the sound is coming from the farm direction. If I get a chance to take a photo, I'll use the camera for better definition than my 'phone,' Mike picked up his Nikon. 'Have you got that photo handy, the one of the man with the hoody clear of his face?'

Jessica reached into the rear well of the car, gathered a photograph and put it on the dashboard.

A large minibus rocked its way up to the gate and stopped. It was closely followed by another two. The driver of the first vehicle alighted and removed the padlock and chain before pulling out onto the road and waiting. The two other vehicles followed. The driver of the last minibus re-locked the gate and walked back towards his parked vehicle.

'That's him isn't it?' Mike snapped away. 'Are we going to follow them?'

The three vehicles then drove off into the mist.

'I think not. We might give ourselves away. I reckon there were the best part of forty people in those buses, they'll be off to work vegetables somewhere. No. I think we'll leave the car here and take a walk through the woods, or even up that farm track now they're away. Grab the rounders' bat that's under your seat. We don't want to end up like the vicar's girlfriend if we are discovered, but put it under your coat.'

Ten minutes later, after climbing the gate and following the track, they sighted an old farmhouse, three barns, and a number of open lean-tos housing a dilapidated tractor and trailer. Two overgrown tracks led off into the woods on the far side of the farmyard.

'No sign of any dogs, yet,' said Jessica, heading for the first barn.

Mike quietly opened the door, 'It's like a dormitory, Jess.'

Along the two long walls were beds, each with a cheap wardrobe. Many had photographs stuck to them.

'Family, I'm sure,' Mike commented.

Behind a partition were wash basins and toilet cubicles. The second barn was similar, but slightly tidier.

'I reckon this is the girls' room.'

There was a deep racking cough from one of the beds. A woman with long black hair sat up and looked at them.

'Are you all right, dear?' Jessica asked.

The woman looked frightened.

'Plis go way,' she cried, and then broke into a language that neither Jessica nor Mike could recognise.

'Do you want help?' Jessica tried again.

'No help. Go way,' the woman was getting distraught.

'Come on, Jess,' Mike called. 'We're clearly upsetting her.'

They went outside.

'I don't think we'll chance the house, but whilst we're here, let's have a look around the rear of the barns.'

Jessica led the way. At the far end of the third lean-to was a dark blue battered transit van.

'Pity it's not green,' said Mike. 'However, there's an interesting smell, like cellulose. Looks like it's been re-sprayed, it's a battered vehicle under the paint, but the paint looks pretty fresh.'

He tried the rear door handle. 'It's not locked! Hey, just look at that. I'll have to use my 'phone for a photo.'

Whilst the outside had been re-sprayed, the interior flooring was still worn wood, with a ring of red paint and signs of building sand.

'We've got 'em, Jess.'

'Take a photo of the number plate as well.'

Just over an hour later they were back in their office settling down at adjacent desks. Mike uploaded his photographs into the company computer system.

'I'll have to notify DS Bills, but I'll see if I can get some goodwill in exchange: accompanying the police on a search and arrest trip, in exchange for the further intelligence that we will have provided.'

66

Theatre Street car park in Swaffham was dark and wet in the early morning. It held a motley collection of vehicles.

Unusually, it was swarming with police. Jessica shook the worst of the drizzle off her waterproof and dropped it into the rear well, next to a passenger, as she climbed into the driver's seat of her Vauxhall, quickly closing the door behind her.

'Sorry, Charlie. Hope I missed you there. We're off at four-forty-five. The Norfolk DI wasn't too pleased to have us, but since we've supplied the initial intelligence and photos, he's OK'd it, provided we keep to the back and don't hinder them. Time for a quick snack, Mike?'

Cub reporter Mike handed around bacon sandwiches to Jessica, and to Charlie, the photographer, who sat in the back.

'Right as far as I can make out the convoy will be headed by Jack Bills, his DC, and his DI, Sarah Briscoe, in an unmarked car, followed by 5 Suffolk uniforms in a minibus. Jack has a bolt cutter to deal with the padlock chain. How about the coffee now, Mike? The Suffolk lot will go via the main entrance that we watched. They'll be followed by an Immigration Service minibus. We'll follow them. The Norfolk DI and his two colleagues will go via one of the back entrances accompanied by a dog handler in his van, and the Norfolk uniforms in their minibus will go via the second back entrance. They're planning to start up the three drives at the same time, five-fifteen. There's also a Norfolk prisoner van.'

Ten minutes later the convoy headlights came on one by one.

'Pity we haven't got an aircraft frequency radio,' Charlie said from the back of the car.

'True, but I think that listening in on police frequencies is illegal,' said Jessica. 'Right, we're off. We follow the immigration minibus.'

The convoy headed north to the centre of Swaffham. Then the Suffolk and Immigration contingent turned west onto the Kings Lynn Road, whilst the Norfolk police headed out on the Fakenham road. Twenty minutes later Jessica pulled to a stop as their convoy halted where she and Mike had kept watch two days previously. The burly figure of Jack Bills walked up to the Worthington Farm gate carrying long-handled bolt cutters. After a couple of minutes, he was back in his car, with the gate wide open.

'They'll be waiting for the Norfolk lads to be in place at the rear entrances,' said Mike.

The sky was starting to lighten as a few minutes later the start signal must have been given. The Suffolk detectives' car moved into the wooded drive followed by the Suffolk police and Immigration Service minibuses. Jessica followed in her Vauxhall. Periodically the car caught a pothole filled with water, jostling them. It was a quiet approach otherwise. No flashing blue lights, surprise was the priority. The Norfolk contingent arrived just after them. Police vehicles blocked each exit.

The Norfolk uniforms and two Immigration Service men headed for the men's barn, the Suffolk police and two Immigration Service women went for the women's barn, and the two groups of detectives headed for the farmhouse. A uniformed male sergeant soon emerged from the first barn and signalled Jessica and Mike.

'Can't see any of your chaps in here. Would you come and have a look?'

Inside were twenty or so men sitting on their beds or sorting through their belongings. All looked very concerned. Three central tables held the remains of a meal. Immigration officers were checking each worker's papers. Jessica and Mike moved around quickly but were unable to spot any of the men they had seen in the Somerleyton pub. Frank took the opportunity for a couple of photographs.

'No. Can't see them.' The journalists headed outside.

They could hear the Norfolk detective sergeant on his car radio organising a police helicopter. The dog handler and his Alsatian were running towards the back of the farmhouse, accompanied by DC Amiss.

Jack Bills and two of his Norfolk colleagues emerged from the farm house shepherding three familiar-looking men in handcuffs to the secure van. Jack walked over.

'We've arrested three of your chaps on a holding offence of bribery. A chap who looks like your thug in the hoody unfortunately gave us the slip and disappeared into the woods via the back door. However, the Norfolk helicopter was on standby at Norwich airport and should be over here in a few minutes. Where was that van you saw?'

Mike led the way round to the rear of the barns whilst Jessica headed towards the women's barn. She was in time to hear a woman constable talking to DI Briscoe.

'Mam, I've called for an ambulance. There's a very sick female in bed. She has a temperature, is coughing and sweating. I'd guess she has pneumonia.'

Two hours later Jessica was listening to a debriefing from DI Briscoe, with strict instructions as to what she could report.

'Thanks for your intelligence. We have arrested three men on suspicion of bribery and immigration offences. I've just heard that the fourth man has been captured, he will be arrested on a similar basis and also on suspicion of assault. We have fifteen foreign nationals with satisfactory immigration and work papers and nineteen who will be held on suspicion of illegal immigration. There's a forensic team coming over to search the farmhouse. It seems that two of the arrested men were registered gangmasters, one for horticulture and one for civil engineering and building.

There's another immigration bus on the way over and also a flatbed truck to recover the resprayed van. We expect charges for criminal damage in due course. There's also a very sick woman. She's probably an illegal immigrant so they wouldn't get medical help for her in case her status was revealed.'

Jessica and her party hung on until the forensic teams and the immigration coach arrived so that they could take photographs of potentially illegal workers climbing onto the bus clutching their few possessions. Charlie also took pictures of forensic staff removing bags of evidence and a computer from the farmhouse.

67

Some several months later, alone in the abbey, in my evening service intercessions, I reflected on the past happenings. One way or another the ancient building had interacted with the lives of many since I had started work here. Outside, a considerable part of the land towards Lake Lothing had been sold. There was to be a promenade and waterside area, further towards us a children's area would give way to a small park with a maintained wild conservation area where butterflies enjoyed rare vegetation. A notice board would give details of the abbey history, whilst a coloured plan and photographs would relate the stone remnants to the structure of the early monastery. The Bishops of Southshore had not moved, neither had Simon Fellows and the Brandon Arms. Max Archer and his wife decided to stay put in their bungalow, helped by a goodwill payment from Gregor Blacke.

From my stall in the chancel, I looked across to the new inscribed dark blue floor stone that protected the remains of Boudica, Queen of the Iceni. The bishop had led the service of re-interment. Local subscriptions and a National Lottery grant had secured the books and communion plate discovered behind the coat of arms. They now resided in the county museum in an appropriate controlled atmosphere. The coins, crown, and sword remnants had raised money that was split between the parish, as landowners, and the school and student Ian. Grants had again been found to purchase them for the county. They were currently on display in Ipswich museum.

Some of the money raised resulted in a new flexible parish centre. The parish of Coxton St. Giles was combined with St Mary's. Probably as a result of all the publicity and finds, our congregation had grown considerably. The congregation target set by the archdeacon when I was licensed was passed. The archdeacon herself was spared legal proceedings but resigned her position and was appointed as communications advisor to another diocese. Our rural dean Alistair was invited to accept the archdeaconry but declined, preferring his more local pastoral role.

Two gangmasters and their henchmen were sent to prison. Mitica Dalca, the bully in the hoody, was sentenced to a much longer term in respect of the grievous bodily harm to Marie. Fifteen immigrant workers were found to have legitimate papers. Nineteen hadn't and were 'repatriated.' The sick woman, who was legitimate, died in hospital of complications from pneumonia. I felt very sorry for all the immigrants, the illegal ones in particular. It turned out that they all had to pay considerable sums for their travel to the UK, and had been blackmailed to work for very low wages. The two gangmasters and their henchmen were consistent in claiming that Councillor Jackson had approached them to offer consultancy on employment law. He had discovered the illegal immigration and employment and had been blackmailing them for some time.

Chief planning officer Clive Lewis and councillor Jackson admitted accepting benefits from potential council contractors without declaring them. They lost their positions and went to prison for contravening the Local Government Act.

Marie's stepfather, Gregor Blacke, admitted providing hospitality to council officials, arguing he was trying to help local development. However, police investigations revealed a number of payments and benefits to councillor Jackson over many years. Gregor broke down in court when admitting that he had been blackmailed by the councillor over drinking before the accident which had killed Marie's mother and put himself in hospital for several weeks. Gregor was given a suspended sentence. Councillor Jackson received a further prison term in respect of blackmail.

Besides the issues of sale or no sale of the abbey, the lives of the people in the parish went on. Lucy Baines' fertility treatment worked. Lucy and Matt became very proud parents of twins, a boy and a girl. Matt stopped playing rugby but took an RFU coaching course and became involved in passing his skills on to junior players. Then he found he was in the early stages of prostate cancer. His prognosis was said to be good.

June Bills saw her grandson born. Her son and daughter in law were not churchgoers but came the abbey to have young Harry Bills christened. June worked for several months and then became progressively unwell. Jack took an early retirement. They were supported by their daughter Chloe, a local midwife. June had died two months ago, leaving Jack devastated and a pastoral challenge. The abbey was packed for the funeral, with many work colleagues from the supermarket. I reflected on how much shorter a life June may have had, if she had taken Dr. Marshall's prognosis to heart.

A vicar's life can be a lonely one. A good church warden can make a massive difference. Jim had proved a worthy holder of the position, a tireless servant of the parish and a great friend. Shortly after June's funeral, he collapsed during a service. He was rushed to hospital and diagnosed with a heart attack. He had surgery and made a slow but steady recovery. He continued to be a member of our parish council but stood down as church warden, a massive loss to our community although his friendship continued. Don Coates was elected to take over as warden.

Sasha and Danny had become more involved in the life of the parish. Their wedding was well attended. Sasha's bookshop friend, Anne, was bridesmaid. A few months' later, Sasha's father retired and the family moved to Carlton Colville, on the outskirts of Lowestoft. With grandparents nearby, Sasha returned to a four-day working week at the bookshop.

Marie, Moses, and I — aah, but that's another story.

Author's Notes

Readers who wish to follow up John's claims about healing and the power of the mind may like to consult the following references:

Luparello, T.J., et al. (1968). Influences of suggestion on airway reactivity in asthmatic subjects. Psychosomatic Medicine, 30: 819-825, in Battino, R. (2000).

Battino, R. (2000). Guided Imagery and Other Approaches to Healing. Bancyfelin: Crown House Publishing.

Koenig, H.G., et al. (2012). Handbook of Religion and Health, 2nd. Edition. New York: O.U.P.

Printed in Poland
by Amazon Fulfillment
Poland Sp. z o.o., Wrocław